NOTES FROM THE EDGE

NOTES FROM THE EDGE

A Historical Novel Based on a True Story

LAUREN STATON

YOUCAXTON PUBLICATIONS

OXFORD & SHREWSBURY

Contents

For my mother, Jean May Cornell

Acknowledgements

To my sister Heidi Jane Tibbles who spent hours looking for family connections and long lost relatives. To my cousin Jenny Cornell who worked on the timeline and supported me in writing about skeletons in the cupboard. To Mags and Steve Andrews, Derek Roberts, Tracy London and others who joined in the Havelock group. To my friend Caroline Riggs for her expertise on mental health when writing about the asylum. Rose Lane from Brighton. To Peter Birch for putting up with my endless questions on WW1. To all my family and friends who contributed to the Kickstarter campaign to make this publication possible and finally to my children, Sam, Joseph and Megan who have supported me in bringing Harry's story out in the open.

Prologue

THE PURSUIT OF TRUTH can be an addiction, particularly when you only have small parts of the story. Perhaps there is enough information to fuel your interest so that it would be easy to romanticize and fill in some of what you believe is missing; easy possibly, but your desire to find out what really occurred is far more gripping than what your imagination tells you to create. The actuality is far more worthy of attention than the invention; it sends you out on to a mission of discovery and then the search for a true story begins. The tale grows from a small amount of information, scribbled down in note form. It grows like a beanstalk, stretching out towards sunlight and as more stories connect and each leaf unfurls, more questions are asked. You are hooked and you want to know more.

This story is hindered by the fact that our main character, who was real and existed half a century ago, carried a dark shadow of delusion; his personality, we are told, inclined him to steer away from the truth and to seek the excitement of wrongdoing. He suffered a mental disorder and ended his years in a mental asylum. Already we do not trust what he tells us and we warn ourselves that we should doubt what we read - so we read again and study the facts. My own instinct is to believe that there is some truth here but am I reading delusions as well as lies?

The notes held in my hand shout up from the paper. The writer needed to declare that his words were worthy of attention and the blurred pencil lines were once written with precision. Written as a record of events on the eve of WW2, they are a transcription of words heard over a transmitter from a small room in South West London.

Harry Cornell, regardless of the consequences, had written them all down

Very little is known about Harry. This intensifies my passion in pursuit of the truth. I offer redemption in a sense: these notes that he wrote down for us to find, have at last escaped the strictness of the times they were born in and are now in the possession of a generation that will cast no judgment and is not responsible for any of his actions. My intention is simply to follow the sequence of events as the evidence unfolds and make some sense of it.

There is part of this man in all of us. Without his actions and mistakes, many of us would not be here now.

There is evidence in the notes that he suffered from *shell shock*. I also learn that there was disbelief within his family regarding his condition. Not surprisingly given what he got up to, he was known as a liar *before* he went off to fight for King and Country. Should we believe him? It would be difficult to lay the blame for his misfortune entirely on a war neurosis. There was a family-feuding over issues of long ago, secrets were left to fester and they fed resentment. They were not amenable to be cured by time and I am not sure as yet if they deserve to be resolved.

I have found myself trying to confirm the facts in minutest detail, pushing my way through the layers of misrepresentation and grasping after a real truth that comes from all sides, an arduous task and at times frustrating as with any story steeped in mystery. The story, enigmatic as it wishes to remain, controls the information it wants us to reveal. Harry was mixed up in a world where people used aliases. Some have been difficult to track down and perhaps never existed; some truly did exist.

Harry Killbuck, a nickname he would come to earn, was a father and a husband and yet he was not talked about nor discussed after his death, nor even during his later years. His very existence only came to light when, on clearing the house of my grandmother following her death in 2002, my sister and I found a green laundry-box that had been placed at the back of an airing cupboard. The box contained loose papers in no set order.

Some items purposely remain hidden, they wait for years to be discovered, either placed carefully in dusty attics or tucked away at the back of cupboards. None more so than this laundry box. I have wondered why it remained in my grandparents' possession. They had moved house three times and it had travelled with them from house to house - yet it was never discussed with anyone. None of my immediate family were aware that it existed. My grandmother had denied any real knowledge about my great grandfather. All my grandparents would admit was that they knew he was an artist and that they had a couple of his pictures in the attic. Any brief mention of him was conveniently brushed aside.

We were told that my grandfather, Jim Cornell, had grown up in the Warren Farm Orphanage in Brighton. There had been a brother and a sister but contact had been lost years before. The orphanage is long gone and all that now remains of it is a memorial garden that looks out over the Sussex South Downs. My grandfather's ashes are scattered there somewhere, as too are my mother's.

When we were small, we would have a day trip to Brighton every July on the anniversary of my grandfather's death. We would be taken to the hillside where the Warren Farm Orphanage used to be. It was called The Happy Valley. We would take flowers and then my mother would drive us to the town so we could go shopping in the famous Brighton lanes. My mother was drawn to their charm, as was I. How little we knew then about the significance of that place!

Following my grandmothers death I spent a day at her house helping my sister sort what remained of her possessions. My uncles had already cleared most of her belongings: her furniture, pictures and collection of ornaments - mostly gifts from her family - had all been boxed and taken. My mother had sadly died young in her forties, some years before, and this was why the task of clearing my grandmother's clothes from her bedroom had been left for my sister and me. We found the laundry box at the back of her airing cupboard, which was situated in her bedroom. I looked around the room, where things of no insignificance had been left like litter by my uncles. There were old receipts and bank statements strewn on the pink carpet. Raffle prizes and un-wanted Christmas gifts were all still in their wrappings and stacked in the corner of the room. The surroundings portrayed tawdriness, as did the rest of the house. My grandmother had tried to gift-wrap her home with floral curtains and cheap ornaments, pink shag-pile carpets and white fluffy rugs. None of them achieved a style of class but they made her happy.

I always thought of my grandmother as someone who was unconsciously trying to climb the class ladder by accumulating bright adornments but her naivety of mind just could not carry it off. In my younger years I could have been accused of not being as close to her as perhaps I should have been and I felt very little warmth towards her. Today is different; having delved into this past of social history, seeped in poverty and hardships, who am I to deny her the happiness she may have gained by coloring up her surroundings in a way that delighted her? Her family had kept her cocooned in her childlike existence and she never grew away from it. She felt safe in her house and had remained in it since my grandfather Jim died, thirty years earlier, leaving her with a grief that she selfishly used to hold her family together to protect her - and they did.

Lifting out the box from her airing cupboard, I knew it did not belong there. My uncles had dismissed it as of no interest and said it was probably just rubbish. Maybe it should just be thrown away? There would not be time here to go through it all and we were in a rush to get finished. I decided to put it in the back of my car and then my sister and I could go through it at my sister's house. I gave it no further thought nor questioned why it was there until that evening when my sister and I sat on the floor of her living room.

We laid out the documents and started to study them. The words on the lined notepaper were written in pencil and had faded. They were difficult to read at first. I read aloud the first sentence, which stated that 'they' were going to move a woman's body from Lillington Street in SW London. We were intrigued then captivated; a story began to unfold. It is now amazing to think that what was contained in that box would open up a cupboard so full of skeletons and hold a story that so many needed to keep hidden, a suffering story simultaneously detached and yet linked to the nerve endings of some inherited gene that I still possess within my own emotions.

It is the story of a man I was about to get to know and to judge as a young tear-away and as an incapable husband and father. To judge but also to feel for because I would find myself fearing for him as a soldier who did not want to go and fight in a war that did not concern him, a war that damaged and wounded him and then brushed him away because of his lifestyle, his craziness and his lies.

The notes are hard to bear. They tell how he suffered from shell shock and was stripped of his pension - more controversially they tell how he was linked to the murder of a man and five women in a forgery gang in 1939, the same month that England declared it was at war with Germany for the second time. They read as if he is reporting on some wrongdoing. He wants this story told so badly but nobody will listen. I sense his teardrops on the brown notepaper and hear a crazy tale of voices in his head with nowhere to go.

What is the truth of it all? It seems there was never a crime reported and without the criminal evidence we are left to wonder if his story is fact or the figment of a fractured brain in turmoil. Was Harry delusional, had he lost his mind or had he been committed to a mental institution at the command of others who would prefer that Harry should be out of sight and not listened to? Was Harry saying too much?

Harry was a broken man, when he was writing these notes, he was a down-and-out who slept rough on the streets of London, a pavement artist and engraver, a man who wanted to find his children so he could get to know them but was pushed away un-forgiven. He was seeking answers and crying out for someone to believe in him.

I am sure for some it would be easier to let sleeping dogs stay dead in the grave but in his death, as, I am told, in his life, Harry Killbuck could charm the birds out of the trees and that is what he seems to be doing now as he tugs at my arm to tell his story.

Photographs

HENRY HAVELOCK CORNELL

THE HAPPY VALLEY AS IT WAS CALLED BY THE FAMILY AND
PAINTED BY HARRY CORNELL

7

HARRYS PAINTING OF THE GYPSIES

HARRYS PICTURE OF EVE AND THE GARDEN OF EDEN

EVELYN ANNE

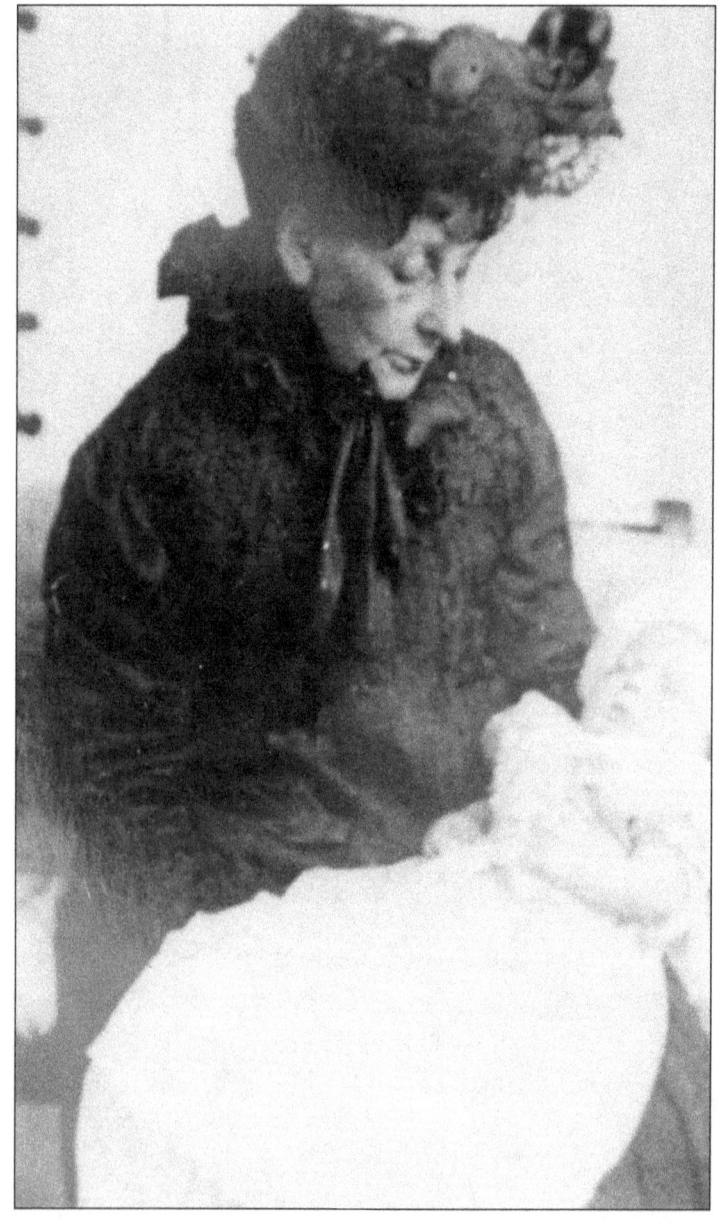

MARY CORNELL (NEE) JUMAN, HARRY'S MOTHER. HOLDING
THE BABY PATRICK.

PATRICK CORNELL, HARRYS SON

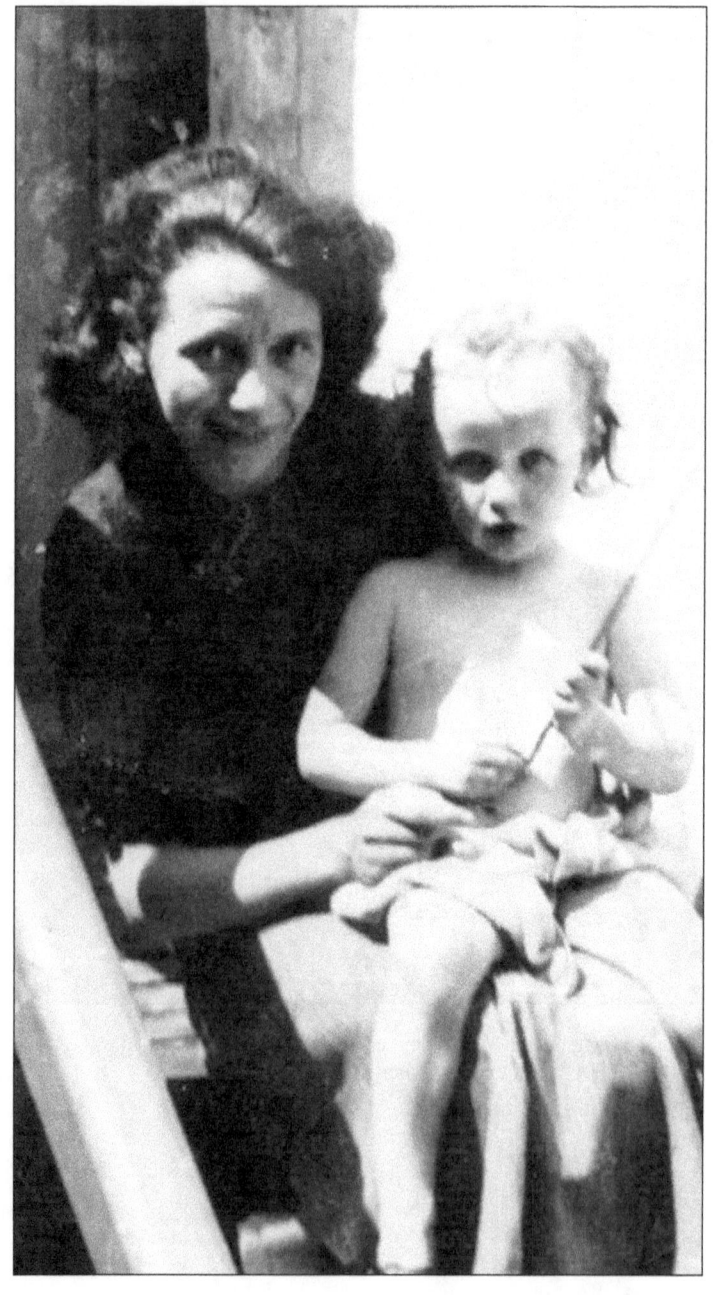

MAY CORNELL WITH THE AUTHORS MOTHER

JIM CORNELL, HARRYS SON JUST AFTER HE LEFT THE ORPHANAGE

ADA QUINN, AROUND 1930

1. West Park Asylum, 1952

A lone, middle-aged figure hurriedly walked along the covered walkway towards the swing doors that formed the entrance to a long corridor. Spring rain pattered onto the roof, drizzling down the panes of glass on either side, onto the black and rotting window ledges.

Jim Cornell pushed the doors, apprehensive of feeling intrusive, wishing he could be more confident. Clutching his car keys and a small notebook he entered the asylum hoping his footsteps would not echo in the silence.

He hated these places. He hated all institutions. He noted the poor condition of the place. The walls weeping and wretched with shards of green flaking paint that hung loosely off the overly-painted walls. He looked up at the cracked windows draped with thin cloth; they fed shreds of angled light, crisscrossing shadows over the floor. Breathing into his fist, he tried to diffuse the rank smell of the place but to escape the smell was near on impossible.

The hospital asylum took him unexpectedly back to his childhood. It reminded him of the institution where he had spent his school days. He had put those years behind him and blanked the memories but the memories were now flooding back into his mind and they produced a bad taste in his mouth.

The corridor seemed to go on forever. Dropping his car keys into the pocket of his jacket, he used his hand to smooth down his thin, windswept hair as he walked. There was no going back. He was walking the halls again, entering the musty damp den of some extinct animal lying dormant, the slightest sound, a cough, a familiar voice or spoken name would awaken the beast of many memories and there would be no escape.

The smell of urine-infested floors, reeking from years of vomit stench and unable to be washed away with disinfectant and carbolic soap detergent, filled the air. He remembered the boys in his dormitory when they had wet their beds and how they cried out when Matron had no choice but to give them three lashes. He remembered the cold draughty rooms and his red sore fingers, poking through the holes in his woolly gloves. He remembered the punishment he had received for tampering with the boiler in the middle of the night, when he had crept into the basement and had tried to get it to crank up. If he could just get it working, he had told himself, all the boys in his dormitory would be warm as toast. He was a master at fixing things but he still got what they said he deserved - three lashes with a cane across his hands.

He brought his mind back from wandering and focused on a solitary, grey, metal bucket at the entrance to one of the wards. The bucket belonged to an inmate, rewarded with the duty of mopping the long and never ending corridors that lead to even more corridors. This inmate appeared out of nowhere and walked towards Jim to claim his bucket. The mopping was meant to give some self-worth. The inmate stopped and saluted but Jim had no desire to acknowledge the greeting. He quickened his pace and kept his head down to avoid any eye contact.

The inmate was sorry, there was no sense of worth in a place where rusted window latches were firmly bolted, imprisoning the pungent odor to remind all who entered of where they were, where glossy red tiles clambered half-way up the walls holding on to the fingerprint smears, which remained like magic ink, put there by the first inmates that walked these corridors back in 1920.

Jim became aware of the cold sound that his footsteps were making on the tiled floor. The echo was enough to take him back to a persistent memory of the time for lights-out in his dormitory. Mrs. Hollindale, Matron at Warren Farm Industrial School, would pace up and down outside the boys' dormitory listening to the sullen silence of troubled boys from the lower classes, boys, weary from a day's graft, attempting to cloak the hunger-sounds deep within their bellies.

The sound of a radio playing from the end of the corridor wiped the memory away. Jim recognized an old war tune. Would they ever stop playing those tunes? The war had been over for seven years. Was Benny Goodman trying to lighten the air? These days of nagging patriotism made him sigh. Jim never made it into the army. As a boy he had contracted scarlet fever, which had left him with a heart problem and therefore he could not be accepted into the Forces.

The war had taken so much from so many people but he had managed to survive it, as did his marriage and the wellbeing of his four children. He had kept them all firmly together, relentlessly sticking to his values and facing many of his own battles at home. The Institution had taught him much when it came to survival.

He passed more wards and noticed the grey and unshaven faces of old men as they wandered and paced aimlessly between tattered armchairs, arranged in no set order. He peered at their tongues, churning loosely and dribbling saliva over their chins. *Poor old sods* he thought to himself, *locked away and out of sight in their own lives of turmoil, within the walls of this building.*

The crumpled notepad that he pulled out of the baggy and misshapen pocket of his brown jacket, had 'room 21c' written on it. He had scribbled the number down earlier that morning. The door of 21c was slightly ajar and he gently tapped.

'I'm Mr. Cornell,' he announced uneasily to the charge nurse in the white coat leaning against a filing cabinet and casually chewing on the end of his pencil. Jim coughed to clear his throat and tried to shake away his apprehension. 'The superintendent called me about my father, Harry Cornell?'

The charge nurse took a moment to react before ushering Jim towards a chair. Jim shook his head. He felt better standing. The charge nurse pushed back his shoulders and tried to display some authority. The white coat they had given him on the day he was offered this position had made him full of his own self-importance. Jim averted his eyes towards the space behind the charge nurse. The thought of receiving any signs of judgment from this young man would only add to his feelings of humiliation. He had already spent the morning justifying to his wife why he should visit the asylum and he had almost run out of reasons –even though the voice that was chattering in his head told to be there. He had asked his wife to come with him but she had flatly refused.

'I can't understand why you would even think about going,' she had grumbled.

Jim was a compassionate soul and feelings of guilt overwhelmed him. How could he feel guilty over something like this? It confused him and made his stomach queasy.

'Your father's belongings are ready for you, do you need to speak to the superintendent?' The charge nurse was polite but his body language demonstrated youthful arrogance.

Jim took his hands from out of his pockets and nervously patted his legs.

'Well he called me, so I suppose I must have something to sign.'

'I'll fetch him.' The charge nurse was clearly irritated and moved past Jim towards the door. 'Can you wait here please?'

Dr. Alex Howard was a short man with dark hair greying at the temples. His white coat was less than sterile white and did not fit over his suit. He greeted Jim with a limp handshake and a supercilious smile when Jim entered the room. Dr Howard felt uncomfortable when meeting relatives of patients; they invaded his routine.

'Pleased to meet you, Mr. Cornell, I looked after your father.' Dr. Howard called on his polite and confident manner, the manner they had forgotten to teach him about at medical school that always seemed to do the trick and intimidate the relatives. 'We tried calling your elder brother but unfortunately he's no longer at the address we have on our files.'

Jim looked puzzled.

'It's the address your father gave us,' said Dr. Howard, 'but unfortunately wrong because your brother left a few years ago. Your address was also on our files, along with a Mrs. Ada Quinn.'

Jim explained that he had not heard from his brother Patrick for four years.

'I believe he was in Ireland working. But I appreciate you calling me; I had no idea my father was here. We lost touch I'm afraid.'

This was a lie. Jim remembered how his father had stood on the doorstep that day, overwhelmed by his heavy overcoat and brown trilby. He had wanted to meet his grandchildren, he said. Jim's wife had refused to be courteous and would not let him near them. His father had left reluctantly, unwelcomed

. That was over twelve years ago. His father had died alone and maybe that was all he deserved. He certainly would not be missed.

'We lost contact with him a few years back, we were not very close. You see - my wife had trouble getting on with him.'

Dr. Howard gave no reaction. Jim realised there was no point in trying to justify why he had not been to visit his father. He had no wish to explain in any case.

'So what happens now, do you need me to identify him?' he asked.

'I'm sorry Mr. Cornell. Your father passed away two weeks ago. We've already buried him in Horton Cemetery.'

Jim was shocked.

'Oh - I see.' He bit his lip. *Just get this over with,* he thought - but more questions began to arise in his head.

'Your father was with us for twelve years, sir.'

Dr. Howard explained how Jim's father had contracted TB.

'I'm afraid it is quite common within the hospital. We did everything for him that we could.'

Dr. Howard had been conscientious over the care of Harry Cornell but now that part of his job was over and he had no desire to offer any condolences or sympathetic gestures. He liked to keep a professional manner about him and he thought it best to keep his distance concerning the personal details of a patient. To deal with a troubled mind was one thing, but to feel any empathy would just drag you down a path with them. He would spare Jim the details whether he wanted them or not.

The charge nurse returned to the room with a large brown suitcase and a laundry box containing books and papers.

'There are these as well.' Dr. Howard pointed to some unframed canvasses wrapped in brown paper and held together with frayed string. 'They're Harry's pictures, the ones he painted. He told the nurse they came from his studio. Would you like some help carrying things to your car?'

Jim declined and the young charge nurse looked relieved. He remembered he had to inform Dr. Howard that a situation had arisen in one of the wards and would he come as quickly as possible. Jim became aware of a commotion and heard faint, hurried footsteps, and then a pierced screeching and a woman's voice wailing from a distant side ward. Dr. Howard shook his head and left the room hurriedly after the charge nurse.

Standing motionless he looked towards the flustered Dr. Howard as he quickly informed Jim that Horton Cemetery was signposted by the entrance to the hospital.

'Follow the signs past the chapel and the mortuary.'

Jim picked up the brown, well-worn suitcase and the green laundry box containing his father's possessions then he carefully balanced the pictures under both arms and walked out into the corridor, towards the long, covered walkway with the broken windowpanes, back to the road where he had parked his car. Placing the suitcase and the laundry box in the boot he squinted at the road sign, which read 'Horton Cemetery', then he manoeuvred the paintings on to the back seat. For just a transient moment he saw himself kneeling beside an unmarked grave, saying the words he was supposed to say and then it came to him: he had nothing to say. Battling with the decision of whether he should go and visit the grave of a father whom he had turned his back on, his emotions gave no indication of how he was feeling, apart from the festering in his stomach which added to his faint nausea. He sat behind the steering wheel as a tear triggered his eyelids to blink. He lifted his hands up to his face, pressing it into the palms. He took a deep breath and stared in front of him.

What a morning.

The phone call from the hospital yesterday had caused commotion over his supper and at breakfast earlier. His wife had objected to his plan to come to the hospital.

'For pity's sake,' he told her.

'Please, don't go, Jim.'

'I must.'

Why the hell did I come? Maybe she was right in her own way. Now in the back of his car were his father's possessions, the man he had turned his back on for the past twelve years and never spoke about other than in shallow whispers. Now there were people who would link him to the man whom he had tried to eradicate from any memory of his past, that day when he had walked away from Brewer Street in his beloved Brighton.

In the back of his car, were all of his father's belongings stuffed into an old brown suitcase. The handle that had once felt his father's fingers gripping the leather, just as Jim's had done only moments before. He felt his father on his skin and his thoughts became haunted with the last memory of him standing on the doorstep twelve years before.

As a small boy, growing up in the orphanage at Warren Farm, he had conjured up images of a father who would one day come and take him home, only to be let down later when he discovered that the family that lived a mere stone's throw away and had abandoned him as if he never existed, at ten months old when he was left with a woman at the Elm Grove Workhouse.

He was never be given the chance to get close to his elder brother Patrick, gone into the care of his Grandmother, or May, his elder sister who had gone to a family and been adopted and cared for. Jim had known nothing of either of them until he got his exit papers from Warren Farm School at the age of sixteen. So really, what was he doing here? He had belonged to this man once but he had never been there for him. Not even on the day he was born. His genes ran through his blood and that made Jim feel sick.

He turned the key in the ignition. The engine took a while to get going. The rain did not help.

There was a mother as well of course but he had no idea what had happened to her. He never knew why she had left him in the workhouse and he had no desire to talk about her. When he had finally met his elder sister, May, she had spoken of a brief memory of her.

'None of it matters to me,' he had told her.

A group of inmates walked down the covered walkway toward the hospital. Shuffling together in a group they were ushered into a doorway by a nurse. One male patient, wearing brown trousers tied together with a piece of tattered rope, turned and smiled. It was the same man who had saluted Jim before in the corridor. All at once this man broke from the group and waved his hands in the air joyfully. He carried a paper bag, which he clutched as if it contained something special. His greasy hair clung to the side of his unshaven and gaunt face. The man raced towards him, shouting as if he had just seen his best friend.

'Harry! Harry! Give me a ride in your car?'

Jim wound up the window of the car and the young and impatient nurse ran over, grabbing the man's hand.

'Tommy, come and stay with the group.'

Jim revved up the engine and pulled away. He drove down the lane as fast as his car would allow. He drove past the sign of

Horton Cemetery and indicated left in the opposite direction, back to the main road and back to his reality, back towards his home in Watford.

The seats of the car felt cold and tacky as he pulled into Estcourt Road; the heater had broken again. The lace curtains at No. 11 flickered and he somehow knew that Morfydd has seen him from his mother-in-law's window and any minute now she would be throwing her coat around her shoulders and hurrying back to No. 7. For most men it would be disconcerting living next-door-but-one from your in-laws, but his wife was glad she could keep an eye on her elderly parents so this made Jim glad too.

The little wall at the front of the house bordered hardly enough space for a front garden; Jim would have loved a big tree or a lawn. A front garden could be so welcoming. A winding path, some hedges and some spring bulbs popping their heads up to greet him would have made putting the key in his front door so much more bearable today. It was usually pleasure to come home to his wife and her Welsh sense of humor but not today. She often recited poems to the kids that none of them ever understood. They must have had some moral tale, supposed to help them understand their hardships.

They were not a well-off family, not that it mattered; Jim valued the bond that ran between him, his wife and their four lovely children. They were blessed with a daughter Jean and three sons, John, Jimmy and David. He knew he was lucky to have them. His life could have been so very different.

His children would never need to understand what his childhood had been like. He had aspirations for all of them and would give them anything they needed. He worked hard to provide for them and he knew how his wife hated feeling like the poor relation. Her sister Gladys had it all: a detached house and a front and back garden. It was the bane of Morfydd's life, knowing her sister had managed to find a man to give her the position where she could blossom into the dutiful wife who did not need to work. Jim was not fussed about possessing a dutiful wife; he strived to be the father that his children would respect.

With this remnant of his father's possessions stuffed into the boot of his car and he felt ashamed that he did not have any memories of a childhood that he would be proud to pass on. While Morfydd recited Welsh tales, telling stories from long ago, Jim would remain silent. He had nothing of his own to give; there was not one story he wished to share with his children about his own growing-up years.

He looked at the wrapped pictures on the back seat and wondered what they were paintings of. Then he saw Morfydd at the window. She would soon be bringing him back to his senses with all of her nonsensical trivia, inconsiderately pulling him back into her own existence. *Thank god for her* he thought. She had no understanding of anything tied to emotion other than her own and that suited him; he was happy in her world because it helped him escape from his. Her black-and-white reality was all that mattered to her and there was no room for anything she found difficult to comprehend. Her Welsh upbringing was clear and concise. Her coldness could be mistaken for naivety and Jim tolerated it because he loved the child in her. She would never understand what was going on in his head and was not going to try, and that suited him too.

She had made her feelings perfectly clear the night before and again when Jim had stormed out at breakfast. *That man*, as she referred to Jim's father, was not welcome in her house. He had made her flesh crawl. When, the morning the call had come from the hospital, she had objected to the notion of Jim going there. He had felt uneasy but thoughts of duty floated into his reasoning to battle with other thoughts of *why should I go?* He had convinced himself that this would be the last thing he would ever do for his father, that it would close and erase a chapter in his life for good. This would be closure for him and he hoped his wife would be compassionate eventually. He wanted it all gone, right down to his earliest memory. But unconvinced, Morfydd had objected and pleaded with him. Just as he had done years ago, Jim's father might come between them once more. His name was not to be mentioned and she certainly was not going to speak about this to the children.

But Jim's car was loaded with all his father's belongings. How was he going to take them all into his home and where would he put them?

Daughter Jean opened the door. She was dressed to go out and was wearing a dirndl skirt she had made for herself. Jean liked to sew and paint; she had a creative gift and was the artistic one of the family. She often appeared in their front room showing off in something she had created. Morfydd would tut disapprovingly and her brothers would tease and taunt her free spirit, but Jim approved of her bohemian designs and her rebellious nature. She loved anything far away from grey and drab. Her generation deserved some colour, he thought. After six long years of war, it lifted everyone's spirit to see them embrace and consume the freedom they had all fought so hard to keep.

Jean called out to her mother to say Dad was home. Jim wanted to hug her and her relentless energy but just waved with a limp hand as she walked down the path over the red tiles, in her stilettos, barely keeping her balance *Why?* Jim questioned himself, why should she care about the burden he felt sitting across his shoulders. Jean was a delight and he was very proud of her.

He was nearly six o'clock as she was not at work. He refrained from asking her where she was going - probably to meet her girlfriends. A milk bar had opened up on the High Street and it seemed to be the latest place where Jean and her friends went after work.

The evening rain fed the dark green moss that coated the bricks on the wall. Jim heard the kitchen back door slam at the end of the hallway and Morfydd telling David his youngest to put some water on the boil. David ran out to greet his father. His grin lit up his thin face, which resembled his mother's although his eyes were like Jim's, dark and deep and cloaked in self-doubt and dark shadows. You would think they were tired eyes until a spark of humor lit them and the love came pouring through. When Jim's eyes met young David's you knew that there was a special bond between them.

Morfydd called out and David scuttled back to the kitchen and back into his shy boy-like comfort zone. Cabbage smells wafted from next door and made Jim feel nauseous. He walked into the lounge and dropped himself into his chair. Morfydd followed him with a frail and chipped cup and saucer full of weak, watery tea.

'You all right Jim? You're back sooner than I expected. The boys have gone over the fields, Jean's meeting Collette.'

'Saw her.' Jim gazed towards the lace curtains hanging at the front window. 'She borrowed ten bob from the pot, I said she could, she asked me this morning.'

'Well?' Morfydd frowned, 'what did they say to you?'

'He died two weeks ago.'

'Good Riddance!'

'Guess I should say that too. They've already buried him - in the hospital cemetery. They tried to call Patrick but couldn't reach him.'

'Good, now we can forget it.' She made her way towards the door but there were thoughts he needed to put into words.

'I should have gone before. God knows what that doctor thought of me. He gave them my name, maybe he wanted to see me,' he said.

'Only if he wanted money from you, or something like that. I know he was your dad, but you're well rid of him.'

'I feel terrible.'

She picked up his empty teacup in her usual manner when conversations became too emotional for her to handle.

'Katie is coming over; we're going into Watford,' she said.

'Can't she come another time? I have things to sort out.' Jim didn't want to face his sister in law tonight. She would have an opinion - and it would be a Welsh one.

'What things?'

'Just some things that belonged to my Dad. I have them in the boot of my car; I was hoping you could help me.'

'I want to go out with Katie. We want to go to the Odeon. I've been looking forward to going all day.'

'Help me out first; just give me half an hour.'

He called David to help him empty the boot. It had started to rain again, but David was excited to look at all the things his father had brought back from the hospital. He helped carry in the four pictures which he leant against the wall in the hallway. The suitcase and the laundry box of papers were placed on the table in the lounge.

'What's all this, Jim?' Morfydd opened the suitcase,

which was full of clothes. 'It stinks; you need to burn it. Take it out to the yard.'

'I don't feel right getting rid of it. Maybe Patrick will want to go through it. Can't you wash it?'

But Morfydd didn't want those things in her house Sniffing and pulling a face, she pulled out some old vests and threw them into the fire. She was going to have her own way even if she had to fight him all night.

'For Christ's sake, woman, leave off, leave it!'

It was seven o'clock and Morfydds's sister Katie was banging at the front door. She marched up the hallway, making a little joke with young David about his messy hair. The atmosphere was in the room was so tense that she knew at once to keep her mouth tightly closed. Morfydd was mid tantrum and it was difficult to speak.

'Katie,' said Jim, 'will you witness what I have to say? Morfydd you can burn my father's clothes if it makes you happy but his pictures and this box of papers and letters goes up in the loft. I don't want you or anyone else to touch them and I don't want anyone to look at them – and that's the end of it. '

'Dad,' David appeared in the doorway, 'come and look at these pictures.'

Jim stormed into the hallway where David had put the four paintings along the wall.

'This was between them, Dad.' David held out a note pad and a brown envelope.

'They're war bonds,' said Jim after shuffling through them. He handed the notepad back to David and told him to put it back in the laundry box. He tucked the envelope inside his jacket.

'Fetch the ladder from the yard, David. We need it to get into the loft.'

2. Delusional Insanity, 1940

Ada Quinn and Dennis Scully Jnr. had allowed Harry enough time to pack a suitcase and pick up a selection of his paintings. His studio in Lillington Street near Victoria did not contain much apart from a mattress, a few old blankets and his paints. A wooden table with empty beer bottles and tobacco tins sat under the poorly painted sash window.

Harry quickly gathered up his papers and letters and stuffed them into the bottom of a laundry box. He put his notes and the envelope safely between his paintings and tied some string around them. He threw the few clothes he had into the open brown suitcase on the floor. Looking at his pots, paints and brushes he blinked and wiped his brow with the edge of his sleeve. Ada Quinn was standing in the doorway, with her hands on her hips; she still had her key and today she was brazen enough to use it. She had poked her nose around his studio a number of times in the past few months.

'If Ted finds out I am here, Harry, he'll go barmy with the both of us - your woman cleared off then did she?'

It amused Ada Quinn to think that Harry had another woman in his life but just a few years ago she would have been insanely jealous. She had a violent streak, which could match Harry's at the best of times.

The years they had spent together living as husband and wife had been turbulent ones. Determined now to put that time behind her, she took control of the situation. She was not going to let Harry put any of them at risk, not now they had money in the bank.

'Come on Harry, looks like she's not coming back.'

Harry gazed out of the window.

'Mary wanted to go back to Portsea,' he said. 'She always loved it there. We were all going there, Patrick too - but the war ...' He tried to read the expression on Ada Quinn's face. It was her poker face and Harry had seen it before when she lied.

'I know what happened to those other women, Ada. That's why we're going in the car isn't it?'

'Move yourself Harry. Come on love, no sense in crying about it now. We've done this before, eh? More times than I care to remember. You're lucky that Dennis is going along with this. Cavanagh has a car waiting for you outside. He's going to get you some help lovey,'

Harry glanced out of the window. There was not much use in saying any more. They had beaten him and now he worried that his life was in danger. Would it be his body the police would find floating in the cut the next morning? Did Goldwater have a bullet ready to shoot his brains out as he had heard him say over that damn transmitter?

On the street, he saw Cavanagh sitting in the front of the car. Well, at least he could trust the old aristocrat, whatever the others said about him. Cavanagh had never let him down. He had supplied the collection of paint pots and brushes that littered Harry's room. *The Aristocrat believed in me* I larry told himself, and his exhibition at the Royal Academy had been a success even though there was a war on. But Ada Quinn and Dennis Scully Jnr., how could he trust them? They had both crossed the line; they had murdered his wife; they had said so. Harry was still trying to come to terms with that.

Evelyn Anne, the wife he had lost so many years ago. The thought of her gone for good now was more than he could bear.

Dusk gripped the sky and played mockingly with the shadows. It was nearly blackout and they had little time before the towns and the countryside would need to follow the law to the letter and put out the lights. They had to be swift or they would be stranded for the night.

It was too dangerous to stay out in the pitch black, not from falling bombs but from risk of arrest or from driving into a ditch without the help of headlights. The black, shiny Rolls Royce had driven slowly up the long, dark lane from Horton, the leaf-laden branches helping to camouflage the dipped headlights. There had been no bombs dropped on this part of Surrey, which was comforting. The Rolls held the road calmly and smoothly. It belonged to a bygone age of Somerset lanes and stately homes. Now it was winding its way to a different house of grandeur, West Park Mental Hospital stood defiantly awaiting their arrival.

*

Dennis Scully Jnr. and Ada Quinn sat either side of Harry in the back of the car. Scully peered out of the window. Tired of trying to keep Harry out of trouble, he wanted an end to this. He could think of a better way to handle the problem - and finish it for good; with his old man now out of the way, there was no reason why they had to go to all this trouble. But his boss had insisted. *Silly old fool* he thought, but who was he to question Alf Goldwater's motives, Alf Goldwater, who reigned using terror and violence although now his power was diminishing. Dennis Scully Jnr. was disappointed with himself that he had not found the courage to stand up to him. Alf Goldwater had told him that Harry would toe the line, but

Dennis Scully Jnr. knew he was wrong; there was too much money involved and Harry could put them all in danger. The only good thing about this stupid war was that the authorities had plenty of other issues to occupy their minds - Hitler's Nazis posed more of a threat than Alf Goldwater's gang.

Dennis Scully Jnr. glanced at Harry. Would anyone believe this delusional old drunk? A couple of electric-shock treatments should, hopefully, stop him shouting his mouth off, maybe finish the old bastard for good. One could only hope.

*

Harry gripped the edge of the black worn leather seats as the car pulled up in front of the black-painted doors of the asylum. He took hold of Ada Quinn's hand, which she quickly pulled away. Anything that had existed between them before was undoubtedly over now. She wished Harry would let go. She had paid her dues many times. The child in Harry clung to her skirt despite the way she had treated him in the past; he always came back crying and whining. She wanted no more to do with him. Ada Quinn had a new man in her life, a proper husband, and a certificate to prove it. Life was looking up. Harry Cornell was a liability. The sooner this was over, she thought, the better it was for all of them.

Philip Cavanagh sat beside his chauffeur, his aristocratic manner kept the others in their own solitary silence. He felt defeated. Harry had so much going for him but this was the last possible thing Cavanagh could do to keep him out of trouble. The war made other pressing demands and Cavanagh could not let any scandal attach itself to his reputation and ruin his chance of doing his duty for his country. He had been called on to work as a camouflage artist and he knew he could be of great use.

Well respected within the Art world, Cavanagh had helped many struggling artists show their talents in the right places. He enjoyed the challenge but these creative types were likely to go haywire on occasions. It was in their nature and it was this that appealed to him and had encouraged him to dabble on the edge of risk. His association with Harry was now too risky. He was in too deep and he needed to get rid of the problem and this asylum seemed the most correct and humane way to go about it. Harry had been in and out of these places before. Once he was inside, no one would ever question the delusions of an insane artist. Poor Harry, Philip Cavanagh really did have a soft spot for him and had worked hard to encourage his work. The exhibition at the Royal Academy had been a positive achievement. Not many of Philip Cavanagh's protégés had gained such recognition. What a waste, all the work and support he had given Harry before the war, and for what? How had he let it come to this?

Dr. Howard, stood at the top of the steps with two charge nurses in short white jackets beside him; he had been expecting them. He stretched out his arm to shake the hand of his old school chum Philip Cavanagh. They had studied at Harrow together.

After a short conversation Dr. Howard ushered the charge nurses towards Harry to help him from the car. Harry clutched at the paintings that he had tied together with string. Scully, meanwhile, casually placed the battered suitcase on the step then got back into the car.

'You should have just kept your mouth shut, Harry.' Ada Quinn gave him a cold and lifeless hug at the door. She leaned forward. 'Nobody will believe you here,' she whispered into his ear.

Harry felt sick at the smell of her cheap perfume which clung to the hair of the grey fox-fur she had draped around her shoulders. She assumed it gave her a look of affluence. One of the charge nurses took Harry's paintings and his eyes filled with tears.

'How long can you keep him here?' asked Cavanagh.

Strange question, thought Dr. Howard, and one not usually asked by a worried relative. Cavanagh was no relative and neither were the others; that was pretty obvious. When Howard asked them about Harry's next of kin, they said he was all alone in the world, but then Ada said she thought he had a son somewhere in Ireland - and then she said she could be mistaken. Well, Dr. Howard knew a sick man when he saw one.

'Our patients leave our care when and only when they are able to care for themselves,' he said although he had no idea how long he was going to be able to keep Harry. Cavanagh shook his hand and walked back to the car, saying he would be extremely grateful if Dr. Howard could take care of the poor chap. It was all a bit odd. There was more to this situation than they were letting on.

'Ada!' Harry called as she opened the car door, 'tell Patrick I'm here. Please write to him.'

Harry walked into the darkness of the asylum and the two charge nurses gripped his arms and guided him down a long, grey corridor. The car drew away, none of them looking back and all of them thinking this was the best action they could have taken.

*

'They're nice paintings, Harry. You're a talented artist.'
'I like to paint - I'm an engraver too.'
'Where are the places in this picture?'
'Near my home, I used to go there a lot.'

'You fond of the country, Harry?'

'I was - before the war.'

'The Great War, Harry? Did you fight in the Great War?'

'You know I did. I fought in France, I was a driver.'

'What do you remember?'

'Nothing, it was a lost cause.'

'Can you try?'

'Why should I? You wouldn't believe me anyhow.'

'Why do you say that?'

'I told them so many times. I wrote letters.'

'What happened, Harry?'

'If you want to know, the War turned me mad, it made me sick in my head. I was injured and they left me. They didn't care about me.'

'And after?'

'They took the piss.'

'Who did Harry?'

'You know, bleeding government, them at the top- They messed with me, they all did, and left me out to dry I forget the war.'

'What's in your box?'

'Nothing.'

'You don't' want to tell me?'

'If I tell you, you'll finish me off.'

'It's not my job to do that; I'm here to help you.'

'Why? Did they tell you I needed help?'

'Help is what I do.'

'Why would you believe me – about the box and everything?'

'I could try to understand, Harry

'Only the bits you want to understand. Bet they told you it's all lies, that everything I say is barmy?'

'Did *who* tell me Harry?'

'I don't want to say anything, not to you, not to anyone; you won't believe me. You're one of them, you won't listen. We'll all go to prison. I don't want to hang for something that *they* did. I never did any of it; they blackmailed me. I won't answer any of your stupid questions. Just leave me alone! Get the hell out of my way! You fucking know what they did - they told you, didn't they?'

Dr. Howard leaned forward, resting his chin on his clasped hands. Harry waited for him to answer. The silence was painful.

'What did they tell you - what?!'

'They told me you're delusional, Harry. Your friends believe you're having a rough time and you're ill.'

'I know what I am and I shouldn't be here.'

'How much do you drink, Harry?'

Harry looked at the floor. *God I need a drink.* 'Bastards!' he muttered under his breath. Raising his arms high above his head, he stood up sharply and his chair fell back onto the floor. Howard leaned forward and blew his whistle for assistance. Harry was already hitting the wall with his fists when two orderlies pushed their way into the room. They restrained him and forced him onto a bed. Harry received his first drugs - to calm him down and silence him.

Howard returned to his office to fill in the forms that would instruct the charge nurses about the treatment that should be administered. Cavanagh had informed him about the patient's artistic talent and his problem with alcohol. The amount of alcohol he had consumed over the years had probably done damage to his brain and he was obviously now delusional. Cavanagh had also told him that Harry was convinced he had suffered from shell shock during WW1. The ministry of pensions had withdrawn his war pension after someone had written to them explaining that his condition was brought on by his mode of life and not his war service. Harry was very resentful and felt trapped into a life of poverty. Cavanagh had explained that Harry also suffered from epileptic fits.

Dr. Howard knew that epilepsy was another condition often brought on by shell shock. He decided that Harry should be treated for epilepsy and delusional insanity and filled out the forms accordingly. Harry's suitcase and pictures were by his desk. He wrote a note and attached it to the handles of the case with a piece of string from the desk drawer. He called for an orderly to carry Harry's things to the store where they kept patients' belongings.

Once he was finished, Dr. Howard stood in the doorway to his office and took a cigarette from a small, brass case he kept in his top pocket. He did not really fancy one; they made his throat sore. He wished he could stop smoking but now was not the time to give up, not now with the War and everything. All was quiet around him; his patients had no idea of the uncertainty going on outside the walls of the Asylum. They had their own wars to fight within their heads. A struggle for sanity; he feared their pain was more than he would ever understand. Breakthroughs were being made in mental health but the war had halted any advances in psychiatry. He would have to wait, as would the patients lined up in the wards, waiting for Hitler to be dealt with first. Would the world ever get back to normal?

He lit up and walked outside into the darkness. Air-raid sirens started their primitive wail and he stubbed the cigarette out on to the ground. He must do his best to help the over-worked staff lead the patients to the shelter and be fitted with gas masks. The hospital was heavily burdened with patients admitted from nearby hospitals that had given up their buildings for wartime activities. Last week they had moved four hundred patients from Horton in just two days.

Dr. Howard was on a treadmill and it was going like the clappers. His patients welcomed him into their world of insanity, amused and abused with the madness of humanity in the clutches of war. But what should he do with Harry Cornell? The new arrival played on his conscience. One more crazy man. Would he be missed? Would anyone care? *War, or no war, these are trying times and 'needs must'* he murmured under his breath as he helped the first of the patients across the grounds to the shelter.

3. The TB Ward.

'Good morning Harry, did you sleep better last night? I hope you're ready for some fresh air. It's a perfect day.'

Nurse Bridget McCarthy tucked in Harry's sheet and smoothed her hands over the wrinkles in his blanket. She always tried to appear cheerful in the morning; it was a lesson she had learnt as a child. 'It will bring luck to your day, Bridget,' her mother would say and the sound of her little voice was instilled in the back of Nurse Bridget McCarthy's mind. Her mother now rested neatly in a quiet graveyard in Tipperary, a million miles from Epsom, yet that little voice was always clear in Nurse Bridget McCarthy's mind. She missed her brothers and cousins but not her Irish life of poverty, damp houses and wet country lanes.

London was a big city; it made her feel part of a much bigger family. Her patients were her next of kin now. She had never found the right man to settle down with and dedicate her life to; she never had any desire to be a mother and raise children; her job was everything. Her concern over her patients care was next to godliness and if it had not been for her tireless questioning about the reasons for faith of the family priest in Ireland, she might have been swayed to become a nun.

She was portly and fifty years old with neat, brown, curly, bobbed hair. She smiled down at Harry. She had washed his face with carbolic soap and a warm damp flannel and had brushed back the small amount of thinning hair he had left on his head. It was her morning ritual. She produced a thermometer and Harry obediently parted his dry lips. He could still admire her smile even though her clinical mask hid her mouth. It made him happy to know she was smiling at him. He remembered the way her teeth, which were a little crooked, shaped her smile, pushing her cheeks upwards into a cheeky squint of the eyes. Her friendly face beamed down on him, her Irish accent warmed her voice. Harry smelled flowers whenever she was near to him.

Nurse McCarthy was fond of Harry. He would flirt with her on occasions, even though he could barely force a grin or a wink, and she was happy to flirt back; she knew he was flirting when his eyes took on a gaze that gave her the desire to give him a hug. Of course she would not be allowed to succumb to such behavior, not in her profession.

Occasionally some of the old Harry would surface, a typical rant would emerge and up would go his arms followed by a bout of aggressive shouting. Some of the other patients were happy to coax him on. These little incidents were happening quite regularly so she kept a close eye on him. This morning was peaceful fortunately and she hoped it would stay that way. She had overslept and Matron had caught her coming in late. Nurse McCarthy had been at this job for as long as the middle-class, starched, insipid Matron. She was a competent nurse and it irritated her to get a reprimand, even though she knew there were rules and Matron had to be seen to run them all with a strict hand. The hospital needed a strict regime in order to cope with so many patients.

*

West Park Mental Asylum, a huge Victorian red-bricked building, stood silent, like a sniper waiting for your sudden move. Staff and patients shuffled in and out of wards; there was no escape. It commanded your respect; it knew everything about you. There was a file on everything: what time you should eat, what time you should pee. They wanted to know how many brothers and sisters you had and if you had slept in your own room as a child. They asked you your mother's maiden name and where you were stationed during the Great War and the last war. The hospital was your mother; it owned you. Buckets continuously clanked in corridors and patients, both men and women, with eyes like owls washed in pools of transparency, shuffled in slippers unaware of where they were going or why.

The TB ward had fourteen men and eight women patients, separated by a small corridor. All the staff wore white coats and masks. Patients cared not why the TB had come to them but all could vaguely remember a time before it had infested their lungs – though few remembered the time before they came to West Park. Some had been admitted at a very young age, abandoned by families not wishing to be tainted by an insane relative or by a young girl impregnated out of wedlock. They quickly became institutionalized. What chance of a memory from so long ago, blocked out with time? The hospital was their home and to everyone else who was sane, did they really know anything of any other world?

The Asylum was suffering from a shortage of good nurses. It was a problem for the hospital; so many men had been called up for national service that there was added strain for those on the home front. Nurse McCarthy had been doing many extra shifts. She was proud to be in demand but resentful of the lack of gratitude of her employers. Dr. Howard the medical superintendent hardly gave her a nod when she passed him in the corridor. At least, her patients were in great need of her and it made her happy that she could make a difference to the final part of their existence, for that reason only, she was able to keep her composure in check. She knew her place - but only just.

Nurse McCarthy wheeled Harry in his bed towards the terrace at the end of the ward, the winter sun struggling to produce enough light to drench the terrace and bring warmth to her shivering patients. This was one of her first jobs of the morning, after emptying the bedpans and changing sheets. There was usually a porter around to help her move the patients outside but today she was alone. One by one she pushed the beds outside, humming and chattering to the patients in an attempt to keep their spirits up - and hers too.

The treatment for TB was fresh air and lots of it. Harry could endure the cold but today he would not raise a smile. He would have liked to complain but there was really no reason to. There was nothing left to hurt him anymore. His breathlessness caused him to cough. He tightened his face muscles and pretended to sleep. Maybe sleep would come, he thought as he lowered his tired eyelids. He coughed again. Nurse McCarthy placed her hand on his forehead,

'There now, my sweet. The tea trolley'll be here soon and you can have a warm drink, a nice cuppa in the sunshine, eh?'

Harry gripped her hand, pushing it away from his head.

'What is it Harry?'

'They know it's me – they're coming to get me.'

'Who's coming, Harry. Who's coming to get you? Is your son coming?'

'Patrick? - No.' Harry tried to lift himself.

'Harry look, the sun's out. It's going to be a lovely day'

'They have my pictures. They took them all: my money, my blanket, my Mother, and William ...'

But Nurse McCarthy had moved on to another patient.

*

Tommy Carter pushed the mop around within the bucket and pushed the bucket through the wards swinging doors forcefully as if he was driving the motorcycle he was always dreaming about. The width of his grin framed his yellow teeth as he giggled, swishing the grey mop from side to side in an ungainly dance of self-importance. He spotted Harry and moved toward Harry's bed. Checking to see if Nurse McCarthy was watching, he pulled a cigarette from a packet of Woodbines and pushed the end between Harry's dry and parched lips.

'Hey Harry! Got this for you.'

Harry's gaunt eyes delved into Tommy Carter's face, unaware of the cigarette, which fell onto his chin, and there was Nurse McCarthy, muttering something about her back being turned for just one minute. Tommy Carter turned and left, taking his grin with him through the white-painted doors. Harry watched him through the windowpanes and the boy pulled a face. He wanted to make Harry laugh but Harry no longer had the strength. *Be careful, Tommy boy*, thought Harry, *you know what this leads to.*

*

Before being stricken down with TB, Harry had taken Tommy Carter under his wing. He had taken pleasure in knowing that he looked up to him and told him stories of when he was a soldier and how they sent him to France in 1915.

The day Harry had been admitted to West Park Asylum, there was another war raging outside of the Victorian red-brick walls and not very far away either. London was only seven days from the start of the Blitz and the life of the average Londoner was about to change drastically. Five years after that, fifteen-year-old Tommy Carter had been dropped off at the Asylum because his mother had run off with an American soldier and she had no wish to look after her son due to his manic behavior. The asylum gave him security and let her off the hook. When the war was over, she walked away without a care. Tommy Carter had been relieved. He disliked his mother and would shake his head and put his hands over his ears whenever she was mentioned.

Harry and Tommy Carter had got in the habit of walking around the front lawn at West Park together. They made up pranks to play on the charge nurses and other patients. Childish, as they were, these pranks, they made Harry laugh and feel boyish again. Unfortunately, Tommy Carter would often go too far and end up being constrained. The charge nurses, losing patience, would get angry with them both.

Harry knew how to steer clear of trouble but the boy always ended up getting punished. Harry's heart went out to him when, sometimes, three doctors would hold him down, attempting to calm him. Harry would pace up and down nearby with his eyes facing the floor, hands deep in the pockets of his ill-fitting trousers that were frayed and filthy.

'Wasn't his fault,' he would murmur. 'Tommy's a good kid, leave him be.'

His sweaty hands would fumble nervously, deep in his pockets, then he would pull them out to wipe his eyes and the stinging sweat would make him angry. Sitting on a wooden bench outside the ward he would rock back and forth.

'Not his fault,' he would say, over and over. 'Good boy, Tommy, stay calm.'

But Tommy Carter was a schizophrenic and his brutal treatment descended on him as if it was a punishment. The scared little boy within him was confused by this. He looked for a glimpse of kindness but it never came. He knew what came next. Stripped to the waist and feeling drowsy, he would look around the cold, sterile hospital room and at the fat fingers of the doctor as he cleaned the shiny metal instruments and handed them one by one to a nurse, whose cold, grey eyes would peer over the white mask that covered her mouth. Most of the nurses who assisted with this treatment struggled to make eye contact with the patient, aware of their gaze, their scared eyes, frantic and piercing, desperate for a kind face or a reassuring look. The nurses felt them digging for some compassion as their own eyes wavered to avoid the patients' eyes at all costs. Tommy Carter would watch closely as a nurse laid the cold, metal instruments neatly side-by-side in the tray on a trolley beside the bed. Two male charge nurses would add constraints to his arms and over his forehead. His big, round eyes would flicker and roll. He knew what was coming; he knew what happened next.

'Don't let them put the metal in your head,' he had told Harry in case Harry should suffer the same treatment. 'When they put it in your head your brain does a dance, but there's no music, Harry, only a lot of rumbling and then there's thunder and it all goes black until the lightening comes and wakes you and the rain comes through your eyes.'

Harry had seen the marks the doctors made on Tommy
Carter's sweaty forehead and it made him mad. He always got
mad at injustice.

'Tommy's a good lad, you have no right. You leave that boy,
he's a good soldier.'

He would pace up and down, trying to find the right
words to spurt out to the hospital staff. There had been no
need for Tommy Carter to explain because Harry knew what
they were doing; they had done it to him when he first came
to the asylum. It had messed further with his head. When
they did it back then, Harry would hold his breath until he
passed out. For those early treatments, they would insert
metal rods through his eye sockets. It had taken four charge
nurses to hold him down. There was no anesthetic.

He had never forgotten it.

*

Tommy Carter was clanking his bucket down the
corridor. His trousers, tied together with string, were made
for somebody much shorter and his thin ankles were exposed
above his socks and slippers. Nurse McCarthy had pulled her
mask away from her mouth. It sat under her chin as she spoke
to one of the charge nurses who nodded as if in agreement and
made his way towards where Tommy was walking.

Nurse McCarthy returned to Harry's bedside and picked
up the cigarette.

'Don't punish him, nurse. He's a good boy. Please, he was
just being kind.'

She smiled down and he tried to concentrate on his
breathing. He drifted into sleep with the sun shining on

his face. He remembered the sun, warm and shining. If he took himself back there, back to a sunny day on Brighton beach, he might find some peace.

Hmm, I so love the smell of the sea. Mum is pulling me along the footpath by the beach and telling me to stop dragging my heels. But I need to breathe.

'Stop puffing, Harry, stop your dawdling.' She is shouting at me.

Mum wants to get back home. And she's so mad, mad at me for running off. My knees are red like raspberries, all bobbly and bruised.

'I can't breathe, Mum, I cannot breathe. It hurts.' I'm scratching at her wrist with the fingers of my other hand. 'Mum let go!'

'Your father will beat you, Harry, if he finds out.'

I'm sniffing and lifting my chin.

'The sea - can you smell it, Mum? Why does it smell like that, where does the smell come from? Is it from the fishes?'

4. Mary Cornell

The English Channel had its own unique odor and it wrapped Mary Cornell in a security blanket brought from her childhood. She had forgotten the smell of the sea but then a small and transitory moment of nostalgia had painted her a quick glance and she saw herself as a child again on the beach of the Isle of White. Sadly she would never share this with her son Harry. He needed discipline, not molly coddling. There was a bond between them but Harry was a live wire. Trouble found him and stuck to him like tacky glue; it infuriated her that he questioned everything.

'Watch your tongue' his father would say repeatedly but Harry was always determined to have the last word, or at least until he suffered a lash from his dad's belt. Her eldest boy, William, never got lashed but William never needed to have the concluding word. William stood above Harry and refused to bail him out of any trouble. She understood that little brothers could be annoying and it was not fair to ask William to amuse his younger brother and keep him occupied but William's disinterest inevitably lead to Harry running off and sulking.

She would watch him walk, sullenly, to the bottom of Hannover Street then dare himself to venture further. Time appeared to be of little importance to him on these occasions and his siblings had to be sent out to bring him home for his meals. She worried that Harry did not seem to care.

She knew he thought he would be in trouble anyhow. He must be on that beach again skimming stones, she would murmur to herself and that was exactly where she would find him, watching the people wandering free of troubles and hanging around with other groups of children on the beach, building mounds of white pebbles and kicking them over. Harry watched them all.

Be my friend and I will show you how to skim pebbles on the water

Be my friend, or I will spit on the sand and kick you.

Please be my friend

Harry had kicked the painted metal green barrier and pulled himself up on the first rung, filling his cheeks with enough saliva he proceeded to spit as far as he could.

Mary Cornell would catch sight of him and shake her head: Harry the most troublesome of all her children and the one she would always worry over. She would grasp her son's tuft of red hair, shouting:

'Harry Cornell! Get home! You can forget any thoughts of supper.'

Mary found it difficult to physically punish her son of which Harry was thankfully aware but as they reached the gate in Hannover Street and she marched him up the garden path and down their hall to the kitchen, she could never entirely be sure what mood Harry's father would be greeting them with.

*

Mary Cornell was a strong and proud woman; her sparrow-like stature was not to be judged as weak; she had a will of iron and ideas that some thought were above her station. She had chosen her husband, Henry Cornell, because he too had commanding views of morality. After a sheltered upbringing on the Isle of White she had ventured to the mainland and made her home in Brighton. There she could bring up her family, secure in the knowledge that there would be plenty of work for her two sons and she would find strong sailor husbands for her growing daughters. Brighton had a thriving community of fisherman and sailors. She was already mapping out her children's lives. Henry sailed along with this plan and would only air his views to her when someone stood out of line.

Unfortunately for Harry, learning to conform to his mother's aspirations was proving to be a difficult task. He was a bright boy with deep, piercing, grey eyes. Unsure of what was expected from him, he would spend hours dreaming up stories in his head. His elder brother, William, although resembling him in looks, had an edge that Harry did not possess. In the eyes of his parents, William could do no wrong. As with most families of that time, the first son was showered with affection and all those who were born after could only grapple for a bit of the share.

The five daughters who came after the two sons would be groomed to go into service and then hopefully marry sailors and they accepted their destinies without question, but Harry was the dreamer. He started to rebel at an early age, and Mary Cornell struggled to understand what was needed to bring him in line. She did not realize that the one place Harry could lose himself, where no one could outshine him was the creative world where he could draw pictures.

There was little money for paper and pencils so Harry had to use any medium he could find. Unknown to Mary Cornell he stole a pencil from the counter at the local corner shop and took the chalk that rolled under his teacher's chair. A new world was opening up for him but it was one Mary Cornell would never understand. Life was hard and she wanted her son to conform. Harry was a good student and wanted to learn but he had his own way of achieving things. She grew tired of hearing that he had taken yet another lashing from his teacher for doing things in his own way.

'Look at my letters, Mum.' He showed her, rubbing his red eyes, a small slate board that he had stuffed in his school sack. She would only nod and paid little attention even though he craved her approval. She had babies to attend to and floors to scrub.

Mary Cornell clutched at the ribbon under her chin from the satin bonnet perched on the side of her thin face. Tired of hearing bad opinions of her son, she reluctantly agreed with Harry to say nothing to his father and was relieved when Harry announced he had found a job and was finished with school for good.

5. Hanover Street Art

Harry lay lifeless as he looked towards the long, paned windows in the isolation ward. Across the lawns towards the red-brick building of the wards in G. Wing he could see groups of young orderlies gathered together, enjoying a cigarette in their breaks and talking about whatever young lads talked about now the war was over. Was it their girlfriends, the football game on Saturday or war stories? Did they have any or had they blanked them just as he had tried to do? He wondered if young Tommy Carter was having his breakfast. He thought he could hear the clanking of dishes in the dining room and the chattering voices of the inmates, some demanding attention, others standing in line, chattering to themselves and rubbing their fingers together as if they were rolling pills between their fingers and thumbs.

Once he had stood in a similar nauseating line then, year after year he had stood in this one, rifle slung over his aching shoulder, holding a metal plate, greasy in his hand waiting for the mash potato to be slapped in the middle and covered in gravy. The smell was the same. The pain in his thigh was the same - except there was no rifle in the Asylum.

The food stank: cabbage and boiled potatoes, braised beef on Monday's, cold custard and soggy coconut sponge. Harry was agitated by the chattering and the noise. Only now he wished he could be back there. *What a crazy notion!* The drugs and the treatment he had received over the years had taken their toll but the treatment for his mental disorder had now been stopped, there was hardly any point. The only thing they gave him now was antibiotics and fresh air. There was little point in a sleeping pill or any other kind of sedative that would send him into drug-induced drowsiness.

He finally understood that his life was hanging on a thread. Without the medication, his mind was clearing and the anger he had carried around with him all these years could no longer manifest itself in his head. Wafting wistfully in and out of consciousness, his thoughts drifted back in time.

Nurse McCarthy walked past the end of his bed. He lifted his finger and pointed.

'Look - there are mountains and trees!'

'Of course there are, my sweet.'

'Well, bloody look then.'

*

HANOVER STREET, BRIGHTON 1888

'I'm intrigued, mesmerized, captivated! The little chipped stones I'm kicking over the cobbled pavement have made scratches into the sides of the larger cobbles. I'm crouching down and peering closely, rubbing my eyes and then running my grubby little fingers over the images I've formed by the scratches. I'm squinting my eyes and see a face of an old man, then a dog. It's magical as I watch how the images change form the further I stand away from them. As the light changes, so does the image. I stand staring. I'm floating over hillsides. I walk another two paces backwards. In my mind the grey of the stone is now bright green and in between them run rivers, on their way to great white cliffs, standing proud over the coastline.

I think I can hear my mum. Yes, she's shouting from the house and my imagination is interrupted. She's calling me to come in but I'm ignoring her. I don't want to go inside. I'm happy here and locked in my moment. I'm not listening to her.

In my hand I feel the rough edge of a chipped pebble. I run the hard side along our front wall. It makes an uneven mark in the red brick as it scratches into the surface. The line is turning pink. I like that. I'm gripping the pebble tighter and making small sharp upward scratches. They are getting longer as I become more confident as to where I scratch and now I'm walking backwards again in the road. I just see scratches so I'm screwing up my eyes again until they're almost closed and now I can see them - mountains and trees and I'm aware of myself smiling at my masterpiece.

Not bad for a seven-year-old.

'Mum!' I'm shouting enthusiastically, Mum!' I'm jumping up and down on the road. 'Look!'

I want her to like my picture. She's standing on to the front step wondering what the commotion is about. She's clutching her arms tightly around baby Margaret Ellen, who is crying incessantly. Margaret Ellen's cheeks are reddened as she sobs.

'Harry Cornell'! Mum shrieks, 'what have you done to me wall?'

She's clamping her free hand around the tufts of hair on the top of my head and is pulling me inside the doorway.

'You mustn't scribble on the wall, Harry! Go and get a scrubbing brush.'

But I haven't scribbled; I've drawn mountains and trees. I'm crying in my head. I don't understand why Mum can't see them. My head is hurting. She says I'm a bad boy.

'You're a bad boy Harry Cornell.'

I'm returning with the scrubbing brush but I chuck it at a thin dog asleep in front of the house next door. The dog whimpers as the dirty bristles dig and scratch into the side of its wretched and boney jaw. It's looking at me confused and questioning as I am yelling loudly at its stupid face. It retreats back inside the hallway of the house. Serves it right for being there. I let the dog get it, the dog deserves to be punished and it's all her fault, my Mother's.

'Harry, where's your brother William?' My father has a croaky voice but it doesn't stop him shouting at me. 'What are you doing inside boy, go and find your brother.'

I don't know why it has to be me that must go to find him. I don't know why it has to be me, he's yelling at. I'm standing outside our house in Hannover Street, my brother William is talking to a bunch of boys who stand there as if they own our road. They're bigger than me but I don't care.

'Dad says I have to play with you.'

William is pushing me back through the gate.

'Go and find your own friends.'

I hear them talking about going down to the pier. They love to hang out down there. They're planning to go under the pier and throw and skim stones into the sea. Why can't they take me? I want to go with them, I hate the other boys, William is my brother not theirs, I want my brother. I'm demanding they take me.

'Dad says I have to go with you! Take me!' I'm stamping my foot. 'I can throw stones as good as you. I can throw better and higher than you.' I'm shouting, but William doesn't care about me not when he can show off with his mates. He'll be different at bedtime when there's nobody else to make jokes with and we lie awake in the dark making up ghost stories. He likes me then, when I share the stash of toffees hidden in the tin under my mattress.

'Get lost, Harry!' One of the boys is shouting. 'You'll be a nuisance. My mum says you are a badun. Go away.'

'Will!' I'm shouting, 'I'll tell Dad you did something and you'll get a hiding.' I stick out my tongue and spit at him.

Will is looking hard at me

'Go play somewhere else, Harry. If you can't say something nice about someone - don't say anything.'

I so hate him. If I go back home, Dad will shout at me again so I start to throw stones in the road. I'm watching them skim amongst the cobbles until one of them flips back and hits me on the shin. It stings like hell as I rub it. I turn and now I'm running all the way to the end of Hanover Street. I'm rubbing and trying to run at the same time.

I get to the bottom of the hill and sit on the wall outside of the Little Fox Pub. There I am, waiting, killing time, when I see a man fall from the doorway and he's stumbling into the road. He's trying to get on to his cart and I'm laughing as I watch him struggle to walk in a straight line. He attempts three times to grab at the reins but loses his balance and falls down. He'll be in trouble when he gets home. I'm imagining his wife hitting him around the head. I'm laughing out loud. Here I am - all on my own, just me and a man out of his face and a scraggy old horse. He's dropped a penny. I watch it falling, catching the light from the afternoon sun as it spins towards the ground and bounces on the pebbles. Bright and gleaming, it's only me who can see it. I don't take my eyes off it. That penny is mine. I patiently watch him as he makes a calling sound to his horse and finally manages to lift himself onto the cart and pull away. As soon as he's out of sight I go and retrieve the penny. Nobody's around. I'm holding it tightly. Uncurling my fingers, I'm looking at it in the middle of my grubby hand. Luck is on my side for a change and I'm wondering what to do with it.

'A bottle of beer for me Dad please,' I'm asking the landlord who takes my penny and laughs. 'It's for his morning pint.'

'You'll need a bit more than a penny, lad, but tell your dad he can pay the rest later.'

I'm pleased with myself. I decide to take the bottle of beer home and give it to my Dad. The door's still open and I stand there catching my breath. He's shouting. I can hear him shouting at my mum.

'Harry needs to toughen up and mix with the other boys. You're too soft with him woman! You don't see William behaving like that.'

Dad is pacing up and down on the wooden boards of our scullery at the end of the hall. Mum's trying to carry buckets into the back yard. I don't care, what they say, I really don't. Margaret is sitting at the bottom of the staircase crying so I wink at her.

Mum is telling Dad about me drawing on the wall and Dad is saying I'm turning into a Nancy Boy. He says she should knock all of that nonsense out of me. I hate my Dad for saying that and I turn and sit on the wall outside and I'm drinking the beer. I'm drinking all of it so I will not be a Nancy boy. Maybe he'll like me as much as he likes William. I'm drinking all of the beer and I'm feeling dizziness in my head. I'm feeling sick and I'm falling back onto the path. I'm lying there with my arms at my side and the world is spinning above my head.

I don't care; I don't care at all.

*

WEST PARK 1952

The sheets on the bed felt clammy again. Harry tried to push himself into a sitting-up position. The sheets were sticking to him; he could smell his own sweat. Tommy Carter was looking through the side window. He had a cigarette and was teasing Harry because he knew he could not have one. *How I would love a smoke* thought Harry and raised a half-winded smile. *How the hell am I going to get a fag? Just one.* But sleep took over.

*

My knuckles are killing me and I'm pulling my sleeve down over my hand so mum won't see them. Where is she? I'm wondering. Dad's tobacco tin and Swan Vesta matches are on the table in the kitchen. 'Go on Harry,' says the voice in my head, 'it'll be a lark'. Aware of Mum's voice in the yard, I snatch the tobacco. I can roll a cigarette easy.

Next I'm on the beach. The beach is the best place in the world. I'm sitting like a grown man enjoying his tobacco on a sunny day, smiling to myself, glad I've done it.

'What you doing here, Harry?' Uncle Will, the husband of my Aunt Sarah, is looking down on me. I shove Dad's tobacco tin and the cigarette under the stones.

'I said, what you doing here? And is that a cigarette you're smoking?' he repeats. Uncle Will is on the beach with some other fishermen. I'm watching the boats and I'm saying to him 'My Mum said I could smoke if I want to.'

The other men are laughing at me and saying things. I push my hands in my pockets and strut towards them, which is difficult over the pebbles.

'How much did this boat cost?' I ask as I run my fingers on the side of their rowing boat. 'Bet you don't catch much fish in it.'

The small group of fishermen are laughing at me. Uncle Will is looking away.

'How old are you?' one is saying.

'Thirteen, and when I grow up I'm going to get a bigger boat than this.' I am pushing my luck.

'Come on, lad,' says the dark-haired man with the pitted face, 'would you like a ride in our small boat?'

They are taking me out on to the choppy water and I cling on tightly to the side and they are grabbing me and tipping me over the side.

'Let go of me, LET GO!' I'm trying to swim but the shock and the freezing water is dragging me under again and again. Now all the salt water is in my mouth and stinging my eyes. They're laughing at me again, as I'm splashing my arms and kicking my legs in a rage. I hate them. I hate them so much. Uncle Will is pulling me out of the icy cold water and dragging me on to the beach.

'Be careful what you say to fishermen Harry. They're not to be messed with, they don't want your cheek, boy.'

I'm turning my head away, I'm so angry and I won't say thank you. I'm not grateful to him. I could have swum to the beach; I didn't need Uncle Will to pull me out and make me look like I couldn't swim. I could have crawled out if I had really wanted to. I could have swum to the beach myself.

WEST PARK

'My knuckles, they're red raw - bastard teacher whacked me'.

Nurse McCarthy glanced over at Harry and watched him rubbing his hands.

'Harry can I help you? What's wrong?'

'He whacked me for the way I wrote my letters, said they were too fancy. I'm not going back there and nobody can make me, I'm finished with school. Mum's happy, I told her I'm working up on the railway. Yeh, Mum's happy.'

Nurse McCarthy walked over towards the bed and took hold of both of his hands.

'You have strong hands Harry.'

'They looked after me those men up at the railway, they looked out for me. I did as I was told and my Mum was proud. I gave her some of my wages. I worked hard and they looked out for me. You had to be careful though. You towed the line, did what they told you to do. Respect. Not like that teacher, I had no respect for him.

5. Clerkenwell War Gangs 1889

Alf Goldwater swung his pickaxe until the sweat dripped onto his black boots. He had recently been released from prison where the courts had sentenced him to one month's hard labour.

He swore blind this would be the last time he got caught. He was mad with himself, mad with the authorities and extremely angry with the people who had reported him to the police. Harry was warned to keep out of his way but young Harry was intrigued.

'So what did you do then?' Harry plucked up the courage to ask.

Harry raised his eyebrows and Alf Goldwater could not help but admire the cheek of the lad. But he did not scare Harry. Alf Goldwater's dark Jewish features captivated him and he felt he had gone up a notch, by being acknowledged with a response. Whilst other workers stayed in their groups, Harry stayed close to the burly but captivating Jew.

Alf Goldwater picked up quickly on Harry's vulnerability and soon had Harry doing favours and running errands for him. Oblivious to the notion of being taken advantage of, Harry took pleasure in boasting to his brother William about his infamous Jewish friend.

'The other men respect him. You have to; he knows loads of people in Brighton and even London. He thinks I've got potential and I could be useful and help him out with things.'

None of this impressed William and the more he showed disinterest the harder Harry would brag about Alf Goldwater. He put him on a pedestal. He saw him not as a Jew or a hard working fellow, but as a giant with an arm of muscle. *Breathe in his air and you are part of his domain.* Harry felt he could belong and would feel protected.

Alf Goldwater, although immune to Harry's enthusiasm, had a charisma that Harry could aspire to. He stood tall and people feared him, but, more than anything else, he told the young, cocky and naive Harry that he had potential. This was recognition that Harry needed so badly and never received from his family

'You stay where you are, Harry,' his father would repeatedly tell him as they stood out in the yard. 'A job on the railways will give future prospects for a young man.' His father leant against the whitewashed wall, amongst the wash pails and drying nappies. Harry sat on the window ledge, his hands in his pockets, desperate to be set free of this prison of advice that suppressed him. His father's words were lost in the smoke from his pipe and floated upwards and over the wall. Mary Cornell made him smoke outside because she didn't like the smell in her small kitchen.

'The railway is a good occupation for a strong lad.' His father coughed to clear the mucus from the back of his throat. But the advice would not lock into the part of Harry's brain that might have been receptive, the part that would put him on the straight but extremely narrow path that he was steering away from. Harry wanted a bigger road, the one that trailed over the hills and far away.

Nevertheless, he was grateful for the pay he received from his first job. When he handed over four shillings to his mother and saw her beam with gratitude it made him glow inside. He craved her affection and, deep down, she saw the good that was in him. *One day I will have enough to make you proud of me,* Harry thought.

Small groups of men were transported along the line between Brighton and London to work on the railway. The route was of interest to Alf Goldwater; he knew people in London and could easily make contact with them. On more than one occasion Harry had been watching him talk to a strange bloke who arrived down one of the lanes near the track. Harry did not recognise this bloke as one of the railway workers He had seen them speak for a couple of minutes before the bloke would jump back on his cart and drive off, back down the lane. It appeared as if the man was giving Alf Goldwater instructions.

'You, Harry - are coming with me,' Alf Goldwater announced one night as they clocked off and walked down Trafalgar Street from the station. 'Tomorrow we're going to stay on the train till we get to London; nobody will notice us.'

A small amount of adrenalin bubbled in the pit of Harry's stomach. Now he was truly one of Alf's boys, although he knew well enough to keep his enthusiasm tucked under control. When the other workers jumped off the carriage midway to repair track at Hayward's Heath, Alf Goldwater and Harry stayed on the train. Green fields and hillsides rolled past them and, cool as he wished to remain, a small smile of exhilaration would occasionally surface on Harry's boyish face. Harry viewed this as a huge adventure. He had never been to London and had no worries about any trouble he was might get himself into. As they left the Victoria Station they were met by a couple of lads with a cart who drove them to a public house in Clerkenwell.

Harry's first impression of London was awe-inspiring, he became full of his own importance just by being in the midst of it. He liked the buzz; London had edge and Harry was soaking it up. He followed Alf Goldwater into the bar followed by the two lads who had been on the cart. They appeared to be older; Harry assumed they must be about seventeen.

Alf Goldwater pushed open the wooden, painted swing-doors. They creaked and Harry pushed them closed. The wood felt sticky, he wiped his hands on his jacket sleeves. The public house was filled with drinkers and stank of stale beer and sweat. The floor was awash in sawdust, chewed fag butts and discarded bottles.

'We need you to help out,' said one of the lads, who had a broken tooth. 'Alf has told me about you.'

'What you want me to do?'

The boy seemed friendly enough. What had Alf Goldwater told him?

'Just follow everyone else.' The lad adjusted his neckerchief revealing a red neck, scratched and sore from an annoying rash.

Harry nodded in agreement. *Hey no questions asked here.* This was better than the railways.

The boy asked Alf Goldwater when the other Brighton boys were coming up.

'They'll be here by seven tonight, and there's more coming later. Do what you're asked, Harry, and you'll do fine.'

Alf Goldwater left the public house. Now Harry was the lone wolf amongst a pack and he didn't want to stand out.

'The name's John Hicky,' said the lad with the broken tooth, 'what's yours?' He passed Harry a bottle of beer. Harry followed Hicky through to the back yard of the public house where a number of youths were gathering. The ground was muddy and trodden with straw; it smelled of damp, stale beer and tobacco. Yet more boys were hunched together along a bench which ran the length of the wall. Some of the lads were joking with each other, as they were playing cards on the top of a barrel.

'Alf says we're to wait here until the others arrive.'

'What's happening?' Harry asked a lad standing on his own.

'There's trouble brewing with the Leather Street lads from across town. They're goin' to make trouble. We need back up; this could get bloody. Not scared are you?'

'Course not.'

This other lad was called George Powell. He and John Hicky were mates and they both came from Clerkenwell. Thin and scrawny, the hair on their heads was shaved thin. Aged only fifteen Harry still towered over them; the sea air had kept him healthy. The two lads had poverty written into the lines on their faces, put there by the beatings and cuts they had collected along the way. Hicky, Harry learned later, came from a particularly rough and roguish family. His grandmother and father were constantly in and out of prisons.

A number of young girls entered the public bar and could be heard giggling. Ungainly and dowdy, they carried sticks and were smoking cigarettes. They started flirting with the landlord at the bar but he seemed to be nervous of his young customers, both the girls as much as the lads. One girl was wearing lipstick and rouge. Harry had never seen a girl that looked like that before and he could not help staring.

More lads came through to the back yard and greeted Hicky who seemed to be the leader. The new arrivals had Irish accents and were cocky and confident, but although Hicky was young and small in stature, he had craziness in his voice and it seemed everyone including the Irish lads was wary of him.

Another lad grabbed Harry's shoulder.

'Harry is it? Just checking. Hicky says you're to stick by me. We're going down to the end of Mount Pleasant. It'll be quite a walk.'

By now, there must have been thirty to forty lads crammed in the back courtyard of the public house brandishing sticks and belts. Harry took off his own belt and put his foot up on one of the chairs so as to look tough. He took a swig of beer from a bottle.

'No problem,' he said.

In the corner, he could hear Hicky talking to Powell.

'Goldwater says to sort the Italian - well and proper. With a bit of luck he should be closing up about now.'

Hicky waved his stick in the air and, with his belt folded in his hand, he whipped it across a bare table. A bottle on the next table rolled on the floor but he ignored it. Why should he care about a bottle on the floor? He looked as if an electric current was running through his bones and out of the end of his fingers, making his shoulders and arms jerk. He was crazy all right. He took a deep breath then lashed his leather belt across the table one more time.

'Ready for a rumpus!' he sang out.

The crowd shouted back then the lads and the group of girls made their way onto the cobbled lane and the Landlord bolted the door behind them with a look of relief.

*

Audrea Barcino was thinking he had done well today selling ice creams from his cart in Mount Pleasant. The street was now empty because it was nearly seven o'clock. He was looking forward to pulling his cart back to his yard. His thoughts were of his wife who would be at home, singing and chopping the tomatoes he had bought in the market that morning.

George Powell came on to the street first, from a side lane. He stood leaning against the wall watching Barcino. Barcino ignored him but when he looked up again there was another group of lads. Hicky and George Cox strolled up to the cart, Harry following.

'Got some *ice cream* for us boys,' Cox mimicked using the Italian accent.

Barcino lowered the lid on his cart.

'Boys you go home. I'm all sold out.'

Hicky lifted the lid and looked into the cart.

'What! You never saved some for us poor working boys.'

Barcino lowered the lid again.

'I am not scared of you bad kids, go home to your mamas.'

Hicky pulled the lid off and threw it into the road. At that moment the girls appeared, enticing the boys on by whistling. Some of the other boys started to kick the lid of the cart around in the road. Barcino ran in front of the cart to retrieve the lid but Hicky grabbed it and whacked Barcino hard across his back. The Italian was knocked senseless and the other lads moved forward and started hitting him with their belts and sticks. The buckles on their belts chopped into the Italians red cheeks and ears. Harry was happy to help.

Edward Brown, a labourer from Leather Street, was walking down Roseberry Avenue which joined the end of Mount Pleasant. He heard the commotion. Reaching for the knife in his back pocket and giving a shrill whistle, he ran forwards, knowing others would follow.

'Give the man a chance!' he shouted at Hicky.

Hicky had already stabbed Barcino in the back with what looked like a bread knife. Brown lashed out with his pocketknife causing wounds to Cox and to Powell. Harry jumped back narrowly missing injury. John Hicky lunged forward shouting, 'SERVE HIM THE SAME!' and stabbed Edward Brown in the chest and head.

Lads from the area appeared from another street and ran towards them, also shouting. Hicky looked at Harry and the others and, with the knife still in his hand, he scarpered.

WEST PARK

'Run to your mum boy, run with the scum.
Run up the alley boy, you haven't gotta a gun.
Run! Run!' shout the strange lads
I'm following sharply behind John Hicky as he turns into a side alley. There are masses of them, at least forty. They're running, bawling and waving sticks down the street.

'If we cut through here we can catch the others,' says Hicky. I'm picking up a piece of wood lying by a bin; it has a rusty nail poking out of it. There's blood on Hicky and on the others; they're pushing in front of me. My back is pressed against a cold brick wall.

'Move out the way - quick!' Hicky is saying. 'We can get there before they do.'

I'm at the end of the alley; a man is coming out of a back door. He's looking straight at me. He must be a shop owner. He's grabbing Hicky by his shoulder. I feel stunned and then euphoria comes over me. Hicky's pulling a knife and stabbing the man in his thigh and now I'm laughing. The man's on the ground and another younger man has come out. He's shouting for the police.

'Shut up!' George is yelling.

Now I'm going back - back the way we came and I can hear more shouting and whistling. I'm running and whistling as well. My heart is racing;, I can hear it beating; I'm laughing so hard

I can't stop, I smash my stick on the wall and beat the branches of the overhanging trees and the laughter is making my face ache.

I'm at the other end of the alley and something has hit me hard on the back of my head. My knees hit the cobbles and I'm falling, clutching the stick I've found. Blood is running down my face; there's pain in my ears and commotion in the street. I'm thinking about my baby sister. I can hear her crying my name.

'Come home, Harry!'

'Mum?' I murmur to myself. 'I can't hear your voice. Mum, please, say it again and again.'

'GET UP! GET UP! AND COME HOME!' commands her voice in my head. I'm trying to listen to it but the sound echoes in my mind and my thoughts are distorted.

There's so much darkness.

'Wake up Harry!'

I'm in a police cell. My eyes are so swollen that I can hardly see John Hicky and three other boys sitting on the floor with their hands tied tightly together behind their backs.

A London War Gang.

The terrors of a whole district

At the county of London, Clerkenwell yesterday, before Mr Loveland-Loveland QC, the doings of a Clerkenwell 'war gang' was again referred to. The prisoners, four lads of small stature, respectfully named John Hicky, 15, Henry Cornell, 15, described as labourers, George Cox, 17, French polisher and George Powell, 15, Van guard were charged upon an indictment with having maliciously wounded

Audrea Barcino and Edward Brown. Mr H.C. Biron
and Mr Partridge prosecution instructed by Mr T.
McDonnell of the treasury. Mr Symmons defend-
ed Cox in opening the case; Mr Biron described it
as an important one to the public inasmuch as the
alleged conduct of the accused lads had resulted in
three people being very dangerously stabbed. So severe were the injuries that it was more due to good
fortune than any other cause that the prisoners were
not being tried in another court on a much graver
charge. The case was one more instance on the condition of lawlessness, which existed in some parts of
the Metropole and disclosed an extraordinary state
of things, which seemed incredible. It was all edged
that the prisoners were in the habit of going about
together in gangs 20 to 30 in number, armed with
sticks, belts stones and in some cases with knives,
making attacks on inoffensive citizens and rendering
the streets absolutely unfit to be used by peaceful and
law abiding persons. When that sport did not come
their way these young ruffians appears said counsel to
engage in a species of pitched battles with rival gangs
in the open thoroughfare. The prisoners denied that
they were connected with any gang and said they
acted in self-defence. Cornell urged that he was not
there at all. The jury convicted Hicky of wounding
the two prosecutors and Cox, Powell and Cornell
were found guilty of committing a common assault
on them. His Lordship postponed sentences.

Evening News, Friday 18th August 1899.

Alf Goldwater and his trusted sidekicks, Dennis Scully, the Irish immigrant, sat in the Public Gallery and watched with interest as the four boys were sentenced. Mary Cornell and Harry's older sister, Mary Louisa, sat a few rows in front. Mary held her mother's hand as they listened to Judge Loveland hand each boy his sentence. He told the boys that their crimes could have been even more serious and, if their victims had died, they would all have been looking at the hangman's noose. Their punishment was severe enough: John Hicky must serve four years in a reformatory school; George Powell must serve three years working on the training ship *Cornwall*; George Cox must serve two months in prison; Henry Havelock Cornell must serve three months for aggravated assault. The judge hoped that this punishment would teach them that crime did not pay and that they would think seriously before engaging in violence of this nature again.

Dennis Scully looked at the Harry, still young impish, his face swollen from the kicking he had received from the two policemen who arrested him at the end of the alley. Alf Goldwater shrugged his shoulders, tipped his cap as Mary Cornell and her daughter and exited the Public Gallery. The two women were clutching small linen hankies that they used to wipe the tears that trickled down their faces. Mary Cornell carried her son's guilt. Hers were tears of disappointment- with Harry and with his behavior – and with her inability to protect her young scallywag. Why had he brought this shame to her family? What was it that she did not understand? What could she not see in him? Had the devil declared a war on him and entered his very soul? She wondered. Or was it simply the boy's own stupidity that had brought this about?

Over the coming years, Mary Cornell would pray for his sins and ask the good Lord to forgive him. She would ask the good Lord to take away the inch of guilt that she held within herself and tried to justify. Never now or ever would the guilt leave her and she put it down to a mother's love.

Mary Louisa held onto her mother's arm to support her as they left the court. She could not bring herself to look at Harry as he left the dock.

Outside, Alf Goldwater turned to Dennis Scully.

'Make sure they get protection in there,' he told him, 'especially young Harry, he's vulnerable.' Dennis Scully nodded.

'I'll try but I can't guarantee it.'

'Get a note to Fred Allen; he is in for a stretch.'

Alf Goldwater walked straight into the nearest pub where he waited for Dennis Scully who had a quiet word with the policeman standing by the horse and cart that was waiting to transport prisoners.

Meanwhile, Harry could only endure and harden his heart. He shrugged off any desire within himself to change, thereby muddying the waters for all that were to be affected by knowing him in the future. If he could have looked into the future would he have stopped and changed direction? Would he have opened his eyes and let some colour into the world of his existence? Who knows? The next three months were going to put a stamp on the character of Harry Cornell. They would be three months of slamming doors, of bolts banging, of iron locks turning, three months of cries in the night and of moonlight hitting the floor as it squeezed through high, slatted windows, too high to reach or look out from, three months of long days' hard laboring, of going nowhere, of clinging to the cold iron of the treadmill with greasy blackened hands, three months without mountains or trees or seagulls squawking, without the smell of bacon from his mother's kitchen, with no ball to kick in the street at Hanover.

No matter how hard he tried the memories would prove impossible to erase; the boy who wanted to paint a picture had entered hell and would have to find a way to survive it.

6. The Duke of York (By Royal Appointment)

'How was your night, Harry?' Dr. Howard's manner was matter-of-fact, as he listened to Harry's chest through his stethoscope and checked the notes on the board at the rear of the bed. He had several patients to see that morning. Not wishing to be overly concerned, he gave Harry little time to reply.

The treatments he had prescribed for Harry during his first few years in the asylum had calmed Harry's delusional outbursts. ECT, *Electric Shock Therapy* seemed to calm him although it left him confused. For a time, he was also put through the ordeal of facing a lobotomy, a brutal procedure that the hospital thankfully decided to cease using. Dr. Howard had reached a point where he questioned his own decision to give Harry ECT. If the therapy had been beneficial to his patient, would Harry have lost his will over time and learnt to give in to his delusional outbursts? Perhaps the images and tales Harry conjured up from within his deep and tormented mind would have been forgotten anyhow.

And now, Dr. Howard was becoming nervous. From the time not so long ago when Harry had contracted TB, he had become more delusional and had started recalling some of his old, far-fetched tales. Had they been festering away deep in the back of his mind, had Harry been unable to voice these thoughts, no outlet? Harry was certainly delusional; he talked of such unbelievable nonsense. But the mind never forgets; it just sleeps. The ECT was not a cure, merely a procedure to close down the memory. The friends who admitted Harry back in 1940 had claimed that the memory was lost already. It had seemed at the time that there was no choice but to calm him and deal with his instability in the appropriate manner.

'How was your night, Harry?'

Harry heard him but did not bother to reply to Dr. Howard because it took all of his strength to speak. Nurse McCarthy held his hand. She knew he liked her to and Matron was not in sight. Both of them enjoying a swift, rebellious moment as if they had just ran giggling to the back of the bicycle sheds. Dr. Howard said nothing. He respected Nurse McCarthy's theories on end-of-life care. He admired her ability to convey humanness while maintaining her role, but he himself remained cloaked in the formal bedside manner he considered appropriate and kept his thoughts to himself, unwilling to discuss them with a mere nurse

'Let it all be,' Nurse McCarthy muttered to herself. Some of Harry's delusions were almost plausible:

'The Duke of York let me paint the pavements outside his house. He liked my pictures; I was an artist by royal appointment. He asked for me, and when the copper moved in on me, his Royal Highness the Duke of York saw to it that I got my place back. Bloody coppers always poking their noses in they were. His Royal Highness ... he told him to leave me alone and then I got my paving stone back.'

Nurse McCarthy had been amused by that one and Harry enjoyed repeating it. He told it to her and Tommy Carter many times, over and over, about how proud he had been when they wrote about him in the newspapers.

'I had tuppence and I couldn't decide whether I should get myself a drink or buy some chalk, so I bought chalk and then I could earn enough to go down the pub,' he would laugh.

Harry had become a down-and-out vagrant in the years after the war. For a short time in 1935 he had spent his nights amongst the homeless in St. Martin's Crypt. He had seen other artists earning money from their pavement art, thought he could do better and found himself a really good spot in Piccadilly, outside where the then current Duke of York resided with his wife and two young daughters.

'Then the Colonel from Guernsey saw me and he bought me some paints,' he told Nurse McCarthy and Tommy Carter. 'He saw my paintings on the pavement and he asked me to paint him a picture that he could hang in his home. He had a grand house. Course, Ada had gone back to Chatham by then - Ada and her fancy bloke. I never liked him.' Harry would moan and grab Nurse McCarthy's arm at this point. 'Don't you let Ada come 'ere, not with 'im. Ada never liked my paintings. She was jealous I could make pictures; she stole them from my room.'

'We won't let Ada come here, Harry. Don't you worry, my sweet.'

'No,' Harry would whisper. 'She wasn't my Evie.'

Nurse McCarthy would try and reassure him. Clear in thought, Harry expressed the emotions that leapt into his dialogue. As the drugs left his system, his muddied mind began to clear leaving it scarred and tender and then, as if half asleep, he could drift back to a disarray of words, mixing people and places.

There's not enough time, he thought in his silence. He always had something more to say, the words popped into his mind, randomly painting small pockets of memory.

How did love just slip through my fingers? I had no idea, Evie, no idea at all, what you meant to me. In the idle stillness of time you were there, just perfect and I let you go.

Dr. Howard sat in the seclusion of his un-inviting office, a paper calendar from the Horton Cluster friends' committee hung slanted on the wall behind his desk that was dominated by a large, black, Bakelite phone. He had previously pulled out a file containing a stack of medical notes concerning Harry Cornell. He had pulled it from the long filing cupboard that graced most of one wall of his office. There was no reason to look back through these notes other than a mere interest that the day had stirred in his mind. He tried to recall the faces of the man and woman who, with his old friend Cavanagh, had brought Harry to the hospital. It was such a long time ago and he had forgotten the details. Glancing through his admission notes, he reassured himself that he had done nothing wrong.

So why did he have this bad feeling? His brown, leather chair swiveled back and forth as he pulled the papers from the file. It had been at the beginning of the war and the hospital had been in a state of chaos. His medical team had been pushed to their limits due to an overcrowding issue and the continuous air raids they had to deal with, if he remembered right.

His notes said Harry suffered from *anxiety neurasthenia*, from the (First) War, a term that described shell-shock. Reflecting on this, Howard considered how this might have contributed to Harry's condition. He flicked through the treatment record. Harry was admitted with delusional insanity, probably brought on by shell-shock, mode of life, vagrancy and drunkenness, said the record. Dr. Howard remembered that Harry had been an alcoholic and somehow scared when he arrived.

Sighing, Dr.Howard pushed the papers together and shoved them back into the brown, glossy file, tying the cotton tabs together.

Oh well he thought, *whatever this man went through is bye the bye. He's not long for this world now anyhow.* He placed the file in his brief case.

BRİGHTON 1901

Evelyn Anne was a skilled seamstress. She had grown up amongst pincushions and silk cloth, helping her German father who was a tailor in his small workroom. Now her fingers were red and sore; she was tired of Madame Grace and her continuous complaints. If it had been in her, Evelyn Anne would have cursed her father who had organized this position for her at the Empire Theatre; he had thought it would broaden her skills.

Madame Grace, a middle aged actress and music-hall performer was a difficult woman to work for and asked the impossible from the young Evelyn Anne. In her last performance of the afternoon, Madame Grace had caught the heel of her shoe in her skirt and she blamed her, accusing her of loosely sewing the hem.

Evelyn Anne was sure she had measured it correctly but Madame Grace had insisted on a different petticoat at the last minute and there had not been enough time to make the adjustment. Standing by the stage door of the Empire Theatre, she pulled her shawl about her shoulders as the doors opened at the front of the theatre. The noisy matinée audience descended onto New Road. *Father is going to be so angry with me*, she worried.

Harry saw her as he left the theatre. He apologized to a couple of friends and told them he would see them later in the pub. Striding up the alley at the side of the theatre he noticed she had been crying.

'I know you're not an actress but you should be; you're pretty enough,' he told her.

That was the afternoon that changed his purpose, the afternoon his selfish tear-away attitude encountered another emotion. A battle began and if the love of a woman could challenge him, Harry was at least going to give it a try.

'She's something special, that is what she is, my Evie, You know that don't you Dennis Scully, so keep your leery eyes off her.'

'You have that look again Harry. It'll get you in trouble. Who are you trying to impress? If you want to court her you'll have to get past her dad.'

West Park

Harry woke slowly from a peaceful sleep but the smile on his face soon disappeared and his face became contorted.

'That bloody fucking German, poking his bleeding nose in all our business! He knows nothing! Nothing, I tell you.'

The energy had swelled within him like a volcano. It erupted as if from under the floor. Nurse McCarthy could not explain where else on the TB ward it came from. Small beads of sweat appeared across Harry's grey, pale skin. Holding out the handkerchief, he coughed into it, his chest reacted and he felt as if he was back in a straight jacket.

'Sorry,' he whispered, 'sorry, nurse.'

He laid back and stared at the white ceiling.

'Sorry, Evie,' he said to himself. He closed his eyes again.

'You're a daft one,' Evie's flirting with me. 'What would the Queen want with the likes of us in London, Harry?'

'You could go on the stage, Evie; I'd listen to your sweet and charismatic voice.' Hah, I love to tease her with long words; I'm grabbing her waist and twirling her over the wooden, slatted walkway, pulling her down towards the beach.

'Harry, you're a lunatic,' she's shrieking. 'Papa would never allow me on any stage. I'm going into service, Harry. Papa has found me a position with one of his clients.'

'But then I would never see you would I? And you'll end up marrying some lord.' I'm kneeling on the pebbles. My hands are in a pleading position. Evie is smiling at me.

'I know my place,' she's saying, looking down on me.

'Yeh, and where's that Evie, my precious girl?'

She's holding my face in her hands. She doesn't have to say anything because I see what she feels. I'm looking into the depths of her love and we feel joined like a lock and key; we fit together. I feel right with my Evie and I know she cares about me. My love for her has no boundaries. Listen to yourself, Harry Cornell; you're love-struck.

'I have something for you, Evie, look. It's a portrait of your face. I've drawn it and written my name just there. You're all mine, Evie, all mine till the end. We matter you and me.'

We hear the music coming from the fairground on the promenade above our heads. The pebbles are crunching underneath our feet, the sun is going down and the night is warm. I watch the surf sprinkle over the stones coating a luminescent tint of blue over them. She's putting her arm through mine. It makes me feel proper when she does that, like we're a proper couple; we're walking like a proper couple up from the beach towards the promenade.

'Let's get hitched, Evie.'

I hold out my arm to guide her off the stones and onto the slatted walkway. People are passing us, eagerly making their way to the pier. Two girls swish past in their striped frocks, ice cream dripping onto lace gloves. Family groups, try to stay together but are separated by other walkers coming towards them, weaving in and out, on their way back, looking for a tea shop. The lights come on and the Palace Pier is awash in illumination. Some strands of her hair hang loose from her straw boater. The breeze blows it into the air. I want to touch her hair; I want to touch her.

'Come on, girl' I'm saying. 'What about it? We should get married, shouldn't we?'

WEST PARK.

Harry stirred and dreams of Brighton lay buried between the clammy sheets and mingled with the sound of clanking buckets filled with tepid grey water. The asylum had failed to erase the lost life that Harry once revelled in; it slapped him across the face and pushed him down where hell was waiting. Any dreams that he once had were now discarded. The image of Evelyn Anne, on the pebbled beach, clutching her hat, drifted away; she was long dead and buried, he thought, well rid of the man who did not care enough to hold onto her.

Harry was agitated; he wanted a cigarette

'Tommy!' he shouted to the man in the next bed. 'Has Tommy been here? But the man ignored him and did not move. 'Stupid old git,' Harry murmured with a frustrated need for a bit of nicotine. 'You not dead yet?'

Brighton 1902

Evelyn Anne felt nervous. She was picturing the face of her father, Wilhelm, because he would probably protest against Harry's proposal of marriage. Pushing the image away from the forefront of her mind, she tried to be positive. She preferred to stay happily in this dream, this moment. She felt warm. Harry had charmed her to the bone. With him she felt all was possible. Was this not how love was supposed to enthrall her?

'Evie, it's out of the question!' her mother, Annie, tried to reason. 'Your Papa will never allow it, and we don't even know this boy.'

'He's really sweet on me, Mama, and he's asked to talk to Papa. He wants to do this properly.' She hoped her mother would pave the way for her to mention Harry's intentions to her father. But Annie was not at all excited about the prospect of marrying off her daughter. She knew her husband, Wilhelm, would object and she wanted to avoid being caught up in endless discussions about who would make the perfect husband for his daughter. Evelyn Anne was his favourite. She had inherited his German stubbornness along with a sense of duty and a good work ethic.

Annie was another matter; she possessed a languorous personality and had found a way to disguise it using manipulative excuses - and Wilhelm fell for them all. He was a gentleman with a forgiving nature. When Annie had treated herself to one too many glasses of gin, he would say she had been 'doing too much', she should 'slow down and rest'.

Evelyn Anne persuaded her mother to help her. They organized a meeting in a small coffee house and let Harry work his charm. Annie was taken in when Harry pulled out a chair for her to sit down, Harry was good at this; he knew instinctively how to use his manners to win over his future mother-in-law. So Wilhelm was persuaded by his wife to meet young Harry, but things did not go as Harry had wished for. Their house was small and sparse, there was no welcome sign above the door, and no bacon smells wafting up from the kitchen - only the smell of starch and lavender water. Wilhelm stood stiffly by the fireplace. He was a tailor and he eyed Harry's misshapen pockets and creased collar with distaste.

'Men like you are nothing but trouble,' Wilhelm said in his broken English. 'Vay vould I give you my daughter's hand in marriage? Young man you vill refrain and you vill haf nothing to do with Evie. We haf forbidden her to walk out vith you, sir. She vill be going to work in service from next month. You are a bad sort. I have been told all about you, young man.'

*

'Harry! Harry! Fetch and carry,' Evelyn Anne sang as she teased him under the Palace Pier, her shawl blowing in the breeze. Harry chased her and she picked up the fold of her skirt and ran over the pebbles. He tried to catch her as she stumbled.

'I have to be back soon,' she told him as she laid down on the stones stretching out her arms.

'Not yet,' Harry said, 'I'll walk you back to the house at eight.'

'If Lady Muck catches me coming in late she'll have my guts for garters.' Actually, Evelyn Anne was enjoying her work in service. It was easier for them to see each other without her father interrogating her. Her one full day off every three weeks was their special time together, the one thing Harry could look forward to.

'Let's get married, Evie. I'll book the church in Kemptown.'

'But Papa, Harry - you'll never convince him. We'll have to wait until I'm twenty-one - then you can make an honest woman of me.'

She pinched his cheeks and he grabbed her waist, and Evelyn Anne held on to her little straw boater to make sure it was secure.

'Harry! Behave yourself!'

He walked her back to her employer's house and she let him kiss her on her cheek. On his way back home he walked into a pub in Trafalgar Street. Two hours later he staggered back to his mum's house, slamming the door behind him.

*

Evelyn Anne was looking forward to meeting Harry and a hot day in June was no deterrent for her as she stood in Brighton Station. She wanted to make the most of her day off. Her primrose dress, heavy with layers of cotton and linen, caught the sunlight. It had been a present from her father and she was eager to show it off to Harry.

He had told her that he would be clocking off at six o'clock. She was a little late; the clock in the station said ten past. She looked around to see if she could spot him. Railway workers hung around in small groups. They were beginning to make their way down Trafalgar Street, tired, weary and smoking cigarettes, looking forward to a hot meal and a comfy chair where they could take off their boots. She made her way over to the tearoom and peeped through the window to see if her Harry was waiting for her there. There was no sign of him; perhaps he was still on his way along the track. She sat down on a bench to wait and smoothed out the creases on her skirt. With hands clasped together, she watched all the busy business travelers disembark from the London train. After an hour she summoned enough courage to ask a railway worker if he knew of Harry Cornell and where he might be. The railway worker smelled of diesel and smoke and the contrast between his clothes and her yellow dress made him feel intimidated. He mumbled something and moved away and she apologised, grimacing when he finally smiled with a grin that exposed his missing front teeth.

'You'll probably find him in the Railway Inn.' He pointed to the right.

The breeze that ran through the great arched roof of the station was brought up from the sea. Evelyn Anne was grateful, it cooled her as she walked out of the station and looked to the right. Beyond the aroma and beauty from the flower vendor, in contrast there was Harry with some fellow railway workers. He was laughing loudly and had a pint glass in his hand. *He has forgotten all about me,* she thought. Too timid to confront him, she turned and walked back towards the station lump with in her throat, clutching her return ticket and wiping away a tear.

Harry, oblivious, was enjoying his after-work pint. If he had another two there was just enough money left to give his mother another extra shilling for the week. Walking down the hill with some of the other men later, at eight o'clock, a fight broke out at the bottom. Harry could not resist getting involved. When a policeman tried to confront him, Harry gave him back a mouthful of bad language and the policeman arrested him. Harry got fourteen days hard labour and lost his job on the railway - again.

WEST PARK

The hospital ward was freezing with all the windows open. The spring weather fought against the cold wind. Harry looked at the curtains blowing in the window. The memory of Wilhelm Gaebel's biting words still rang in his ears. He felt the same feeling in the pit of his stomach as he had back then. He had so wanted to be good enough for his Evie.

'Nurse McCarthy,' Dr. Howard called from down the corridor, 'step into my office please - when you've finished your shift? I'd like a brief word.'

7. German Place

Wilhelm Gaebel was a proud man. He had come a long way from his Potsdam origins, seeking a new life of strong values. His family was his life and his purpose. When he found out that his precious daughter had been carrying on with Harry Cornell he was disheartened and silently, in his own space, had shed a tear. Wilhelm did not trust Harry at all.

'Zis man is a young thug and he has no proper trade,' he complained to his wife, Annie.

Annie was more trusting of young Harry who had already used his charm on her but this further infuriated Wilhelm, especially since he had been making enquiries. Harry was known around town as a drunk and Wilhelm had been shocked to learn about Harry's jail conviction in a London court.

Annie in her calm and aloof manner suffered the ranting of her husband but got him to agree that if Harry could be persuaded to find regular employment then Wilhelm would at least consider the prospect of the marriage.

'I'm not a man, to be rigid in my judgment,' said Wilhelm. 'I vill always give a man a second chance.'

Perhaps he knew of Harry's brother William because he was a tailor's apprentice. Maybe Wilhem could convince Harry that tailoring was an honorable trade to enter into.

'He has to be able to support you, Evie,' Wilhelm told his daughter as they walked around their tiny garden in the spring of 1903. 'I want you to be happy with a good, strong man. Papa will not always be around to care about you.'

'He does care for me Papa, really he does.'

*

On every street corner in Brighton there was a public house with double-fronted doors enticing you in from whichever direction you happened to be walking. For most working-class men the enticement took them over the threshold to the rosy-blushed cheeks of a round and voluptuous landlady, her husband polishing brasses, rolling barrels in the cellar or still sleeping from some merriment of the previous night. The landladies welcomed the likes of Harry with arms stretched open and a come-inside-my-lovely smile. Genuine or not genuine, to Harry they were all offering the maternal mothering he craved and, so long as he continuously fed their purses with his pennies, he could be at their breasts.

Mary Cornell did not like her boys going into the pubs but because her husband worked for the brewery it was difficult to stop them because they were eager to enter where all the men were so frequently to be found.

For Harry the pub was the place to be and the taste of strong beer had long lingered on his taste buds, ever since he was high enough to push his cheeky chin on to the level of the bar when one of the old brewery workers would persuade the landlady to give him a few sips of beer. As he grew taller, he knew how to charm the landladies - until he got barred for going a notch too far. Harry, always a charmer, would move on to the next street and the next pub.

As soon as he started earning wages, they went, without question, into the purses of the landladies who were happy to serve him and take his money. This carried on night after night until he stumbled out of the double doors, angry with those who got in his way. But now there was something new coming along and Harry would have to think about spending his money on other things. Love was in one corner and the pub was in the other and who would win the fight?

After Harry had lost his job at the railway, Alf Goldwater had given him a few errands. Alf Goldwater gave him his first cart and the loan of his mule to make deliveries. There would be good wages coming his way but he mustn't let his drinking spoil his chances. Alf Goldwater didn't want him spouting his mouth off about his carryings on.

'I'm a lucky devil,' he had told Evelyn Anne. The thought of saving enough money so they could get married soon was at the forefront of his mind. His father reinforced the message.

'Be careful of the drink Harry. When you're a married man you'll have a wife to care for.'

But Harry was only nineteen, he didn't understand about responsibilities. All he knew was that married men received more respect. He didn't want any more lectures, not from his Dad or Wilhelm or anyone. He was just proud that his Evie wanted to be his wife and that was enough.

*

Harry was over the moon. He had managed to get work again from Alf Goldwater on the promise that he would not ask any questions. Alf Goldwater gave him a wad of notes down under the Kings' Arches where the fisherman brought in their catches. Harry strutted along the tread boards and up the steps, jumping two at a time with both hands in his pockets. After that, Wilhelm reluctantly gave his blessing for the marriage and fashioned a lace-and-chiffon wedding dress out of French muslin for Evelyn Anne.

She wore it on the 20th June, 1903 at the Church of St. John the Baptist in Kemptown. Her sisters Louisa and Pauline were her bridesmaids and there was a wedding breakfast in the small garden at Nelson's Row, where Annie and Wilhelm Gaebel lived. There was no room in Hanover Street for Harry to live with his young bride, so Harry went to stay with Wilhelm and his family until it would be possible to find their own lodgings.

*

'Men like you are nothing but trouble,' Wilhelm reminded Harry.

Harry left by the back door and slammed it behind him. They were barely a month into their marriage and Harry had come home drunk.

'You'll never change!' Wilhelm shouted at Harry's back.

A staunch Catholic, Wilhelm forbade Harry to re-enter his house because he hated the effects of alcohol. Evelyn Anne locked herself in her room mortified. Later that night, a policeman who bought him home asked Evelyn Anne to sober him up.

'I suggest, sir,' the policeman said to Wilhelm, 'you tell the young man to stay off the drink for a while. We picked him up on Carlton Street; he's been fined 5/-.'

*

'I have to leave Papa. He's my husband and it's my duty.'

Wilhelm was concerned. Harry had found lodgings for him and Evie at 5 German Place. It was a four-storey building close to the sea front and Marine Drive. Harry could stroll easily down to the arches from there, where he would hang out with Alf Goldwater and Dennis Scully. Evelyn Anne was excited. Harry had found enough work to put by two months' rent. The room had a large, sash window that looked down on to the street. Harry put his arm around his young wife's waist as they peered out.

'You can smell the sea from here, Evie.'

Dennis Scully and William, Harry's brother, appeared at the door carrying a wardrobe that they had struggled up the stairs to reach the first floor. Harry held the door as they negotiated it into the room. There was already an iron bedframe. Mary Cornell had given the young couple a new mattress. The old one leaned up against the wall on the landing, stained and lumpy.

Two young boys from the family who lived upstairs knocked on the door.

'Me mum wants to know if you're throwing away the mattress and can we have it?' they asked sheepishly.

'Tell her we want sixpence for it.' Harry laughed and the boys ran upstairs, their boots echoed down the hall. 'They'll be back,' he grinned.

Three other families lived in the house and all shared the privy in the small yard at the back of the house. The water came from a tap on the end of a copper pipe that came out the ground in the yard. It shook as the water coughed and splattered into the enamel jugs they used for carrying it up to their rooms.

*

Evelyn Anne looked pale and tired. She looked out of the window to see if she could see Harry coming up from Marine Drive. It was getting dark and she had not eaten since breakfast.

There was no bread or jam left and she was hoping Harry would bring a piece of fish home for his tea.

As Harry turned the corner she saw he had something wrapped in newspaper. She assumed he had stopped off in the pub for a drink because she heard him shout at one of the kids from upstairs.

She put the kettle on the little stove to make him some tea but when he entered the room he had a bottle of ale in his hand. She took the fish and laid it on the table.

'There is no money for potatoes,' she complained.

'You have the fish.' Harry said. 'You need nourishment for the baby.'

WEST PARK

Nurse McCarthy stood at the end of the bed with both hands on the metal bedstead.

'I'm off home now Harry, you sleep well,' she said.

She was like a caring mother tucking in her child before saying goodnight. The night staff were not so compassionate. Harry felt vulnerable when she was not around. The electric light cast faint shadows over the pale green walls. He watched her as she walked towards the swing doors and became aware of the sound her footsteps made out in the corridor. She knocked on Dr. Howard's office door.

'You wanted a word with me, sir?'

'Ah yes, it's about Harry Cornell. Is he talking much?'

'He's saying quite a bit, sir but he's confused. Is there a problem?'

'Just wondering, that's all. I don't think he has long poor chap.'

'Yes sir, is there anything else - only I don't want to miss my bus.'

'No, you run along. See you in the morning.'

But Dr, Howard felt uneasy. He left Harry's file in his briefcase.

'You have a little son,' Mum is telling me. 'Come into the room, Harry, come and meet him.'

My Evie, you're so pale. I'm kneeling by the bed and, in the flickering candlelight, I look at his little face, his pinched nose.

'Patrick, this is your mummy,' I'm saying as I kiss her on the forehead.

She says nothing; she looks grey, grey as the sheets that cover her tired body.

Mum is fussing and wrapping my son in some linen.

The doctor says he'll be back later if we need him to,

'Your wife must sleep now,' he's telling me.

I'm so proud of her.

*

Oh, how Patrick cried in those first few weeks.

'I'm sorry woman, but I won't be home tonight or tomorrow, Alf needs me to help him out.'

'Harry we have no food.'

Evie is crying; Patrick is crying; the bloody kids in the hall are crying; the fucking street is crying. I am slamming the door again as I walk down to the beach. Past Bola Bucchis restaurant. That fat Italian, he makes me feel sick.

I am looking at the small boy with an ice cream. Will I ever be able to afford to bring Patrick here one day. I walk down to the sea and sit on the stones. Out there is France, out there is. ...

BRIGHTON 1904

A year later Evelyn Anne gave birth to a daughter, May, a sweet, frail child with brown, curly hair. Harry would make her chuckle as he teased her but Patrick clung to his mother's skirt. He sensed the dark side of his father; he felt his aggression. Evelyn Anne wrapped her skirt layers around him and he felt safe in the folds of cotton.

She had to fight Harry to stop him spending his pay in the pub. Harry was full of excuses about where the money went. Deep down, she knew he loved her. He used his charm and she always forgave him. He noticed her, he commented on her, from the colour of her eyes to the opalescent glow on the little necklace she wore that had been a gift from her father. But was it enough? she asked herself. *Why was Harry so difficult to love?* When he was drunk he was a monster.

Harry was not keen on domestic bliss. He loved his family but hated walking in - to a constant reminder that he could not support them. Any money he earned went either into the pub coffers or a fine for being drunk and disorderly in the street.

A month after May was born, on a cold January evening, Maggie, Harry's younger sister stood in the doorway of a pub in the lanes of Brighton and yelled.

'Harry, come home, our dad has died.'

*

Harry folded his arms against the back wall in the yard of Hanover Street and cradled his head. His brother William stood in the doorway of the kitchen, his Mum and sisters were assembled in the front room.

'Do you think it's right bringing the kids to this?' William, always the giver of righteousness, puffed on his pipe and tried to make small talk with his brother. Harry put his hands in his pockets.

'She wanted them with her; it's just to pay respect William, that's all.'

'Got much work have you, Harry?'

'Enough. Yes, Dad would have approved.' Harry stepped past William into the kitchen and William followed him.

'Mum wants you both,' said Maggie lifting her chin up so she would not cry. Not one for emotion, she wanted this day to run smoothly. Her father deserved respect and there were people gathering in the road waiting for the hearse.

'Leave off him, William,' she added, 'just for today,'

After his father's funeral, Harry was back in a pub and drowning some unpleasant memories of his childhood. He had listened to the hypocrisy of the family as they reminisced over his late father with glory tales and fond recollections. Harry better remembered the harsh words that crushed his aspirations and the beatings with a belt across his bare legs. Mary Cornell looked on as he picked up young Patrick and put him on to his knee. The boy flinched and ran to Evelyn Anne. *Like father like son*, she thought.

WEST PARK

'Put the restraints on,' the orderly was saying to the night nurse. 'He's flapping his arms again and he's in danger of falling out of the bed.'

Harry grabbed at the nurse's mouth-mask. His eyes were fiery and angry.

'Get off me, copper!' he shouted. 'I'm going home. She's waiting, is my Evie. I need to go home.'

'Come on, Harry,' the orderly said pushing him back on the bed. 'It's all okay; you're as home as you ever will be.'

'I'll get him a sedative,' said the nurse and re-positioned her mouth-mask.

'Mr. Cornell, I have no choice but to sentence you once again to fourteen days hard labour and order you to pay 5/-.'

How stupid am I?

'I've no money for coal, Harry!' Evie is shouting.

I'm telling her to go and borrow a few bob off Dennis Scully, down at the Arches.

'Tell him I'll pay him back.'

She won't go, not my Evie, she's much too proud. I'm telling her to say they can take it out of my wages but she just looks at me and shakes her head. Patrick is crying again.

'Two weeks, that's all Evie, two weeks.'

BRIGHTON

Evelyn Anne walked down to the arches, leaving Patrick and May with the family upstairs. Alf Goldwater stood towering over a couple of fishermen.

'You looking for Harry, woman?'

Evelyn Anne felt sick in her stomach; she was apprehensive of a man like him with such dark eyes. She avoided coming to this place. It was a hot day and she needed to cling onto the metal handrail as she descended the steep, stone steps onto the pebbles.

'I was looking for Dennis Scully. Doesn't matter.' She turned and started to climb back up the steps.

'Evie! Wait!' called Dennis. He came out from under one of the Arches, his shirtsleeves rolled up over his elbows. Trying to be respectful he rolled them down. He could see she was distressed. He followed her up to the promenade.

'I came to tell you that Harry won't be able to do any work for a couple of weeks. He's in jail.'

'You okay?' asked Dennis Scully, lowering his voice.

'I'm fine -but I've no coal for the stove.'

Dennis shook his head. He detested the way some men treated their women. He felt sorry for her; she did not deserve to be put through all this hardship. Harry was out of control. Getting himself arrested again would only infuriate his boss and bring attention to their dealings under the Arches

Alf Goldwater was too sharp; Dennis knew he was going to have to cover for Harry yet again. He had a son of his own, the same age as young Patrick. Kids should not go hungry.

He pushed a few coppers into the palm of her hand.

'There, go and buy some coal. If you need anything, you come and find me. I'm here for you till Harry gets out of jail.'

*

What makes a man re-offend? The policeman shook his head as he grabbed the arm of the drunken man whom he remembered was only let out of prison a month previously. And here was the man again, a broken bottle in his hand and blood running through his fingers.

'Cornell, what do we have to do to get through to you?' the policeman demanded. 'Tell me, but for the grace of God there's no helping you.'

*

The punishment was always the same. The crime hardly changed and the wheel of destruction just carried on turning. Harry believed this drunk - victim or culprit, name him as you choose - was who he was and, despite the frequent words of wisdom rammed down his throat by well-wishers and others, nothing could change his belief. And nobody listened to the cries of Harry Cornell himself. The reason within him that made any sense had been trampled on many years before.

*

'If the rent isn't paid by tomorrow we have to leave here, Harry. We can go to my parents.'

Evelyn Anne was heavily pregnant with their third child. Harry detested the idea of having to go back and live with Wilhelm, but, in the summer of 1909, they borrowed a mule and cart from Alf Goldwater and turned up at Nelson's row. Harry, full of rage, felt he had failed his family. The rage took him back in front of a judge following an attack on a man in a Brighton pub with a broken bottle.

The hammer went down hard on the bench

'Three months on prisoner ship, *The Argyll*,' pronounced the judge. 'Let's hope the prisoner will think about his actions in future. I'm tired of seeing your face before this court, Mr. Cornell.'

Evelyn Anne did not go to court. Dennis broke the news to her later that day as she sat on the wall outside her father house in Nelson's Row.

'This can't go on, Evie.' He handed her his handkerchief to wipe away her tears.

*

Baby James William Cornell was born at 4.00am in the morning, two weeks before Harry finished serving his time. Wilhelm was worried about Harry coming back. Annie could not cope with all the children and the crush in the house and she took seclusion in the back privy with a bottle of gin. She was little help to Evelyn Anne.

Harry knew that the atmosphere would be strained in Nelson's Row when he returned so he took refuge at his brother William's house in Brewer Street. William had married Florence Botting, another Brighton girl, and was trying to settle down to respectable, married life. Meanwhile, Mary their mother, announced that she wanted to sell her house in Hanover Street now that her husband was dead. She moved later that year to run a small guesthouse in Grosvenor Street. William's house in Brewer Street had plenty of room and, due to force of circumstance, Harry started to spend a lot of time there.

Harry was extremely jealous of William; it seemed he had everything. Harry wanted to return home to be with Evelyn Anne and the children but he found it hard to cope with the children and gave her little money and Wilhelm was hostile. Wilhelm did what he could to help Evelyn Anne but all the extra mouths to feed stretched his own finances.

Evelyn Anne's sister, Louisa, had married an Ernest Moore, a small jolly man from Newhaven. Young Patrick had taken a shine to him and the sisters would watch them playing in the garden.

'It should be Harry out there spending these precious moments,' Evelyn Anne said one day. 'A boy needs a father.'

Harry was spending ever more time in his brother's house, the reason being that Florence had a sister who had taken a shine to Harry and his charms. Bertha Botting was chubby and voluptuous and nourished Harry's ego with her flirtatious giggles and naive responses to his little jokes and innuendos. He allowed her to walk with him in the park on Lewes Road, sometimes even daring to take a tram down to the pier where they would promenade. He would leave Bertha on the sea front and walk back to Nelson Row via a pub or two on the way.

Evelyn Anne dreaded him coming through the door. It was often on a Sunday morning when Wilhelm and Annie were in church that Harry would appear and the ranting would start and it was always the same. Harry would storm off later via the Arches, a couple of pubs - and back into the welcoming arms of Bertha Botting.

8. Sordid Liaison

Harry cared little for the affections of Bertha; her sister Florence cared little for Harry and told Bertha what she thought of him.

'For one thing he's married. This can only end in tears.'

But Bertha was besotted and believed everything Harry told her, as he strung her along in his tiresome game of lies and deception. Empty of any compassion for his marriage to Evelyn Anne and the welfare of his three young children, Bertha stayed smitten and selfishly melted to his lurid affections to the embarrassment of Florence and William.

Harry had stepped over the threshold, away from the loyalty he had felt for Evelyn Anne, His feelings for her were fast fading so he went all the way. Why the hell not?

It happened in the basement kitchen of Brewer Street, where earthenware milk jugs were hurriedly removed from the scrubbed-pine table top. He had no care or respect for this space; it did not belong to him but only to his actions. He shoved her back on to the table, which squeaked as the wooden legs rocked back and forth against the quarry tiles underneath, where clutching at each other's clothing Bertha begged Harry to say that she was the love he desired. Her chubby fingers fumbled through his red hair pulling at his ears and digging her nails into his neck. Harry screwed his eyes shut and was repelled at the thought of her even as he embraced her, as she tried to leave her mark on him. He hated her lavender-scrubbed, plump skin.

Bertha welcomed his sexual aggression as a sign of his desire for her, but Harry's need was only to release his frustration. Bertha arched her back across the table as Harry used his forceful advances to show he was in control, gripping onto both of her legs. She allowed him to push up her petticoats and let Harry do whatever he needed to do. There was no passion, only sexual fulfillment.

As soon as it was over, he pulled away and left her to adjust her clothing. He walked into the backyard, washed his hands and face with water from the tap and felt - angry. He was not entirely sure of who he was hurting the most - Evelyn Anne or himself - but certainly it would end in tears for Bertha. He did not care tupppence for her feelings.

Evelyn Anne endured Harry`s endless verbal abuse and his aggressive behavior, holding her head not in shame but with strained dignity that stung his gigantic ego. Like a child who is not allowed a toy, he threw it and broke it. She was his toy. He knew he could not keep her so he hurt her. He would not show Bertha any want or desire either and that evening he crawled back to Nelson Place where Evelyn Anne laid rigid in the iron bed huddled to the baby James. She sensed he had been with a woman. She could smell it on him and this time the smell was not disguised by the putrid odor of ale.

'I love you Evie,' he said pathetically.

She lay with a stillness that dared her not to breathe a response.

WEST PARK

I smell your hair and push my fingers through the tangles of it. 'Evie are you sleeping? I've done something bad. I don't know why. Evie are you sleeping? Please don't cry, I'm not worth it. I've been so bad to you. Please Evie, love me like you used to.'

I'm putting my hand on her cheek. It's pale and transparent. 'Evie you're cold, ice cold, why won't you wake up?'

'They've killed her!' Harry yelled at the top of his voice. 'They've murdered her in her own bed. Now they're coming for me. I need to get to her; I need to go home to Brighton!'

'He's off again,' said the orderly and put his hands on Harry's shoulders, shaking him to wake him up, but Harry's eyes were already as wide as a barn owl's, his feverish forehead was covered in sweat beads as the nurse cooled him with a damp flannel.

'He'll wake the other patients and set them off,' she complained. But who was she to care about anything other than a quiet shift so she could continue doing her crossword, now crumpled and un-solved on the desk at her station? Who was she to Harry? Her starched and crisp uniform came from a later time, a time belonging to Bill Haley and the Comets, linked to milk bars and twirling poodle skirts, nothing to do with his world. She cared nothing of love and pebbles on beaches, of mountains and trees, a mother's smile from underneath a black bonnet, a brother's word of whining wisdom. Her hair neatly combed, she knew nothing about bolts slamming across wooden prison doors, mud in the trenches of France or cold nights sleeping on a pavement with London rain beating down on your damp overcoat, trickling down your back.

Harry coughed. Tiny splatters of blood spat down on to his sheet.

'I'm not changing that tonight,' she said. She cared not a penny for what was contained in the head of this man. Sitting back in her chair she picked up her pencil. *Seven across, nine letters, 'intervene', yes!* she grinned to herself.

Harry stared at the ceiling, worrying about Evelyn Anne.

'You okay now, Harry?' asked the orderly as he walked past the end of Harry's bed. Harry wanted to reply but the words would not come. His memory struggled to contain the simple things he was told from a few minutes previously, but back in Brighton all those years ago his memory produced a clarity that was as clear as any Sussex sunny day.

1911

For months, Bertha had been trying to hide the swelling of her well-rounded stomach. As her waist expanded under the folds of her skirt, the waistband of her cotton apron sat creased, crumpled and squashed under her large and swollen breasts.

Harry had not touched her since that day in the basement kitchen. His avoidance of her suffocating attention became evident to Florence, who was increasingly irritated by the situation. Why Harry still came to visit them was beyond her belief. For Harry it was all part of his game of retaliation at life's blows. His ego strutted and flaunted in front of William as Bertha displayed her affection for all to see. Harry ignored her advances but to no avail; he was not able to deter her.

One day Bertha brazenly announced she was going to have a child and Harry was the father. He was appalled and denied everything. Of course, he was unable to get away with his lies. Those who were close to him were tired of trying to keep up with his slanted versions of the truth. The news reached Wilhelm Gaebel who decided it was time to protect his daughter in the only way he knew how.

Evelyn Anne had found out about his liaison with Bertha and she confronted him. His guilt pushed him into a corner and the only way to escape confrontation was to lash out, so he punched her.

'Can't they all see I want nothing to do with her?' He ranted. 'The woman is all over me.'

Unfortunately for Evelyn Anne, and her children, they were forced to witness his rage, in the tiny room at the top of Wilhelm's house. Wilhelm closed his bedroom door gently turning the key in the lock. He patted his wife Annie's hand as they listened to the raised voices, followed by sobs then a painful silence. They could not interfere. His heart was heavy with sorrow and he closed his eyes, wondering how this was all going to end.

Harry left Evelyn Anne crying silently into her cotton sleeves, slamming doors behind him as he walked out into the small lane of Nelson's Row. He stood motionless, in the light drizzle of the early evening rain. The gaslights from the Palace Pier beckoned him to walk down the hill and through the myriad of lanes where there was a pub on every lamp-lit corner. His escape - onwards he stomped on the cold cobbles, each step cursing, each drink another drowning of despair. The thought of her crying stabbed him like a poker through his heart. He didn't make it to the Pier but turned right and walked towards Brewer Street. Not to see Bertha but to see his Brother William to confront him.

By morning when Harry at last turned up at Brewer Street. William stood in the front parlor of 11 Brewer Street with his hands in his pockets. Florence sat anxiously in the chair beside the fireplace.

'Someone better let him in,' said William eventually. Their mother, Mary Cornell, was visiting to discuss the forthcoming marriage of her daughter Maggie to a Christopher Redman, a sailor from Chatham. She was excited that her daughter was to marry but upset because it meant Maggie would move away. Harry's loud banging on the door shook the house. Mary Cornell who was in the hallway moved towards the front door.

'He's drunk William,' said Florence. I don't want him in my home please, William.'

Mary Cornell felt she had to open the door to her distressed son. She knew what was going on in his head. She saw it in the look he gave her, just as she had seen it in his eyes the day he was convicted and stood in the dock at Clerkenwell. She knew he was guilty but at the same time she heard his inner, child-like voice crying out to be understood. *Nothing has changed Harry*, she thought to herself, *and I still don't know how to help you.* Unable to offer arms of comfort nor to allow tears wept onto her shoulder, Mary Cornell kept her Victorian composure, her chin as rigid as rock and her eyes tensed with tears that were locked away behind aching eye sockets and closed bedroom doors. She had once hoped Harry would find a way to reach out to her, but she also knew that he had given up on her affection years ago.

Harry stood on the step.

'William! Can you hear me, you fuckin' told him, didn't you? You told him I'm the father of Bertha's baby. Get out here, William, and tell me what you said to Wilhelm!'

A door opened opposite on the other side of the street and neighbors looked out to see what all the commotion was about. Harry kneeled on the steps and clung on to the handrail leading up to the front doorway. He hung his head over the iron railings and looked down towards the open window of the basement.

'Mum!' he shouted, 'tell William he is a fuckin' liar. I don't love that bloody women. I never touched her.'

'I'll deal with him,' said William to Florence. 'I don't want the whole street witnessing this.'

Mary Cornell looked down at her son, sobbing on the black-and-white checkered steps.

'Where - is - he?' he asked her, his husky voice spitting out the words like darts hitting a dartboard. 'Where - is - William?'

'Harry, calm down.' Mary Cornell opened the door wide for him to enter.

'Let's sort this out in a dignified manner,' said William from the hallway, blocking the way.

'Why?' asked Harry. He pushed past his mother and dropped onto the bottom of the stairs putting his head into his hands. 'Why did you tell Wilhelm, William?'

Florence appeared in the doorway with her hands on her hips.

'It was me, Harry, not William,' she said. 'I told Wilhelm about your sordid liaison with my sister - and I told him to tell Evie.'

'Tell your woman she's wrecked my marriage,' Harry shouted at William.

'No, she's not,' said William, 'you done that yourself, Harry. Now please, you'd better leave.'

'Go back to Evie,' said Mary Cornell, 'try to save what you have. Think of the children, Harry.'

Harry walked towards the door. He shook his head in disbelief.

'Look at you all here, all warm and cozy, look at you, Lord God, look at you.'

*

Dennis Scully handed Evelyn Anne a bag of potatoes when they met in Nelson's Row

'Evie, has he lied again? Has he punched you?' Dennis whispered. 'He's a spineless drunk and this needs to stop. You know it.'

Dennis Scully needed to know what Harry was doing; his store of that sort of information was what kept him protected on the patch, the one Alf Goldwater ruled over. He followed Harry's movements as intensely as any other business that linked him to Goldwater. Evelyn Anne sat on the wall outside her father's house and clutched her arms about her knees. Her striped skirt was threadbare and trailed unevenly on the cobbled path; her cheeks were flushed and reddened from the tears that had streaked down them. Tilting her head back, strands of her blonde hair fell listlessly behind her ears. The smell of cooked cabbage and potatoes filled the early evening air and kids in the Row were being called in for their tea.

'I can't say, Dennis,' she said, looking at the ground. 'It's probably because I know about what he's done to Bertha and now my father knows too. I'm scared shitless. Harry can explode at the slightest problem.'

Dennis Scully checked to make sure nobody was watching them then clasped his fingers around her chin.

'Evie, what is it?'

She stood up and walked towards the lines of washing zigzagging across Nelson's Row, they walked through drying nappies, tea cloths and workingmen's flannel shirts.

'He went over to William's causing all sorts of fuss; he went round there going barmy, all the way over to Brewer Street, and now the whole bloody street knows what he did. Worse, he accused William of telling my Dad. How will he be able to stomach this? He's really angry.'

Her shaky voice trembled.

'There's more, Dennis. The night before last he had a go at Patrick, hit his head against the door. I'm frightened for my kids. What if he touches the baby? Baby's crying all the time. I can't calm him down, I just can't. Harry has really lost it this time and he's telling me it is all my fault. I can't take this anymore.'

'He's a bloody idiot, and it is not your fault, woman.'

'Please, Dennis. You can't tell anyone else.'

Dennis Scully walked her back to her front door. He put his arm around her shoulder but Evelyn Anne just stared ahead. As hard as she tried to contort her face, her mouth tightened, then her eyes filled up.

'I wish I could just run away from him, Dennis, but my parents couldn't take the shame of it and who am I to ask them to lie for me? He'll kill me, Dennis. Next time he'll kill me, I know he will. And then my kids will see their dad hang. I can't bear the thought of the workhouse. I'll not take the kids there, he'll find us anyway and never let us go.'

They sat in silence for a moment. Dennis Scully felt sick in his stomach, thinking of Harry, drunk and out of control.

'Evie, you have to leave. If I promised you I would take care of it and get the kids to a safe place and sort you somewhere you can hide - would you do it? Would you leave him?'

'Don't do anything stupid. Harry has a good soul deep down. He doesn't mean it; it's just the drink; he can't help it.'

'I'll take care of it, don't worry.'

Evelyn Anne stood up and he watched as she limped over to the baby in the perambulator. She lifted the sleepy little boy and cradled him in her arms, holding him to her breast.

'I need to feed him in case Harry gets back. Thanks for the potatoes, thanks for everything. I'll be okay now, I promise' She wanted him to go. She did not want her parents to see her weeping and she could hear their voices in the kitchen.

Dennis Scully left and, as he left, he planned in his mind what he could do. He had known Harry long enough now to know what he was capable of, especially when he was drunk. He had seen him in punch-ups when they worked on the railway. Harry had received his fair share of beatings, and when he had downed a few pints all reason went out the window.

Dennis thought about Evelyn Anne back in the days when they all met up on the West Pier. Her big eyes, they were as round as the moon itself. Beautiful little Evie that Harry had become besotted over and Dennis Scully had to painfully witness - painfully because he had loved her too from the first moment he had laid eyes on her. He sighed; things were complicated. He remained loyal to his own wife and his little boy who shared his first name, fondly known as 'Dennis Junior'. He held loyalty close to his heart where it sat high in the ranks of his warped morals. Now he had made a promise to Evelyn Anne and that was good because he could at least pour his love for her into keeping his word. He walked to the end of the Nelson's Row and up to where he lived on Carlton Hill. The sun was going down. All these difficulties - he thought about turning back down the hill, to get a pint in one of the many taverns that lined the bottom by the Lewes Road. As he turned, he heard hooves clip-clopping over the cobbles and the wheels of a cart. It was the mule and cart that belonged to Alf Goldwater.

Harry was guiding the cart into Nelson Row.

Harry, drunk and with a bottle in his hand, fell down on to the path outside his house. Dennis Scully could just see the back of Harry and he was on his own. He was still angry and anxious for Evelyn Anne. His fingers grasped around the bone handle on a penknife he carried. The street had no gaslight and was empty. Just for a fleeting moment he visualized himself lurching forward. *This could all be over in a moment, why not?*

Dennis Scully froze to the spot at the end of the lane. Even he was not prepared to hang for the murder of a violent but damn stupid drunk, he would find another way to finish this. He needed to find a way to protect her and the kids.

Finally Harry made it through his front door. Dennis Scully waited. He wanted to make sure Evelyn Anne would be okay, he wondered if he should linger in the shadows outside, but then he convinced himself it would be better to walk away. He knew he would only make the situation worse if Harry found out he had been there.

Harry sat on the end of his bed and watched as Evelyn Anne tucked Patrick and May into the small bed they shared at the end of the landing. The baby was sleeping soundly in a wicker cradle at the bottom of their bed. Her parents slept in a room downstairs and had taken their meal separately, Harry did not care about them but he did care about losing his wife.

'Where were you?' She plucked up courage to ask after they had eaten.

'Looking for work,' he said. 'I've got Alf's cart again. I done a couple of jobs for him.'

'You got any money, Harry - for the children?'

'If I did, I'd give you. I'll get some tomorrow.' He had managed to buy some beer and cigarettes. Evelyn Anne resented that.

The drink had made Harry's head swim. He needed to lay back on his feather pillows. Scrunching up the coarse, brown blanket and the eiderdown, he closed his eyes, breathing heavily.

Evelyn Anne undid the laces on his boots and set them down by the fire that was still flickering in the hearth. The warmer months were coming but the nights were still cold. Coal was expensive but she had managed to get some with money she had saved from taking in some mending. Not scared of hard work, she kept the room and her children as clean, warm and well fed as she could manage. She had developed a skill for cooking and producing meals made from very little. The mash potatoes they had eaten that night were a real luxury, cooked with gravy that had been left over from the Sunday roast a few days earlier.

The food had sobered Harry and he had been in a fair mood. As the atmosphere calmed, Evelyn Anne worried less. There had been an episode two nights before when she had struggled with Harry when he had pushed Patrick against the door and held his hair scrunched tightly in his fingers, Patrick had lost consciousness for a couple of seconds. Evelyn Anne had panicked; she had realised Harry was oblivious to what he had done. She lay still as a board on the bed next to him and only fell asleep after she heard him snoring. *What's going on in your head Harry, should I leave you? We can't stay here. When did it all go wrong?*

*

Early morning mist dampened the wooden, slatted seating that faced the fish market. Barely visible through the dim light were the grey and scarred arms of men carrying wooden crates, stacking them ready to be filled with the catch of the day. Their idle chatter as they hauled the crates over their shoulders filled the damp air along with the salty smell of the sea in the background.

Dennis Scully leaned forward on the bench, his huge hands clasped together as he stared at the ground deep in thought. You had to be careful down there; it was a meeting patch for undesirables, and it was not often that Dennis sat alone. He had his own ring of mates he could rely on, he had many favors owed to him and it was time to call in a few. If it was up to him, Harry Cornell would be facing a nasty accident and there were plenty around who could oblige him in performing such a deed.

Alf Goldwater sat down beside Dennis; he was munching on some bread and salted beef. Alf Goldwater had his own pitch at the fish market down by the King's Road Arches, which he shared with his brother in law Alf Gunn after they both left the railway. He commanded respect and he knew how to exert pressure when things got in the way of business deals he was involved in. Dennis Scully had worked with Alf Goldwater since he had arrived with his family from Ireland. Alf Goldwater had taken him under his wing and kept the young immigrant out of trouble.

'Bloody Cornell,' said Dennis Scully.

'What's the problem?' Alf Goldwater wiped his mouth on a screwed up silk hanky, pulled from his overcoat pocket. 'Got feelings for Cornell's woman, have you? Probably deserves a good slapping; what's she been whining about?'

'Harry needs teaching a lesson but I promised we wouldn't touch him.'

Alf Goldwater shrugged.

'Harry been naughty has he?'

'A bit, but he still has his uses Alf. He can be hot-headed but he's keen and he won't let us down. I just need some help sorting a few problems.

*

Evelyn Anne stood on the corner of Trinity Street facing No. 11 Brewer Street. It was a Sunday morning and the Congregation was leaving St Martins Church. They spilled out on to the cobbled street. Bell ringers tugged away at the bell pulls, distance bells competed in conjunction with the rattling of trams which trundled past on Lewes Road, taking day-trippers down to Brighton.

This was no day trip for her. May tugged at her skirt crying and Patrick sat on the kerb, his little bruised cheeks red from the tears. He wanted to go home; he wanted it to stop raining. Evelyn Anne covered the baby's head with her shawl and pulled the kids towards the front door.

'Is she here?' she asked Florence when her sister in law answered the door. 'Is she here?'

Florence was shocked to see her unexpectedly standing there so bedraggled and unhappy.

'Bertha! Look here, these are my children. Do you want them too, as well as my husband?' Evelyn Anne shouted into the house. She pushed the children forward and told them to go to Florence who ushered Patrick and May in through the front door.

'Don't let Harry hurt them, Florence. They're still my children.' She walked back down the street, carrying the baby, towards the small crowd gathering outside the church. At the bottom of the road was Dennis Scully, waiting with a mule and cart. He had known she would go there. He needed to get to her before Harry found out she was there and started making trouble. Alf Goldwater was sorting things and it would not be long now.

Evelyn Anne cried out Berthas name. She saw a hand on the lace curtain.

*

Harry couldn't wait to tell Evelyn Anne that he had taken two rooms in Jubilee Street. He had paid one month's rent. He needed to get her away from her parent's house so they could all be together. If he did this and demonstrated that he could be committed, then this horrible business of Bertha Botting would all go away. It was a chance to make things better. He had made a few extra shillings cleaning and repairing boots. There was enough to give her for some coal and food.

*

Mary Cornell took the hand of her grandson Patrick and they walked towards the Level, the park near Brewer Street.

'Mummy will be back soon,' she told him. 'You're a very lucky boy; you're going to come and stay with your Nana and your Aunties.'

*

Meanwhile, three-year-old May twirled her brown, curly hair around her fingers and held on tightly to the skirt of her Aunt Mary Louisa as she stood in the doorway of Mr.& Mrs. Mayer's in Artillery Street.

'It's just be for a couple of months then Mummy will come and get you,' said Mary Louisa as she tried to console the crying toddler.

*

Evelyn Anne clung to her baby at the back door of the workhouse; he was only ten months old.

'You have to,' said Dennis. 'You can't take this work if they know you have a child. It'll only be for a few months, Evie.'

The plump and tired-looking woman took the infant from her arms.

'There love, just sign here,' she told Dennis Scully. She opened the brown book and wrote, *mother is ill*, in one column. Above was a long list of names and guardians scrawled in neat handwriting. Dennis Scully took out a pen and wrote *Harry Cornell* in neat hand-writing.

'I'll come back soon,' Evelyn Anne said tearfully. She kissed baby James and stroked his cheeks. *Harry can't harm the children now,* she told herself.

The door creaked as Dennis Scully held it open. The women held the infant on her hip and told them it was time to leave and she would take care of everything. Dennis Scully gave her a small bag of coins that she pushed between her bosoms.

Together and without saying a word, they walked quickly down Elm Grove, and away from the workhouse. The cart was waiting. Evelyn Anne had a small brown suitcase and was clutching her purse with the money her father had given her earlier. She hugged him tight.

'Goodbye, Evie,' he said. 'You'll be safe in Eastbourne.'

'When I've enough money saved, I'll come and get them.'

But the night Evelyn Anne left Brighton was a night that changed futures, it was a night that brought darkness over a family, a night that set the seeds that grew into division, despair and hatred, enough to run for decades through the veins of uncles, aunts, cousins and grandchildren. A night that left more questions than answers, those concerned, who could not get their questions answered, choosing to remain silent, harboring their own conclusions.

She never returned to Brighton.

*

Harry awoke in his chair to the sound of a policeman thumping on his door. He had slept in the chair all night long, waiting for Evelyn Anne to come home. Four empty beer bottles lay on the floor where he had dropped them. He jumped up, thinking it was her and the children. As he opened the door he was maddened at the sight of the policeman on the doorstep.

'Bloody coppers what now? I've done nothing.'

'Okay Mr. Cornell, please calm down, sir.'

'Where's my wife and kids? You bastards, you know where they are.'

'Mr. Cornell, we don't know the whereabouts of your wife, sir, but we'd like to know why you paid a woman to take your son at the workhouse. It's against the law, sir. A Mrs. Crabtree has been arrested up at the workhouse.'

Harry took a step back.

'She was going to *sell* your son, Harry,' said the policeman suddenly recognizing him. 'We have him here, and you need to take him.'

Behind the policeman was a woman from the church.

'Is this your son, Mr. Cornell?' She handed him to Harry.

Harry, with tears in his eyes, just nodded.

'Please make sure you look after him properly, sir,' said the woman. 'You really need to find his mother.'

WEST PARK

'Hey kid, do you know me? I don't know where she is so stop yelling. Tiny little one, a bit of me, a bit of her, ha ha. That's it sonny, grab my little finger. You just sleep and I'll be back in a while. Shh... and your ole Dad'll bring you back some warm milk. There that's a promise and I'll go find your Mum eh? How about I go find your Mum and bring her back home with Patrick and May, and a nice bit o' bacon for me tea?'

Nurse McCarthy was back on her shift.

'I hear you had an eventful night Harry,' she said as she changed his bedclothes.

'You need to look after your baby, Evie. He's been crying. I can't make him go to sleep. You've been gone too long.'

'Well, I'm back now, Harry, and I've not got a baby, remember.' Harry laughed.

'Why are you joking with me, woman?'

'I'm not joking. Can you hear a baby crying? No you can't. Well, not on this ward anyhow.'

JUBILEE STREET. BRIGHTON

'What you doing here?' asked Harry.

His Mary Louisa stood in the doorway clutching at her shawl. It was later on the day after the police returned baby James from the workhouse.

'Come to gloat have you?' he added.

'I've just heard about the baby. Come on, let me make you some tea. How could she leave the little mite at the workhouse?' She looked down affectionately at the sleeping infant. 'Patrick's with Mum and I've dropped May off with Mr. and Mrs. Mayer's. They're both safe and well.'

Mary Louisa was due to go off to work in service in a few weeks and now she was concerned about Harry, who was obviously distraught. She feared for him. Who would be there to help him come to terms with this? He had brought shame on the family. Evelyn Anne's reputation had taken a blow too.

'What sort of mother could desert her husband and three children in this way? Little Patrick's crying for his mummy. May, bless her heart, doesn't understand why her mum has left her. There was no room for baby William in Artillery Street, what with Thomas Mayer out on the boats all day long.

'He can stay here,' Harry interrupted her. He put his hand on the crib, 'The kids can all come here. I'll find Evie, she has to come home. There's no way Evie would leave the kids, not like this.'

The house stank of stale beer and cigarettes. The pots were not emptied and Harry needed a bath by the smell of him. Baby William needed changing and had been crying for hours before falling asleep from exhaustion and probably hunger. Mary Louisa put some water on to boil and opened the windows.

Harry felt abandoned, lost in all the confusion; he was still trying to deal with the shock of Evelyn Anne's departure.

'Harry, I'm cooking you up some soup with some bread I've brought from Mum's. You have to eat something.'

She gave him a clean shirt she had prepared for him and he made his way towards the bedroom, stumbling on the bottom step. An hour later, washed and shaved, he was sitting at the table at the front window looking out onto the empty street.

'I have to find her, Mary, and bring her home. She belongs here with me.'

'Harry, she's gone. I don't think she'll come home, not after what has happened.' Mary Louisa averted her eyes. She put her hand across his hand.

'It wasn't me who gave baby James to a woman at the workhouse, I just can't believe Evelyn Anne would do that.'

Harry could not comprehend what had happened. Evelyn Anne would never abandon her children. He would find her and bring her back. He vowed to himself that he would look for her, she was the love of his life and he could not live without her and the kids. He would not give up on her. He would find a better job with regular work. *I will never touch her like that again* he promised himself.

'I have to go now, Harry,' said Marie Louisa. 'I'll come back tomorrow. I've broken some bread into warm milk. Make sure you feed the baby and here's a penny so go and get yourself some coal.'

Louisa left then James woke up and started crying again. Harry knew what he should do even as the anger swept over him, but he picked up his overcoat, took the penny Louisa had left him to buy some coal and made his way down the road towards the pub.

WEST PARK

'Go home you bloody piss head. She isn't here.' The barman is escorting me towards the door.

'Get off me!' I'm shouting, 'let go of my sleeve!' What does he know? Maybe she's gone to the pier. Yes, I'll go to the pier.

It's raining on my back; I can see the lights twinkling through the drizzle. The pier is where she will be waiting for me.

I can hear the music from the fairground; feel the pebbles crunching under my boots. 'Evie! Come on girl! Come to Harry, Come to Harry!'

I'm here waiting!

I'm watching the sun rising, in all its perfection.

It stretches light across the horizon.

'James,' I murmur. I can't breath as I rush home.

Run up the hill, Harry.

Bloody copper at my gate, in my house. 'Evie!' I shout. Has she come home?

The copper has my son James in a blanket. He's yelling at me. 'This child is in a sorry state, Harry. Where've you been?'

'Get your bloody hands off my son, copper!' I'm shouting.

There's a woman at the gate and she's spitting at me.

'You're a cruel man, Harry Cornell, a cruel, evil man.'

'Bring him back!' I'm shouting. 'You bastards! Bring him back!'

9. For King and Country

Bertha gave birth to a son on the 11th January 1912. Still trying to convince all her family of Harry's undying love for her, she insisted that the child was to be named Henry William Cornell. Some days later, she sat at the kitchen table twiddling with the brown strands of hair that fell on to the nape of her neck.

'He'll love him, once he sees him, I know he will' she told her sister Florence who was growing tired of her younger sister's inability to grasp the reality of the situation.

'Harry Cornell doesn't give a hoot for you or the baby.' Florence was annoyed that she could not get through to Bertha. Bertha had ruined her reputation. 'Look what's happened to Evie, and the situation she's in.'

Bertha turned her eyes away from her sister's glare.

'I don't care about her. Harry loves me.'

'Bertha!' Florence grabbed Bertha's shoulders. 'He's not even made time to visit young Patrick, poor little mite, or his mum. Believe me Bertha, it's best you just forget him. Find yourself a proper husband and a father for the baby.'

'He loves me Florence. He told me in so many words.'

'Forget him Bertha – please.'

Harry will never change; love is blind, poor Bertha Florence told herself. 'Bloody Harry,' she said. 'I hate how he's treated you. It's just not fair.'

Harry, adamant the child was not his, was having nothing to do with Bertha. It angered him how they judged him. He avoided visiting his brother and Florence. Meanwhile, his mother

Mary Cornell and his sisters were now living in Grosvenor Street where Mary worked hard at running her small guesthouse to make ends meet. The boy, Patrick, was living with them. Harry avoided them too. *How wrong they all are,* he thought self-pityingly, dragged down again to a low morale. *What makes them so righteous?* Just the thought of them reminded him of his failure as a husband and father.

He turned to what he did best. Any money he earned found its way straight into to tills of the local public houses as he wallowed within his tenebrous lifestyle.

*

By the end of that year, his mother had packed up the guesthouse. It had proved too much for her to cope with. She moved up to Chatham, near London to be near her daughter Maggie and her new husband. Her other daughters, Blanche, Sarah and Amy had already left. Maggie now had a young son and was pleased about the extra help she could expect to receive by having her family nearby. Mary Louisa did not go to Chatham and was working in service at the Metropole Hotel in Christchurch.

*

Six months after the arrival of Bertha's baby, a policeman stood yet again on Harry's doorstep, this time with a warrant for his arrest - not for being drunk and disorderly but for willingly neglecting a child. It was the way the judge repeated the word *'willingly,'* that kicked Harry back, like a shotgun into his shoulder, as he stood in the courtroom. *'Willingly,'* as if with intention. He laughed in his stomach at the stupidity of the word, how it made him want to vomit. He summoned the last of his strength and held it in place with resentment of the establishment. How could the judge could have the slightest idea how he felt? Harry knew that he was incapable of *willing* all this misfortune.

From then on, the only time anything made sense was when he was highly intoxicated, happy to wallow in the chaos and for some absurd reason he could see things for what they were, unfortunately through misted vision. He understood that he had lost control and that he was a puppet in the hands of those who judged him. As he told the policeman when he was led off to prison once again, for one more month of hard labour: 'No need for a fucking prison, copper; I am chained to a life that's a living hell.'

*

Dennis Scully had paid Harry's rent as Alf Goldwater had instructed him. Harry still had his uses and Alf Goldwater needed him in his debt. He still had links to contacts in Clerkenwell and although Harry had only been a kid when he had sent him there, he knew Harry still craved action should the need arise. What made Alf Goldwater nervous were Harry's drinking binges.

'Watch him,' he would say, 'watch Cornell. He'll drop us in it one day, I swear.'

Dennis Scully feared for Harry but thought the he needed a chance to prove himself.

'Stay on the safe side,' he told him in his soft Irish accent, 'for your own sake and your mother's. She's a sweet women so she is.'

Harry could string a yarn, but so far had never breathed Alf Goldwater's name in any of his drunken episodes. One wrong move or a word out of place could end up with him face down in a gutter with a rusty bread knife in his back. He was well aware of the consequences of dropping Alf Goldwater in it.

Grateful to the burly Jew, the only higher source he was prepared to answer to, Harry at least had a roof over his head. If he played Alf Goldwater's game, he could soldier on and stay safe. But sometimes, when music played in the distance, filling the air as it screeched out from the music hall on the pier, and when the sunrays hit the surf illuminating bubbles over the stones on Brighton beach, Harry felt so alone.

Rain hit the grey paving stones in Jubilee Street and Harry squinted through the streaked, watery, sash-windows looking down into the street, the pain in his head added to his difficulty in focusing. He watched the droplets of water as they hit the stones and puddles forming alongside the kerb and how the water collected and worked its way towards the drain hole. He lit a candle to try and bring some extra light into the empty room. The taste of the beer coated the back of his throat as he grabbed a cigarette butt he had placed in a saucer on top of the chest of drawers. Beer was his saving indulgence. The warm feeling comforted him and took away the pain in his head.

The rain didn't worry him when he later pulled on his jacket and slammed the door. On his way to the Arches, he looked in the face of every woman who hurried past him.

Harry felt the over-burdening loss of Evelyn Anne and would turn to Dennis Scully.

'Let her go, for crying out loud!' Dennis would reply lifting up his arms, un-characteristically passionate. 'You need to pull yourself together and stop fretting over her. Accept that she's gone for good.'

'If you know where she is, Dennis, can you give her a message from me? Tell her I'm sorry for the way I treated her.'

Then Harry would would stop speaking, as if someone had slapped him across his weary face and retreat back into his world of self-pity for fear of being out of control, back-tracking on words, shoving them away and burying them deep so they could fester feed and breed on un-clear delusions.

*

Dennis Scully stood with Alf Goldwater and observed Harry standing on the beach and staring out to sea.

'He wants the job in Newhaven,' Alf Goldwater commented. 'Want to go with him?'

Dennis Scully shrugged.

'I'm not happy with it, Alf. He's looking, for his Mrs. He's obsessed if you ask me.'

'Who said I was asking? Just sort it, Dennis. I need Harry back on the patch and he's like a bleeding wet rag. I said he could go to Newhaven. Just need to know when.'

Dennis Scully was right; Harry wanted that job, he wanted to get out of Brighton. He came up with an excuse so Alf Goldwater did not pressurize him into being Harry's minder.

WEST PARK

Dr. Howard wanted a holiday. This was wishful thinking because the hospital laid great demands on him. He found himself counting the days down towards his retirement. When the war finally ended, the running of the hospital was slow to return to how it had been in the old days.

There were new drugs coming on to the market that were very exciting. Some treatments used on the patients in the hospital in the past, had left him feeling uncomfortable. Even though he had convinced himself that they had caused marked improvements in a number of his patients, there were many who had obviously suffered quite badly. There was nothing else he had been able to offer them.

News about the horrors of war and the Holocaust were gathering momentum in the newspapers. Stories had reached him through colleagues about the practices of the Nazi surgeons and although they were classed as un-confirmed speculations, he believed it was possible those horrific surgical procedures had taken place.

What if I had been German he wondered? *Would I have allowed myself to be coerced into these malpractices given what we've had to do here?* The question morbidly intrigued him. Fortunately he was not German and not facing any criminal court. He was relieved when, at the end of the war, they started to learn about drugs such as *Largactil* and *CPZ*. These relatively new drugs helped calm the patients and made his working day easier as well as his nurses'. It frustrated him that there had been another outbreak of TB on the ward. It added extra pressure just when his overworked and restless staff might have expected some respite.

Matron popped her head around the door.

'Can I tempt you to a nice cup of tea, Alex?' she asked.

Dr.Howard welcomed this rare example of one of the matron's human moments. They were few and far between. *Some of us really are sane,* he thought.

'The condition of Harry Cornell - quite worrying,' she said. 'The nursing staff say he's delusional. Is he saying much?'

'Not really; he's mostly jabbering on about his wife.'

'What are you going to give him?'

Dr. Howard did not answer. He clasped his hands together.

'You've thought about it haven't you, Alex?'

'It was such a long time ago that he came here,' Dr. Howard said. 'We should let him die as the man he was. He's not in too much pain. Why knock him out?'

'Is he getting distressed?'

'Just frustrated. None of what he says will make any sense to anyone.'

'Nevertheless,' Matron looked serious, 'would you really want to take the risk Alex? Think about it.'

The sympathetic side of Dr. Howard struggled to reason with himself. His values were versatile but needed justification. He had sailed close to the wind on many medical decisions he had been faced with but wherever possible, he had tried to put his patients first. Harry Cornell had been a difficult one. He had questioned himself many times over how to diagnose him. The man was delusional, probably brought on by neurasthenia, his mode of life, alcohol, maybe even cocaine. But Dr. Howard had wondered about the diagnosis of *Delusional Insanity* that Harry carried with him when he arrived. Truth be told, his acceptance of this diagnosis was not entirely separate from his acceptance of the donation of several hundred pounds made shortly after Harry's admission, a welcome addition to the Asylum funds. And anyway, and with the war going on in Europe, why would he not go with the diagnosis he had been persuaded to enter on the admission form all those years ago? Eleven years ago to be precise. If now he was letting Harry have his say, just before the end, what harm could it do?

I'm watching them carry Wilhelm in his coffin with the polished brass handles.

'Has Evie come? Is she here? She must be here. Have you seen Evie?' I'm asking Annie.

'Go home Harry. My daughter's not here.'

Surely Evie would not miss her own dad's funeral?

'Go home Harry.'

I see her - her black coat and wide straw hat, her hair strands down her back. She turns and looks.

'Harry, I'm Pauline.'

Evie's sister.

'I thought you were Evie - sorry!'

'Newhaven - she's gone to Newhaven.' Pauline's mouthing that to me as she follows the coffin. I think, yes, I'm sure - she's saying 'Newhaven'.

Nurse McCarthy wiped his brow with a soft, damp flannel. She studied his face as he closed his eyes and drifted.

BRIGHTON 1914

Brighton was bracing itself for the influx of day-trippers about to descend onto its beaches for the August Bank Holiday. The headline in the *Daily Telegraph* announced '*BRITAIN EXPECTS EVERY MAN TO DO HIS DUTY.*'

Visitors promenaded Brighton sea front, gaily adorning summer smiles under straw boaters, war was muttered on their lips as it entered their idle chatter. Harry kept his head down and his shirtsleeves rolled up over his elbows, intermingling amongst the happy day-trippers.

Each smiling and giggling group of young ladies in their

fancy summer frocks caught Harry's eye as he studied their faces then moved his eyes down, undressing each one slowly in his mind.

None were his Evelyn Anne. He wanted her soft hands on his aching shoulders. He thought of her lying back on the beach with her hair on the pebbles, he thought of the way he would kiss her face as he held her small waist tight and secure against his body. The smell of her body tucked and molded into his, in the little room in German Place.

He leaned against the green painted railings and looked down on the bathers. Striped fabric awnings angled in the pebbles, sheltering family groups: mothers tightly wrapped up in rickety deck chairs, brothers, sisters-in-law, and family friends sharing ice-cream that dripped down the side of cones and onto starched muslin cuffs. An impatient photographer enticed children to pose with pride as he tried to control their composure, giggling mischievously in their blue cotton bathing suits.

Harry listened to all the laughter and was mindful of music coming from the merry-go-round. The Blue Danube, fitting for painted white horses as they rose up and down on twirling poles, carrying riders in their frilled skirts and petticoats. Boys riding cheekily freestyle on the wooden platform at the base of the merry-go-round before jumping off as a dare, caught Harry's attention and amused him.

Seagulls squawked high above as they circled over his head, controlling the skies. There were always seagulls, their beady eyes watching for a miniscule of food discarded on the walkway. Every bird for himself he thought as he watched the game of survival flying in and out of this holiday chaos.

Harry had never felt more alone, cast out into an existence away from the Brighton beach he doubted if he had ever belonged to. There it was, the beach, stretched out in front of him like a gigantic stage. No longer a performer, he was merely a member of the audience, pushed to the back of the stalls, unable to get a good view. *Where were his children?* He wondered. *Were they sitting down there somewhere in this same sunshine? Was young Patrick throwing pebbles in the sea? Was May crying for her mummy? Could they be playing on the beach somewhere, in front of him?*

He turned his back on the beach. Suddenly, he resented the day trippers and wished they would all go back to their grimy little London slums with their happy, condescending faces grinning at every slightest moment that enhanced their '*beside-the-seaside experience,*' He wished they would stop rubbing his nose in what he could not have any more. His innocence was long gone and he wanted them to feel like he did, why not? *Why did they deserve the happiness he had been denied?*

*

War had been declared at the beginning of August and was slowly gathering momentum. The day was a hot one and the townspeople seemed fixated as they came out into the sunshine. Harry watched the crowd form a parade on Kings Road. This was no carnival; the mood was somber and a drum was beating. The crowd set off in the direction of *The Level*, an open park situated just on the edge of town. Posters had been displayed all over the town and the Mayor of Brighton and M.P. William Crook were going to make speeches.

'He understands the people,' said the landlord in the pub where Harry had called in. 'Crook was in the workhouse you know, and now he's really important, up there with all the bigwigs.'

Mary Cornell had told him proudly that William had enlisted but Harry had already seen him as he left the Odd Fellows Hall in Queens Road. William, in uniform, was walking with Florence and smiling as they strolled together down towards the town. Harry had stood hidden in the shadows of a doorway and watched them.

Would Evie be proud of him, if he was all dressed up like that? He imagined her waving him off to war, running along the platform at the train station, shouting his name and waving her straw boater in the air. He shrugged. He was ignoring all the hype. He was of the opinion that it would all be over by Christmas so best not to take it too seriously. Happy to find a pub on the sea front that was empty, he stood at the bar determinedly civilian. Local suffragettes Dora Miller and her sister Clara stood in the doorway.

'King and Country!' they called out to the townspeople marching along King's Road.

Harry was irritated by their presence in the doorway of his local, He ordered his pint and he sat with his back to the door, his shoulders forward. He looked at his hands and at his fingernails, blackened from his laboring work.

'Thought you would be at the meeting today, Harry,' said the landlady.

'They don't want married men, so no point.'

'Your Evie's long gone mate,' said the landlord lifting bottles of ale on to the wooden surface of the bar, sticky from an ineffective washing down with the grubby grey cloth he now had flung over his left shoulder. 'You should do your duty. You'll get out of Brighton, you might get the chance to leave England, get over to France.'

Harry downed his pint. He did not want to be lectured. He made his way outside onto the street. Dora Miller climbed down from the wall she had been sitting on and nudged her sister Clara, who raised her eyebrows under her black, wide-brimmed hat. Clara straightened her sash over her long grey coat and composed herself.

'Go on,' said Dora.

Clara pulled out a white feather and thrust it in Harry's hand. He scowled at her and threw it on the ground. They were giving white feathers to all the men not in uniform. He carried on walking away from her.

'Hey! Cornell!' she shouted, 'Go and do your duty for your King and Country - you a coward, eh?'

Harry, glared back at her and walked silently away. Later that evening, in a drunken stupor, during an argument in a pub in Jubilee Street, he was provoked into crazed retaliation. He attacked a man with a broken bottle and shouted obscene language at the arresting officer. He was sentenced to yet another three months' hard labour. The sentence was handed down on September15th 1914. Now he could not join the army even if he had wanted to.

Talk of war and news of injuries coming back from France reached the inquisitive ears of him and his fellow inmates in Lewes Prison. There was a thirst brewing, a way to release anger and frustration, a reason to embrace violence. The prisoners had a look about them, it said: *we can do this and for once we can be heroes. It's what we know.*

But not Harry, he had done his time trying to be a hero and where had it got him? He had no wish to serve his King and Country, why should he? He laid his head back on the straw prison mattress, the fleas in the bedding made a meal of his sweaty arms as they bit into his skin, now red from scratching. Suddenly, outside in the hallway, there were raised voices, his door opened and a prisoner stood in the opening.

'Get lost, Delany,' said Harry.

Delany stood with his arms folded across his chest.

'You better watch yourself. Cornell.' Delany rocked forward grinning a sarcastic smile that revealed his broken, jagged teeth. 'Goldwater's been arrested.'

Harry sat up.

'When?'

'Last night, down at the arches. There are a lot of people very unhappy.'

'Got nothing to do with me.' Harry laid back down.

'Your name's been mentioned - something about a job in Newhaven. Know anything about that do you, Harry?'

'Nothing to do with me.' Harry jumped up off the bed and pushed Delany out of his cell. He slammed the door shut. *I said nothing, nothing,* he thought to himself, but in the pit of his stomach he could not be sure. He had been off his face with drink the day they arrested him. He had only one day more to serve of his three-month sentence before he would get out of jail.

*

Outside the prison, Harry moved quickly into the road and jumped onto the back of a moving cart.

'Oi!' shouted the elderly driver.

'Just shut up and keep going old man, I need to get to Brighton.'

The old fella did as he was told. 'Someone after you?'

Harry said nothing.

'There's gratitude,' said the old man. 'Tell you what, I'll take you to the station. This mare is much too old to pull us both to Brighton.'

Harry nodded but kept his silence. He needed to get to his mother; for the first time ever, he was anxious about her safety.

*

'What d'you want, Harry?' Florence stood upright with her hands on both hips.

'Where's William?'

'He's joined up; he's left already

Harry asked Florence for the address in Chatham where his mother and sisters were living and then walked down Lewes Road towards the centre of Brighton. It was cold and getting late. He needed to find Dennis Scully and find out what had happened to Alf Goldwater. Walking up Carlton Hill he spied Dennis Scully's wife walking up ahead of him and followed her to her house. Peeling off before she got there, he followed the lane that ran along the back of the terrace and jumped over their back wall. He waited crouching in the back yard.

'I wondered how long it would take you to get here,' said Dennis's soft Irish voice from the shadows. ''Tis not safe for you here, Harry. I'll be in trouble just for you being here.'

'Fuck you, Dennis.'

'You're in big trouble.'

'What happened? I said nothing, I swear.'

'Alf's been arrested, Harry. You better run. Goldwater's sworn to find you - join the army, why don't 'cha.'

'With my police record?'

'Lie, save your skin. Goldwater thinks you've grassed. He's got men out looking for you.'

'And you, are you one of them?'

'That's for sure. And if he knew I was talking to you, I'd be in big trouble too.'

'So why then Dennis?'

Dennis Scully did not answer. Harry grabbed his shirt collar.

'Why not finish me here and now? What's stopping you, Dennis? Go on, pull your knife on me, and get it over with.'

'Quiet - someone will hear you.'

'Go on - do it!'

'No.'

'And why's that Dennis, you piece of chicken shit? Why not finish it off? I'm just a worthless old drunk aren't I?'

'No.'

'Stick a knife in me, finish the job. What's stopping you?'

'I promised.'

'What's that meant to mean? Who did you promise?'

Dennis Scully hesitated. 'I promised your wife.'

His words hit Harry like a blow to the head.

'When? Where is she?' he almost shouted.

'Lower your voice.'

'You fucking bastard. You know where she is don't you? Tell me where she is, Dennis.'

Dennis Scully wished he had controlled his words. He had to find a way to shock Harry into shutting up. He was in danger of Harry gripping onto every word he said, and that scared him. He decided to go for broke.

'She's dead, Harry, She died.'

Harry staggered backwards.

'No you're lying, you bastard, not Evie.'

Dennis crouched down and cradled his face in his hands. He was softer than he should have been and he did not want to see the pain in Harry's face. Harry looked like a living corpse, his face white and blank. His emotions seemed to have left him. With an obvious effort of will, he straightened his back.

'Join the army you say - join the fucking army!'

He leapt over the back wall and disappeared into the darkness.

10. Larkhill camp. Salisbury Plain.

Carefree are we to exist this way.
Falling leaves scatter on our paths.
There are words in you.
I hear what you say.
Scared is the night, dare you ask.
I dream I am leaving to faraway lands.
You will wave from the gate that is locked.
Your fingers stay limp as you lift up your hands.
And time stays behind - tick tock tick tock.

BRIGHTON 1915

As the London train pulled away from Brighton, he held his head down. He did not want to see anyone waving farewell. They were all strangers to him and any connection he had previously felt was now diminishing, leaving a feeling of emptiness lacking in sentiment.

The train, laden with other local men from Brighton and Hove, pushed slowly forward, there was a whistle and steam filled the platforms, people ran alongside waving.

Moving out onto open track, the train shunted forward. He saw the railway sheds he had once leant against with pickaxe and shovel, on those weary days as a young lad with Alf Goldwater and Dennis Scully and the rest of the boys. He pushed his thoughts of Brighton and what was left behind to the back of his mind and leaned his face against the window. The train wound its way through the Sussex countryside.

Mountains and trees - just memories he thought to himself, amused that his mountains were just rolling hillsides, blown all out of proportion when he was a kid. He observed the other men on the train and listened to them chattering amongst themselves, talking of duty and honour as they attempted to light their pipes and then posed in a style that they imagined gave them their masculinity.

Bloody kids, he thought, He watched their repeated attempts to stuff tobacco into the end of their pipes, clutching at their braces with the other hand as the train clumsily jolted over the track. The train carriage became filled with a fog of smoke and he added to it by rolling and lighting his own cigarette. He crouched against the side of the carriage and was glad he had taken a seat by the window. The way it rattled rhythmically against his shoulder gave him comfort. For added protection, he folded his arms and crossed his legs and kept his eyes looking out of the window. He wanted to avoid any conversations with strangers; he had nothing to say.

Keep your head down, Harry, and go with the flow.

He reached Chatham later that evening and sat with his mum and his sisters drinking weak tea. Patrick sat on his grandmother's knee and she wrapped her arms around his small, frail body. Patrick had Harry's red hair. Harry was relieved that his mother avoided the subject of Evelyn Anne, and he was happy to see the boy and his sisters again.

*

The men in front of him stood impatiently in the November drizzle, pulling up their collars of their heavy overcoats to keep their ears warm. Queuing was something Harry hated.

'Get it over with eh?' he overheard the man in front of him saying as he stubbed out his fag on the pavement. 'Your wife sent you down 'ere?'

He was not sure if the cocky Londoner with the crooked smile was talking to him so he ignored him and shuffled forward. The copper who paced up and down the queue looked at Harry for a brief moment while Harry averted his eyes and allowed the other men to jostle him forward. They huddled together, eager to get through the door of the recruitment office.

'Move along, sir,' a uniformed soldier instructed, clutching his clipboard. Harry made his way towards one of the tables. The men around him did not look very fit as they stripped off for their medicals. The smell of sweaty bodies polluted the air as they folded their clothes, exposing hairy chests and tattooed arms. Harry breathed in as the examiner listened to his chest then checked his eyesight and took measurements. He was glad to put his clothes back on; it was freezing.

'A1 here, you're through, sir,'

As if he had won some prize, Harry grunted back.

The medical officer handed him the slip of paper. Harry made his way down stairs to where a uniformed officer asked him to sit in the chair with polite authority. Harry sat with one leg stretched out to the side and leaned back in his chair. The officer knew his sort; he started to fill in the enrolment form.

'Can you read?'

'Yes, sir.'

'First time in the army?'

'Yes, sir.'

'Married?'

Harry took a moment. 'Widower, sir.'

'Religion?'

NOTES FROM THE EDGE

'Catholic, sir.'

'Know anything about horses?'

'Lots, sir.'

'Ever been in prison?'

'No, sir.'

The officer looked up then jabbed the form with his finger. 'Sign here. Report to Woolwich tomorrow, 09.00.'

The army did not really want a man like Harry, but right now they would take almost anyone male with two arms and two legs. How long it would take them to find out about his prison record, Harry wondered, amused by how easy it had been to go through the process.

*

The smell of bacon and sausage filled the cramped back-parlour of the small house in Chatham. Mary Cornell busied herself as she prepared for another goodbye. Two sons away fighting, what was the world coming to. *William can look after himself, but Harry what about Harry?* she thought, *no one will look out for him.*

Harry looked through her with his glassy, grey eyes. They cried out to her, helpless as always. There was no way to reach him. How could she let him know that she cried for him, her tears attached to guilt that hung on her heart as heavy as sin? Mary Cornell could never understand what she had done wrong, only that she must have done something, otherwise why would Harry block her? She prayed a lot more than any of her children were aware but her prayers for Harry were ignored. Harry had a brick wall around him and this time it was bigger and stronger than ever. She sensed it the day he appeared in Chatham.

'The boy is running scared,' she told the Virgin Mary. 'Please, help my Harry and bring him some peace.'

She saw it in his eyes, so much fear flickering that he could barely look at her and it scared her. It scared Harry too. He could not see a future and feared to believe in one. *Day by day* he told himself, n*one of it matters now.* Angst-ridden, Mary Cornell remembered how she had seen that look when he was a small boy.

'It's just a bloody war, mum, stop fretting,' he snapped. 'They say it won't last long.'

Mary Cornell slapped bacon and sausage between two doorsteps of bread and placed his breakfast front of him. Candlelight flickered, illuminating the dingy, meagre kitchen

'I can't see if it's raining out,' she said. It was still dark and it would be a couple more hours until there was daylight. Harry said nothing. He wiped grease off his chin, where it was running down his shirt.

'Shall I wake Patrick, Harry?'

'Nah, leave the boy sleeping.'

Mary Cornell wanted to thump him on his chest. She wanted to shout but kept the words silent in her head. *He's your son, Harry. What if you never come back from this war? Can you not even say goodbye to him?* Her exasperation left her feeling empty and cold.

'Look after yourself, Harry,' she said at the door as he was about to leave. She gave him a gentle hug.

'I will mum - who else is going to look after me, eh?'

That hurt her even more. Mary Cornell wiped her tears with the corner of her apron.

'I'll be waiting for you, son,' she said. 'We all will.'

'Yeh, well you take care, and look after the boy and tell

him his mum's not coming back for him. You can be sure of that now.'

She put her head to one side questioningly.

'Tell him,' Harry said, 'when the time's right. I'll leave it to you, Mum. You know best.'

'Please write to us Harry. Write to Patrick at least.'

But he was never going to: no letter of affection, no card, no word at all. Harry left and went off to Woolwich to train to fight in a war he cared nothing for, not for King or Country and neither for his family. To stay alive was all the motivation he had, and he was not even sure how important that was any more.

WEST PARK

Would you like some dinner Harry?' Nurse McCarthy stood beside the bed. 'There's shepherd's pie with some tasty gravy.'

'Not hungry today.' Harry was finding it difficult to breathe.

'But you like shepherd's pie - just try a small amount?'

Why wouldn't she go away? Harry had no desire to eat or talk. It was getting dark outside and he could see a group of doctors walking together outside the window, walking quickly to get out of the rain. He saw young Tommy Carter marching behind them, wearing a cloth cap and jacket.

Left! Left! Left! Basic training they called it, for the sloppy bunch we were. Greengrocers, coalmen, railway workers, labourers, clerks - brothers, sons, fathers husbands, what did it matter? The army was the place to lose your identity.

Left! Left! Left! Lose your cloth cap, waistcoat, shirt and old jacket. Piles of uniform on the ground. Sort what you need, he said – poking his stick in it all. 'Make it fit you, lads. This is what you wear now; this is your army clobber, stand proud lads.'

'You are dreaming again, so you are,' said Nurse McCarthy to bring his attention back. 'Come on now, let me help you to eat something. There, this will put some hair back on your chest.'

WOOLWICH, MARCH 1915

'It's so foggy out there; I couldn't see the RSM and only a couple of lines in front. Anyone need to see the old bugger?' said a soldier on a nearby bunk.

'No,' said another one, 'but his voice was like a bleedin' foghorn.'

Harry was tired of barrack room chatter, He was no stranger to being yelled at and the very fact of being on the receiving end told him the old Harry was emerging again.

The regimental sergeant was not fond of soldiers who did not give a toss. Harry endured each day and settled into army life. He was able to shake off the depression that had hung over him. There was no room for it. Army life took over and ate away at any space he had to allow feelings of sorrow. A real man would never admit to feelings of despair, no, a real man got on with it. When he struggled to cope, and it still happened from time to time, he would find a way to get drunk.

Russell Cooper sat on the end of his creaky wooden slatted bed, aching legs stretched out in front of him, leaning back with his arms folded behind his head. He was looking forward to a spot of leave and the subject his best pal, eighteen-year-old Edward Forster, would repeatedly bring up.

'Well I'm done with drill practice, I have leave on Friday, my Emily will be waiting at the station for me, looking like a picture,' said Ted as he was known. Ted talked too much, especially when the subject was his sweetheart. Harry took pleasure in teasing the young lad.

'It's amazing what can happen when she's not seen you in over five months,' he said. 'If she's as pretty as you go on about, she's probably found herself a nice country bumpkin, like you get up there in Hertfordshire. Someone who has no wish to be a hero eh?'

But the lovely Emily would never do that, thought Ted. Ted explained how his sweetheart had remained loyal to him since they were fourteen and how they met one Sunday morning in the village church. There was not a day that passed when he had not been sure of her love for him.

'Of course,' piped up Russell Cooper messing with the mop of shiny hair on top of Ted's head, 'the lovely Emily...'

Harry was not taking any leave. He had no wish to travel to Chatham. He did not want to visit his Mother nor his son Patrick – and a return to Brighton was not a sensible option either. Other soldiers back from leave described time spent with sons and adoring daughters, picnics in parks, visits to picture houses, hugs on stations, gifts exchanged, tearful farewells and talk of King and Country. None of this was for Harry.

The months passed quickly and basic training was thrust into every waking hour. Harry began to ache to escape from the monotony of drill, physical fitness and the eternal lines of men in order of rank and repetition. Similar to prison, the army offered a sense of security and Harry clung on to it. He was getting his belly filled, he had a bed, and a blanket and he didn't need to make decisions or be responsible for his actions. The army did that for you. Each day was a tiresome treadmill but Harry had no wish to fight against what it offered him. At night this false sense of security wrapped around him like a woolly blanket, a blanket full of holes, holes that were the memories of Evelyn Anne and the children, memories that he tried to forget and erase. In the middle of the darkness he would hear a baby cry and wonder for a second if Bertha's baby was anything like him. Such thoughts angered him and he would shake them away and never speaking about any them. If he buried his past deep enough he could learn to believe that none of it really happened or mattered.

Russell Cooper had worked him out.

'He must be some sort of ex-con,' he told Ted. 'Look how he watches the door and jumps when anyone enters. He's a bag of nerves. He's living on the edge. I wouldn't trust him.'

But Ted however saw another side of Harry, the side that those who judged him, rarely saw. Ted and Harry connected even though Harry still refused to let his barrier down, indeed it was impossible to break it.

An officer entered the barracks and they all stood to attention. Ted, with his large chin lifted a little higher than the other men, this infuriated Russell Cooper but amused Harry. They were both aware what Ted believed - that God would keep him safe from harm - just so long as he played by the rules.

'Work hard and all will be well,' Ted's father had told him when he joined up. Those were Ted's values too and he was keen to stick by them and do his duty.

'At ease, men,' said the officer. He walked up and down between the beds. 'Whilst on leave, I expect you to keep your noses clean. This is not your chance to get a belly full of ale lads. Say your goodbyes and don't be late back on Monday. We mobilise at 12.00 in the drill hall. Pick up your passes from me after tea. After the weekend, be prepared lads - we're on the move.'

'Do we know where, sir?' asked Russell Cooper.

'Can't tell you yet but, sorry, we'll not be seeing any action just yet.'

Sorry? thought Harry, sniggering to himself. *I'm really gutted.*

Ted, Russell Cooper and the others waited for the officer to leave before relaxing. One of the men had a VPK, a small pocket Kodak brownie.

'Shall we organize a photo then? Could be the last time we're all together.'

They grouped themselves outside the barracks. The soldier with the camera attempted to set them in order but the men made jokes and fooled around. Harry was reminded of a photographer on Brighton beach who with arms outstretched used to try to group families and friends together who refused to stand still.

'Harry, you're the oldest bloke here, can you crouch down at the front?' asked the frustrated cameraman.

'Can we get copies to send home?' Russell Cooper asked. 'Only there's a few girls I know would like one.'

Russell Cooper stood with his legs apart and his pipe in one hand while he grabbed his crotch with the other. The other men chuckled and made lewd gestures. When the photographer had finished, he asked Harry to take a picture with him in the group. Harry took the small camera in his hand. He'd never taken a picture before nor held one in his hand.

*

'What time you leaving, Ted?' Harry asked later that afternoon.

'Seven o'clock. I get a train into London and then to Tring, I'll be with my Emily, tomorrow morning. Why are you not taking leave, Harry?'

'No reason. Ere, give your sweetheart this.' He had been sketching earlier, on the steps of the barracks, a sketch of two doves entwined.

'Ah thanks, Harry. She'll love that.' Ted put it in his pocket.

Harry didn't like it when anyone praised his work.

'All a bit silly really. Tell her you drew it, eh?'

Russell Cooper walked up. He tugged at Ted to leave and get some refreshment.

'I could do with a beer,' he said. He did not invite Harry to join them; Harry gave Russell Cooper the creeps. 'We got stuff to talk about, young Ted,' Russell Cooper added and nudged Ted with a cheeky grin.

Harry laid back on his bed without comment. In less than a week, they would be out of here and at some other artillery training-camp. He was going to make the most of this bed.

*

News filtered through that huge numbers of casualties were arriving back from the Western front. Many men from all ranks were losing their lives. The men waiting in the training camps could not be sure of anything and rumors were all that many had to go on. For most British people it was becoming clear, as change descended upon them, that their lives would never be the same. This war made demands not only on those fighting at the front but on the people at home too. Nobody had a clue what the next four years was going to bring; most thought that it would soon be over so were biding their time and enjoying the best bits. The call on humor was immense and there was plenty of it flying around. Newspapers talked of the glorious soldiers giving their lives for freedom. 'Freedom' - Harry had forgotten what it meant.

*

Over two-hundred uniformed soldiers crowded chaotically on Amesbury station. The men jostled as they queued to get tea which was being handed out from a trolley that had been wheeled on to the platform. It was mid-afternoon and a light drizzle of spring rain freshened the air. The men were facing a four-mile trek up to Larkhill Camp on Salisbury Plain and tea was welcomed.

'Here, Harry, I got you one.'

'Thanks, Teddy Boy.'

Ted and Russell Cooper held their fingers clumsily around their cups, warming their hands.

'I actually think you may be winning some gratitude there, Ted.' Russell Cooper dared to be sarcastic but Harry really was grateful for the tea.

'Better get in line,' he said, directing his eyes towards Russell Cooper, who knew he had overstepped the mark. Harry walked off, not wishing to engage further in conversation.

'Take no notice of him,' Ted apologized.

The sun came out as they marched. It was a fine day and Russell Cooper whistled a tune. The villagers in Amesbury came out and waved white handkerchiefs as they passed. Some of the soldiers waved back. By the time they reached Larkhill Camp, the sky had turned cloudy. They marched down the open track, over chalky ground still soggy from a wet winter.

WEST PARK

My teeth are chattering.
I can't stop the shivering.
The rain on the tin roof keeps me awake.
I need the toilet, blast. I'm not getting out of my bed.
The pillow feels damp; sod this I need to pee.
Sorry lads, up at five, jump to it soldier - but I'm freezing
Sargent Major.
This isn't right.
This is bloody torture.
Push him a little, just enough to make him mad.
Old Harry, don't mess with Harry.
So we nicked more coal from the back of the store.
Evie! I've got you some coal. It cost me a penny.

'What you smiling about this morning, Harry?' Nurse McCarthy asked as she entered the ward and started to open the windows. He smiled as he gazed out on to the terraces. 'You warm enough?' she asked '- Harry, can you understand me?'

'It's bloody freezing,' he said. 'It's damp and my socks are damp.'

She pulled his blanket up to under his chin.

'You're not wearing any socks, my love.'

'I have some coal,' he said.

'Yes, Harry.' Nurse McCarthy pushed his bed towards the terrace door. 'Of course you have.'

11. The Whores of La Havre

Rain was hitting the tin rooftops of the wooden huts that stood in endless rows, high up on Salisbury Plain. Many thousands of troops were billeted here and not one of them would be escaping the noise of the rain that night as it hit the tin like fireworks exploding overhead.

Harry was trying to ignore it by drawing a picture of a cathedral. His pencil was getting shorter than his stubby fingers. His pencil was a necessity and without it there was nowhere for him to escape to. He took out a small penknife and meticulously cleared around the edges to expose more lead. He enjoyed creating detail but his drawing lacked any true perspective. His cathedral was perched at an angle with the spire reaching to the top of the envelope he was using to draw on. The light coming from the candle was not enough to see properly and he had begun to squint. He placed the pencil on his bedside table and pulled out the neatly folded letter from inside the envelope. He had read it earlier and wanted to read it once again before he went to sleep.

Dear Harry,

I am writing to tell you I have now moved in with Mum, Patrick and Amy. I am finished with service and the hotel. I think it is best, what with the war on.

We haven't heard from you in months, and it has been worrying mum. We only need to know that you are okay and keeping out of trouble.

Patrick is a good boy and growing up fast. He has his own room now and is going to school. William is still away fighting and we heard they have sent him to France. We received a letter to say he is well and in good health. He sent Mum a lovely piece of embroidery, which apparently the men are doing to keep themselves busy.

There's still no word from Evie. Mum won't talk about her in front of Patrick. I've heard that May is settling well with Mr and Mrs Myers in Brighton; we're going to visit Florence and the children next month. I'm afraid I have heard nothing about baby James; nobody has heard anything but I am happy to make enquiries if you would like me to.

What with so many men away fighting, we all have to do more. I've started working at the ammunitions factory and my skin and hands are turning a lovely new shade of orange.

Please Harry, if you are well can you take a moment to write to Mum? It will mean so much to her.

My candle is burning low so I must end now. I trust in God to keep you safe
Your ever-loving sister
Mary Louisa.

In the darkness he saw their faces, talking to him all at once. It confused him as he tried to decipher who said what. If Evelyn Anne was dead, why was it not common knowledge? Harry was troubled: *could Evie still be alive?* Maybe the story of her death was a mistake or a lie? But why would Dennis Scully lie to him? He laid back pondering in thought. Should he write to Annie her mother? She would know the truth, and, if Evelyn Ann was really dead, would it not be possible that the police would be looking for him? After all, he had left Brighton in such a hurry. Surely they would have traced his whereabouts by now. *What a stupid mess. Dead if I run; dead if I don't.* If Evelyn Anne were alive then why had she not come back for the kids? She would never abandon them.

Where are you girl? I love you so much it hurts. Where, where, where are you? A tear slid down his weathered cheek as he lay in the black of the hut surrounded by the heavy breathing of soldiers asleep, perched on a hillside with the rain pounding down on the tin roof before running like a shower into the chalky slime ditches outside. It poured into the miles of false trenches that hundreds of men had been digging on the vastness of Salisbury Plain. This place might as well be on the moon, he thought. It was a crazy, pointless place of madness.

Could it be possible that Evelyn Anne was alive and sparing a thought for him tonight?

*

The rain evaporated into morning mist and spread like a blanket over the horizon.

'An amazing picture,' said Ted as he saddled up their horses. Harry patted the beast and looked out over the view, squinting at the morning sun.

'It'll it will be man-made mist in a couple of hours, when they start firing fourteen-pounders.'

'She seems a bit jumpy today.'

Harry patted the horse. 'She'll get used to it, she's a young'un.'

'D'you think she knows Harry?'

'Knows what?'

'D'you think that she knows there's danger out there?'

'Daft lad! Don't let it get to you. They have a job to do just like we have. The horse needs to feel secure; it needs to know you're looking out for it. It knows as much as you and I – which is bugger all.'

For a fleeting moment, Harry had seen fear in young Ted. It was wheedling its way to the forefront of the boy's mind. *Poor kid, doubt was rising up.* It had always been there but now Ted must learn to face it. It had probably been there, Harry imagined, when Ted had said goodbye to his sweetheart back then on the platform in Tring and told her he would be back soon, a slither of doubt turning in his queasy stomach as he fought at remaining positive while he hugged her.

Harry was aware of Ted's anxiety. Ted had confided in Harry on a number of occasions. Ted wanted to trust his officers, the generals and the politicians to make the right decisions, to keep him safe, but doubt was twisting amongst his bravado

Harry could see what was on his mind right now and broke his thought.

'The reality is - nobody knows,' he said, 'nobody knows anything, not much. It's your job to keep this beastie under control and, out there, when it comes to it, it'll be your mates that take care over you. You have some good friends with you, Ted - come on or we are going to get yelled at.'

They attached the horses to the limber, laden with all the heavy ammunition. Harry wiped his forehead on his cheek and pushed his shirtsleeves up over his elbows.

'Phew, it's going to be a hot day.'

The tracks were thick with soggy chalk. It would take a lot of sunshine to dry them out. By the evening they would both be covered in a chalky-white dust and would be scrubbing it of their boots - again.

The horses laboured, pulling the wooden wheels along the track. Empty shell cases lay all over the place, the boots of the marching soldiers pressing them further into the mud and chalk. Voices echoed across the wind as ammunition was loaded and fired from the heavy artillery over the rolling hillside. This training filled Harry with a new sense of purpose. As each day passed they were getting closer to being sent over to France. He had dealt with fear before and had learnt to numb that emotion.

In the hut at the end of a long day, the men chatted about their families and homes, they talked about dying and of the glory of it because they could not comprehend any other way to make sense of it, but Harry just shrugged: *what will be will be.*

'Don't you worry about how your mum will deal with it if you die, Harry?' Ted asked.

'Like any mum I expect.'

'I hate thinking about it,' said Ted shaking his hands as he lifted them out of the cold water trough. He had been so full of enthusiasm, caught up with the flurry of propaganda, fighting for values, for his country. Time out here on Salisbury plain had given him a sneak preview of warfare; he was beginning to see a truer picture.

Harry had placed a broken piece of mirrored glass on the window ledge and was attempting to shave.

'There is no point worrying about it,' he said.

'Someone will shed a tear for you, Harry.' Ted knew he had touched a nerve and stepped backwards. Harry wiped his chin on his towel and pushed past him into hut. He cared little about dying, it was just part of the process; one day the good Lord would send him to the gates of hell anyhow. He had imagined the blackened iron, burning hot, the finials glowing red. He imagined how he would fight to wade through, as they taught the men to survive a gas attack. Hell could smell his fear and sensed it was calling him.

Harry half-believed that France would be his end. If France offered him death he could walk happily forward, mocking it along the way. He had rehearsed this walk many times. It had started as a young fourteen-year-old in a cold and damp prison cell, when, in the darkness, he saw his mum standing in the shadows, unable to reach out and hold his hand, unable to offer him her chest to bury his face in as he sobbed, and him walking forward but unable to reach her. He saw himself walking towards the gates of hell but the steps he took never got him any closer. They were in his sights but always out of reach.

Russell Cooper tapped Ted on the shoulder and Ted flinched.

'Leave the old sod alone,' he laughed, 'he's a weirdo.'

*

In early June of 1915, Harry's battalion boarded a train to Southampton whence they sailed to Le Havre, arriving at midnight. The crossing was smooth and the men sat back-to-back on the deck in the eery moonlight unaware of the danger from German submarines in the Channel. As the boat pulled into La Havre they could make out the silhouettes of damaged vessels moored in the harbor, awaiting repair. By 8 a.m. the next morning they had the order to disembark.

Harry guided the horses with care as they nervously set foot on French territory. It was his first time on French soil as it was for most of them. A strange and warped excitement that ran through the groups of tired men. There was no turning back now. They had all been handed a printed note from Lord Kitchener. They were to consider the note confidential and ordered to keep it with their active service pay book. It read:

You are ordered abroad as a soldier of the King to help our French comrades against the invasion of a common enemy. You have to perform a task, which will need your courage, your energy, and your patience. Remember that the honour of the British Army depends on your individual conduct. It will be your duty not only to set an example of discipline and perfect steadiness under fire but also to maintain the friendliest relations with those whom you are helping in this struggle. The operation, in which you are engaged, will for the most part, take place in a friendly country, and you can do your own country no better service than in showing yourself in France and Belgium in the true character of a British Soldier. Be invariably courteous, considerate and kind. Never do anything to injure or destroy property. And always look upon looting as a disgraceful act. You are sure to meet with a welcome and to be trusted; your conduct must justify that welcome and that trust. Your duty cannot be done unless your health is sound so keep constantly on your guard against any excesses. In this new experience you may find temptations both in wine and women. You must entirely resist both temptations and while treating women with perfect courtesy you should avoid any intimacy.

Do your duty bravely.

Fear God.

Honour the King.

As if they would not respect the virtues of the flirtatious mademoiselles, a popular topic of conversation at the training camp.

Harry took a moment to reflect amongst the crowded men and the chaos. On horseback, and feeling the heat generated by the nervousness of the horse's body, he patted the beast, reminding it he was in control. He turned his head to look back. The ship that had brought them was sailing back out of the harbor, back to England across the Channel. It struck at Harry, something he had previously refused to believe - he loved his England, his mother, his Evie, his children, the lights of Brighton even. His heart was there and it belonged there. He had a home after all; he was part of it and whatever he had done, he vowed he would come back and say he was sorry. He took a swig of whiskey from the flask in his rucksack. It felt comforting on his chest.

'Onwards,' he thought, 'let's get this over with.'

They were told they would be marching for at least half of the day and it was shortly after midday when they reached the rest camp where they pitched tents and watered and organized the horses. There were eight men to a tent. By mid-afternoon hundreds of tents covered the fields and supplies were passed along the line. Harry, Ted and Russell Cooper were in the same tent.

They were to remain there for nearly a month.

West Park

Harry turned his head towards the dim light. The night nurse sat behind her desk. The light shone under her chin, illuminating her rosy cheeks and her painted, red lips. Her blonde hair was cut short in a bubble cut and her fringe neatly curled under her white, starched cap. She checked the watch pinned to the corner of her apron.

Claudette, I'm placing my money on her little table.

'Arry,' she's smiling at me, showing red lipstick on her teeth, 'we 'av meesed you.' She's pulling her silk shawl higher up on to her shoulder, only it has slipped back down again.

'You like my money madame, I can tell. You're running your painted fingernails over my three coins. Got a drink for me Claudette? Only I need the taste of whiskey before I go up.'

'Arry Arry,' she's whining, but I'm not paying any more money for her scraggy old whores.

I'm asking her about Eloise. She's laughing, her eyes are directing me upstairs.

'Hey, you old hag,' the soldier behind me is shouting. 'You need to check his pecker before he goes up there.'

There's a whiskey glass in my hand. She's watered the whiskey down again. I'm grabbing the bottle from her table and climbing the stairs. Eloise, in her black silk chemise, is opening the door. I'm ignoring her welcoming gestures. Are you not proving to me, Eloise, how tiresome this charade has become? bereft of any music or introduction, this performance will not receive applause or a standing ovation. She's pulling back the curtain, there are no gold tassels, only faded, frayed lace.

I stand with my whiskey in my hand. She grabs at my crotch with both hands and is helping herself, tugging and grunting, lowering herself ungainly. I sip my whiskey slowly. Eloise is sipping slowly too. She knows what I like, but she's talking too much. I don't like her talking such shit.

'When the Germans come I will tell them, Arry got here first,' she's saying. 'I will tell them you invaded Eloise, you 'ave the Victory. Rule Britannia!'

Stupid cow, she thinks we've invaded her bloody country. Kitchener needs to tell the French why we're here. We're welcomed in the whorehouse so long as we have the right amount of coins. The army encourages it for married men. The army understands their needs, but I don't expect the wives at home will.

Eloise is laying face down on her bed of crumbled grey sheets.

'Come on soldier 'Arry. I will tell ze Hun you are ze perfect Eenglish gentleman.'

I'm pouring my whiskey in the small of her back then sipping it. I can taste the cheap, stale perfume. It taints the sides of my mouth. I'm tugging at her hair and pushing her face into the mattress.

'Sleep tight little whore; there's a line of eager Tommie's at your door waiting to push back the curtain.'

I'm lighting my cigarette as the next soldier pushes another lad in front of him into Eloise's grim excuse for a room. 'Share and share alike,' he's grinning.

I care nothing. I don't know why I bother coming here, well some of us have needs and I like the whiskey. Claudette, Eloise, all of the mademoiselles, their compassion is reeking with lies and self-gratification. French, English, Belgians, Canadians and maybe soon, God forbid, the German Hun Bastards, they'll all pass through these rooms. When our trousers are around our ankles and our braces are on the floor, we're all the same. Those little tarts know it and that makes me feel sick. The look on the face of Claudette tells me she holds power over my comrades. All these soldiers, you know what faces them, don't you, Claudette? This is the only pleasure they may experience. You know that death is lurking in the shadows waiting for them, maybe in the next village, tomorrow or at the weekend. And when we slap our coins down on your table, Claudette, do you think of this as your duty to the war effort?

Hey Claudette, give them a drink, get your girls to lift their skirts, suck their cocks, slap and pinch their spotty arses. Whatever you do, they'll never write home about you, they'll never speak of you with gratitude or remember you fondly, not when they drink tea in their front parlors with their mothers and sisters. Neither will they think about you tomorrow or at the weekend when lying injured at the front or in some bombed-out church. No, not a thought about you will they write within the lines of a poem on mud-splattered notepaper. Your only glory is in the moment of a man's groan as he comes over your pale, sickly-smelling skin. That will be your glory, for King and Country, your duty to all men because, as I said, we have our needs. And that's all that matters to men or boys; you may have the power to please us but the sin is yours and yours alone. We are the heroes, the godly and the saved, whether dead or alive, but the sin is yours. You think you have some kind of power over us? You have nothing, French bitch. So take your money and stop, STOP grinning at me.

Harry looked over at the nurse.

'Whore!' he yelled, lifting his hand.

The nurse ignored him.

'You will suffer for your sins, stop your fucking grinning at me!'

She hardly shook her head.

'Go back to sleep, Harry - and watch your language.'

12. Shell Shock

Nurse McCarthy had overslept. It was still raining and she was not looking forward to the lecture she would receive from Matron. The night staff-nurse was already in a panic but she was not able to leave until Nurse McCarthyhad arrived. It had been a hard night and the night staff-nurse needed her sleep.

Harry had been awake most of the night because there had been a thunderstorm and they always spooked him. Lightening had illuminated the sky. It made the patients jittery, worst of all Harry.

The night porter saw Nurse McCarthy running from the bus stop.

'I know, I know I am sorry!' She pulled her rain-hat off chuckling. 'What awful weather. The bus was late; I thought I'd missed it.'

'You're in luck. Matron was late too.' The night porter grinned.

'Don't suppose you could get me a brew?' she asked as he held the side-exit door open for her.

'Go on, girl, sneak in through a side ward. Nobody will notice you.'

'Damn, I didn't see that.' She tugged at her skirt pulling it down, hoping to cover the run in her black stocking. She walked hurriedly behind the nurse's station.

'Please don't have a go at me, Carol. The bus was late.'

Staff nurse Carol just wanted to get home. She handed Nurse McCarthy a clipboard.

'What sort of night did Harry Cornell have?' she asked .

'Well, he's still with us. Here's my notes - all yours now.' Night staff-nurse Carol glanced over to Harry's bed. 'He's quite vocal – he called me a whore.'

'I've been called worse,' said Nurse McCarthy. The night porter put a steaming cup of tea on the desk in front of her. 'You'll need a brolly!' she called after the night staff-nurse who was already out in the corridor.

She put on a sterile mask and walked over to Harry's bed.

'Morning, Harry. Doesn't look like you'll be getting much fresh air today, not with this awful weather.'

He was comforted to hear her voice. It had been a bad night; he had drifted in and out of sleep, the imagery of war still vivid in his mind.

The lights were on in the ward because it was still dark outside and the clanking breakfast trolley was making its journey up the corridor. There was a clap of thunder outside. Thunderstorms are often welcome in England to clear the air of a hot and sticky humidity, but for Harry the clap of thunder and lightning took him back again to France, his whole being torn wretchedly from his bed. In an instant, he was cowering in a muddy ditch and Nurse McCarthy saw it in the look in his eyes, a stare that stretched so far forward that it went right through her. There was no jumping under his bed as in the early days; he could now only lie rigid in fear. She held onto his trembling hand.

'It was a big thunderstorm last night but it's passing. This is the dregs of it. You're all cozy and tucked up warm in here. You're quite safe, Harry.'

FRANCE 1916

He was driving both the horses forward along the ammunition line. It wasn't rain beating down on his back but wet, muddied earth that was shot into the air after a shell had exploded eight-hundred yards up in front. The German gunners knew where they were. It was the same every night.

The ammo-laden limber struggled through the slippery muddy track towards the gun positions. Harry was playing the usual game in his head. It was always the same game: he was not there but somewhere else and he focused on imagining the casual whistle of a man with no worries, a whistle that floated between ground and sky.

The horses, exhausted and weak, had had enough. For the horses, everything was as real as it could possibly be. The left horse was holding back and Harry tried to drive it forward through the confusion of mud and the darkness which tricked the eyes. A flash lit up the sky and he caught the gaze from the black eyes of the petrified beast. It was scared shitless – as was he. The little game in his head was no longer effective. The whistling imaginary man had run for his life and Harry and horse connected. Both were waiting for the moment that would blow them to smithereens although it never came. Only the game of death taunted and played under the thunder, lightning and raining grit and grime that fell repeatedly over their heads and down their backs.

They were taking a gun to replace one damaged the previous night. Six horses were needed to pull the gun and this required three drivers. There were often times when he did not have a full crew and today was one of them. Two drivers had been killed the night before and they were waiting for replacements. Harry had seen both of them as they slid into the slime and mud. The first had been killed by a bullet that took half of his face away; the other was still alive when the mud slid on top of him. He fell into the shell hole and the whites of his eyes stared out through the shower of mud that followed and that finally knocked him under. They had tried to pull him out, but when they did, he was already dead.

With or without re-enforcements the gun was needed and young Ted was all he had to help him drive the horses. The horses, scared, tired and caked in thick mud, were sore from minor cuts and it was not an easy task trying to keep them calm. One slipped and pulled Harry with him into the ditch at the side of the track. The horse panicked and could not recover its footing. Losing his grip on one of the reins, Harry slid further into the ditch. Scrambling to keep his balance, he tried to reach the fallen horse which lay on its side at an angle in the ditch. It kicked out its hoof and caught Harry on his thigh. He yelled in pain.

'Grab my hand!'

Ted was towering above him, carving his silhouette into a backlit background resembling a flickering cinema screen. It took a moment to focus and he could have sworn the boy was grinning.

'Get out of here, Teddy boy!' he shouted.

But there was no fear in the lad's eyes. Ted would not leave Harry, not in a million years. Ted crouched forward and slid on the mud as he stretched out his hand. Harry grabbed on to it tightly and Ted pulled hard whilst still sliding forward.

'Let go of the horse, leave it Harry!'

Harry did not let go. The horse was lifting its head and Harry let go of Ted's hand so he could hang onto the horse to see if he could get it back on to its feet. Ted pulled back and Harry slid further down.

'I'll get some rope!' Ted shouted. He turned and climbed back to the top of the ditch.

The bullet entered the side of Ted's head and exited with such force that the blood was projected through the air and seemed to Harry as if it was travelling in slow motion. The second shot took Ted's head right off and propelled it along the track like a bouncing ball. There was no time to comprehend what had happened. Harry stood in shock. He began to shake from the center of his stomach, connecting every nerve ending that he possessed until all the parts of his body shook with uncontrollable rage. Russell Cooper let go of his horses and appeared at the side of the ditch. Distraught and struggling to stand solid in the mud, he lost all awareness of danger and stood fixated on the body of his friend in front of him.

No fond farewell, or re-union to look forward to, no words Teddy boy of gratitude for you to feel comfort. There are words here in my heart and I'm shouting, but they make no sense. What can I say to a bloody body in bits? What can anyone say? Give me the words to say to you and tell me, what I must say to your lovely Emily. Do I tell her you'll not be coming home now? Do I say you were brave and death came to you because you were trying to help me, a pathetic old soldier who needed to climb out of a ditch?

'Russell! Get away! Get away lad! Don't stare. Let's say a prayer, eh? Yeh, let's say a prayer. We can ask forgiveness. That's what we'll do. See this is all so bad. We're playing a game with the devil and the rules are made to finish us. It's because of me that this is happening. God is punishing me for my sins and you as well. Russell - stop staring lad!'

Russell is staring at the head. It's rolled under a tree. The eyes are looking right through him. I can't make him move. I'm shouting above the gunfire but nothing is coming out. I can't make him move - and the next bullet will be his.

'Russ!' I'm grabbing at his ankles and he's staring at me. His gaze penetrates me like the stabbing of a bayonet. In and out, his hatred pours through me. His hatred of this war is now on my back and I can no longer stand it. I'm no longer a man, just a piece of rotten meat to be eaten by the rats.

Russell is gone. He's walked away. I want him to run but he just walks through the mud and no bullet passes through him. How can that be possible? It's black now and the earth explodes once more and down comes the dirt with branches of trees, pieces of wire, leather and what is left of man and petrified beasts falling from the smoky sky where the fires of hell light up the clouds. It burns onto the back of the dying who lie face down clinging on to their last thoughts of love.

Why do I see mountains and trees?

I see her, my Evie, on the pier, on the back of the painted horse on the merry-go-round. I hear the music. Please don't cry Evie. I'll come home, yes that's what I'll do.

FRANCE. MAY 1916

Harry was not found for two days and then he was taken to a field hospital in the back of a Red Cross ambulance, unconscious and very weak and suffering from exposure and dehydration. He had no serious shrapnel wounds. They cleaned him up and left him to sleep.

It was recorded that he had deserted following his failure to report back. Russell Cooper was repeatedly asked about his whereabouts but said nothing. He had been seen retreating from his post by an officer and had been arrested. The image of Ted's head rolling under a tree still terrorized his young mind as if its ghostly gaze cried out from beyond the grave.

Harry carried the same image. All three of them had endured continuous attacks on the ammunition column. Night after night they had dragged the ammo up to the front lines. Night after night the Germans knew exactly where to fire their shells. They had driven the horses through the dark wondering which shell blast would be their last. There were rest breaks but only for a few days at a time.

The field hospital, once a small village church, was situated ten miles behind the lines. At night he could hear the gunfire as it vibrated through the crumbling stone walls of the church. He asked about the horse; he had grown strangely attached to it.

'It died,' said a soldier. 'It's gone for horsemeat.'

So it had ended up as *plat de jour*, in some Frenchman's stew. The field doctor said he had a lot of bruising on his leg but should be up and about in a few days and would be able to return to duty. Around him the wounded soldiers lay on thin boards covered in thin blankets. It was hard to sleep when the church walls echoed with the sounds of pain and re-occurring terror. The more seriously wounded were sent back to England. Some of them never made it as far as the French coast.

*

Russell Cooper crouched on the cold, stone floor of a prison cell in a small, French police-station, staring at the bars over the window. The image of Ted's white eyes staring at him was locked in his brain. Those two round eyes blinked at him over and over, and every time he saw them his shoulders would twitch. He could no longer speak.

They said he was able to walk unaided, that he had been strong enough to walk away from his post that night in the ammunition column. They said he was young and strong and had suffered no injury from shrapnel or bullets, neither had he been near enough to a shell explosion that might have severed his nerves. They said he must be a coward and that the twitching was the act of someone trying to avoid his duty to serve his King and Country. They said he should be executed for desertion and that he showed no remorse for his action. Harry heard about it shortly after from one of the firing squad. Russell Cooper was shot at 5.15 a.m. on the morning of May 16th 1915. The firing squad of young soldiers had assembled nervously and Russell Cooper had twitched uncontrollably. They thought he was unaware of what was happening to him when the officer put on the blindfold and pinned a white hanky on his jacket to show where they should take aim. He died in a second Harry was told.

Layer upon layer, the confusion over the purpose of war persisted, layering more and more chaos, working it's way into the poems of men trying to make sense of it. Some looked for glory, believing they were there for God and mankind; some did not believe in any cause, laughing in the face of authority, nodding their heads and mocking, to them it was a sick game played on the minds of men. This was what war was - death, disguising itself, using a hundred reasons, gathering souls and gathering madness.

They had told Harry to be nice to his French hosts as he stood on their land amongst their cattle, peppered with blast and without real welcome at their door. Bad manners was one thing, he thought, murder of a young life was quite another.

WEST PARK

Who writes these fucking rules? Why am I here Evie? Why am I still standing? Why me? What does god want from me? Was I really not worthy to die? I'm leaning to one side in that cottage doorway, my rucksack clinging to my back.

The French have shut the door in my face and bolted it.

'Go home, Harree,' they're saying, 'we do not want you here.'

Bloody French. A shell hole is the only place left to hide. It's better to be buried whole because if there's no tomorrow, then why should I care. There's no glory in a death without reason, and I can't see a reason, not even for the Hun, not even for two young boys who have yet to reach nineteen.

The mud is gripping at my boots and here I'll stand, not proud, not with courage but cemented in trembling fear, wet from the sweat and the downpour of freezing sobs from the sky of a thousand men in battle. My hands cup my ears as the blast vibrates through the earth. It rumbles like a monster underground, searching for where I stand.

Pieces of lost men are caught in the wire. I see a finger on a hand gripped to the barbed and twisted metal, a charred finger that once caressed pale skin and soft hair.

'Turn Harry! Run!' A voice is yelling out from the smoke. Run from this hellhole. Keep your head down, pull up your legs and boots and move. The mud will slide and you'll feel nothing. I see nothing, only the anger in my brother's face. I see my father, cold and vacant, because he has no pride there for me. I will never be his hero.

I will not be vaporized!' I'm screaming inwardly, deeper and down as the horror of it all pierces my soul. Each nerve I possess stands taut and alive. I am my very own self alone and I'm naked and exposed for all to see.

'Here I am!' I'm opening the door and letting in the vultures to feast on me, but to no avail. Pick holes in my flesh, vultures, but do not kill me, not unless with a bullet that will make me a hero. The sky is raining mud and I'm cemented. The filth is on me, in my eyes and mouth, layer upon layer. I just let it come.

FRANCE

Against all odds, Harry survived. The earth did not take him; it spat him back out on to the surface, undigested, cast aside but covered in the vomit, spewed from the stomach of war. But would the noise and the mass of flickering lights exploding in the corner of his mind ever leave him? Would he ever sleep again? They had mocked him but they had not executed him, unlike poor Russell Cooper. No man could serve his country who was so dishonourable, they had said; he was a drunk, a cad and unfit for service. He did not care, neither did he try to understand what they meant.

The drink took away the war in his head but it also had a knack of bringing back her smiling eyes and the hope that maybe she had not left him. She gave him strength. He could face the lies the scum said about him, when her hand, cold and creamy, unfolded in his palm. The lies had no substance when Evelyn Anne came into his vision. She would understand and forgive him; she was full of all the love that he needed to be a man.

In his nightmares, the wind would come and blow her away, the crumpled leaves of autumn would dry up his vision and he rub his eyes. His canvas would fall empty onto the ground as leaves float downwards from their branches.

Would somebody tell me where she's gone? 'My Evie,' he

whispered in the corner of his tormented mind. *'When the war's over and I can think again,* I need you to come home.'

He had received a wound to his left leg. Fever had followed and he was taken to a casualty clearing station. He was not sorry when the army eventually agreed that he should be sent back to England. They had been hoping to send him back to the front but the fever had worn him down and his leg was taking a long time to heal. They moved him on to the field hospital at Le Havre where it was predicted he should recover in a couple of weeks.

*

The Red Cross ambulances bumped along the track towards the hospital. Stretchers were unloaded and the walking wounded were met by other soldiers who helped them out of the ambulances and into the old chateau on the edge of the village that was now one of two base hospitals. Large, white tents were arranged in lines across the grounds and the chateau looked down on a chaotic scene where once beautifully landscaped gardens of hedges and weeping willows had purpose and precision.

The patients hobbled and limped across the grass and graveled paths, some sitting in groups huddled together, smoking cigarettes, others walked up and down, talking with their pals, hoping for a miracle - to be sent home - but knowing they would probably be returned to the vile war and pointless violence that had brought them to this small taste of a sanctuary in the first place. There was no beauty or scent left lingering in this French garden, no *'Lavende'* or *'Laurier Rose'* nor neat lines of box hedges; now it was just a place where the army and the war, colored in the fractured boundaries of a once beautiful and charming chateau with khaki, mud and blood stained bed sheets.

Harry took in his surroundings in his mind erased the army, imagining what a beautiful house this must have been. Looking through the trees, he could see grey smoke in the distance, billowing up to the sky. He created a canvas in his mind. By erasing the smoke in his imagination, there on the steps of the French chateaux, he could see the South Downs in the distance, and on the hillside was Evelyn Anne, sitting in the long grass picnicking with his three children. Tears came into his already-wept, weary eyes and he stood frozen for a second. An explosion shook the hillside and Harry stumbled and cursed. A young soldier grabbed his arm, his accent, well-spoken and well bred.

'Steady on old chap.'

Harry pushed his arm away embarrassed. He was able to limp with the aid of a stick. The young soldier told him to follow him into the chateau through the wooden, and rather grand, front doors.

Inside, the cold, grey, marble floor was not very welcoming. Somewhere in the shadows, was there a *petite madame*, tight lipped and looking at the boots and mud on the cold marble floor that she had lovingly mopped and polished. Broken men were piled up together, littering their blood, coughing and spitting so that blood was smeared across the French beauty, grand and austere. Harry walked through to what was once the *grand salon*. He was shown to a metal bunk and given an army blanket. It was cold in the room and he shivered. He wanted a wash and thankfully it was the first thing they offered him a couple of hours later when a young English nurse with a strong northern accent, sponged him down with warm water from a metal pail.

The smell of carbolic soap on the sponge left him feeling nauseas but he was glad to get out of his uniform, which was encrusted in mud and had lice crawling about in the seams. He was given a cotton vest with long sleeves with bloodstains on the cuffs but he was happy to wear it. The fever had left him stinking, the same stench he had smelled on dying men. The nurse took the smell away with her soap and he was grateful.

The hospital was crammed with casualties. There was a battle raging in the Somme and more ambulances arrived continuously. The roar of the guns could be heard in the distance and with each explosion his body tensed so tightly that the beats of his heart would thump through his chest. Wrapping himself in a foetal position, he tried to hide his tears. He understood about what was happening, about the fear that ran through his veins. It could be so bad that he would bite his bottom lip until it bled. But the fear was not going to beat him, he told himself. He had to carry on. He knew the fear; he saw it in the face of young Russell Cooper and yet they had shot him for it. *I'm no coward,* he told himself. *I can do this, I can do this,* he muttered at the back of his brain, determined that the army should not detect his fear. He had already faced enough of death and to be shot or thought of, as a coward was not the way this was going to end, not for Harry Cornell.

The hospital coped with more than just injuries earned in battle. Some men had trench foot, a disgusting condition suffered by many in the trenches from wading through mud and filth, too weary to dry their feet in impossible conditions. The army made each sufferer pair up with a comrade to make them dry each other's feet. It was an arduous task especially when the feet were beginning to rot away. As well as trench foot, men arrived daily with diseases such as dysentery, caught by the lack of clean water and healthy food. Diarrhea had no place to go except into the mud where men walked amongst it. Toilet paper had become a valuable commodity. Then there was trench fever as it was called. This was caught from lice that nibbled through stale sweat into the skin of soldiers as they slept. And syphilis, this and other venereal diseases were seen as 'tickets back to Blighty' although the army was becoming aware that men were purposely catching it. All in all, the health of the soldiers on the front line was pretty dire.

The hospital was rife with sickness and, as the days went by, Harry suffered painful stomach cramps. Gradually he became dehydrated and they diagnosed him with a severe bout of dysentery and finally, they had no choice but to send him back to England.

Finally, he was going home. He was discharged from the hospital and put on the train to Calais. Once across the Channel, they sent him to a military hospital in Kent until the injury in his leg was healed. A month later, in July 1917, he was discharged as un-fit for service. It was all over.

*

Harry went back to his mother's house in Chatham. Mary Cornell had not heard from her son in over a year and was delighted to have him home. She *wanted* to care for him. Whatever Harry had become, he needed her more than any of her other children. Mary Louisa, now married and living close by, was a regular visitor and helped her mother care for him. His leg gave him a lot of pain, and walking or standing for long periods would put him into a bad mood. He carried a small walking stick that he would throw on the ground in a rage as he fell back into his chair, kicking it across the room. They would hurry to retrieve it and place a blanket on his lap. But Mary Cornell observed a greater injury in her son. On the outside, when he wasn't in one of his rages, he could turn on the charm, teasing young Patrick and playing little jokes, but then he would stare into nothing, his grey eyes focusing on empty air. She would have to shake him to get his attention.

The frustrated outbursts, were becoming frequent and although his leg had healed, there was something else going on in his head. He would lose his temper one moment then be lost in thought another, staring at a wall or into his hands. The nightmares that filled the night made him cry out. She heard them and would go into his dark room. He was the troubled boy-child she had known long ago and there was no husband now to tell her how to handle him - nor to make her feel that she was failing him. She could not find the answers to make things right. She turned to her religion. *What was it that he needed in order to find peace,* she asked in her prayers.

'Harry you should pray,' she told him and he tried, but the Lord had no answers so praying was pointless. Sleep deprivation made him incoherent. He lay for hours going over the time before he was buried in the mud where he thought he must have died. He remembered thinking that heaven was nowhere near and how he must be in hell. How it was black, just black. It was the place where he had been told he would end up so many times. He heard the voices of his brother, William, and his Father.

'You will end up in hell, Harry,' and there he was, just as they had said he would be.

During the day there would be periods when he could not speak. The words just would not come and he gave up trying, unsure of what sounds he was making. His sobbing was silent. Mary Cornell and Patrick heard him banging his cane against his leg in frustration. The doctor prescribed rest but there was little rest for Mary Cornell who found it so difficult when Harry had these 'episodes', as she called them. She had coped with his drunken outbursts before the war but this was not the same. His pain was intense but it was not real. How could they take that away? It was like an imaginary cancer, eating at his brain. She wondered if they should send him to the asylum, but she did not want that. She told Patrick his dad would get better soon if they kept praying. Sometimes she thought her prayers had been answered and she thought he was okay again, only to watch his symptoms take over triumphantly, trampling any hope that they were moving forward with his recovery.

The war was still raging but Harry was having the breakdown that he had held back for two and a half years. In the front bedroom of her small, terraced house in Chatham, Mary Cornell took her son's head to her bosom and he cried all the tears he had held back for far too long. He cried out in the night for Evelyn Anne, Patrick, May and baby James, the children he had missed and lost. He cried for those who hid in the shadows where they slept, Teddy boy and the young, confused Russell Cooper, singing sad songs for King and Country. He cried for his sanity through misted vision, hope had become an illusion, a pretend picture of green, rolling, peaceful hillsides, where mountains and trees were just soft sketches smudged on paper and love lived between the lines of war and whiskey.

13. Brighton Manor

For some people, war had refused them a place, reserved only for the heroes and the worthy. For Alf Goldwater, imprisoned inside a Victorian fort of red bricks and bolts, war had been denied and his punishment was empty time. Time made up of minutes and hollow hours but also with resentment. The game outside was a great one and he was not allowed to play.

The day they took off his chains and pushed him outside, he was full to the brim with rage against the world but the world had changed and so had the people. The men who should have been there respecting him, the world of Alf Goldwater, were gone. They lay dead in a muddy patch of grass in some far away field in Flanders. There would to be no flags flying to welcome back Alf Goldwater.

Brighton smiled again as war came to an end. The Armistice faced a confused population, wondering who exactly the winners were but grateful that it was all over and the men were coming home. Goldwater came back to the arches and stretched out on his bench that somehow had remained on Brighton beach. He looked at the remains of fishing boats lacking their lustre through neglect over the past four years.

'You survived then?'

A strong figure stood in front of him in the late sunlight. Squinting, he shielded his eyes to focus. It was the figure of a soldier in the remnants of his greatcoat and war-worn boots. The soldier stood proud and at ease.

So you went off to fight

'I did.'

'You did your bit for good old England?'

'I did, Alf, but I'm glad it is over.'

'Yeah, I guess it is. Enough of bloody war talk, you Irish bastard. The manor needs sorting and I have people to see. You up for it?' Alf Goldwater grabbed his arm.

'I am Alf.'

'It's good to see you again.'

'You too, Dennis. I've missed my old Brighton Manor.'

14. For the love of Ada

'I thought I'd lost you and there you are on the chair again. 'Why are you here? You're telling me the rain has stopped, when there is none outside. I've let it all drift away - no skies, no clouds, no sun nor rain - it's all gone away and now you tell me about the rain, as if I care. Why have you come here? Why now? You must have heard it was me that killed them. You knew I was rotten, you knew, didn't you?'

'Did you tell the kids, Evie? Did you tell them what their old dad did? Did you grip their shoulders and shake them in their sleep to make them understand? When they sleep, are you in their dreams? Because, Evie, they don't know where you are.'

'It's all right to punish me, but the children Evie, why hurt them? Did you not want them because of me? Do you whisper to them in their dreams and tell them you have died? Is that why you never came back - because it's not you sitting in the chair is it? It's not you! Is it! You're not real are you, Evie? Go away from here woman. Get out of here! No more pain! No more of this!'

'Harry?'
'Mum?'
'Why are you shouting?'
'It's William, he was laughing at me again so I hit him. I hit him with the stick when they told Evie about Bertha's baby. No, it's Teddy boy, I'm dreaming about him. He tried to reach me and he let go of my hand and I couldn't save him. Evie was here,

Mum. She was sitting in that chair. She let go of my hand too. She hates me and she's gone away She hates the air I breathe.'

'You must try and wake up. Get yourself together, son.'

'I want to close my eyes.'

'Wake up, Harry my love. Wake up and face your sins.'

Mum is praying to the picture on the wall, but it is not the Virgin Mother that she's praying to; it's Evie, and May is clutching at her skirt. She's telling Patrick to leave the room.

'Get out of here, boy!'

'Dad,' he's calling, 'don't cry daddy. I'll come back.'

'Only cowards cry, then they shoot them. Be brave, Patrick. or they'll tie you to that crooked pole and shoot you. You're just a boy - get out of here!'

'Harry wake up, you're safe. You came back. You're not going back there.'

'Am I dying? Am I dying, Evie?'

'Yes, Harry. You are.'

Mary Cornell cared for her son as best as she knew how. She was the only person left, not to judge him. Whatever he did or had done, she wanted him to know that she would always be there for him.

The world was changing. It was easy to read the faces of injured men who felt lucky to be back on English soil, with no words spoken, families and friends could understand more about what suffering was still being endured by those remaining in the game. The war carried on in their heads. There were still songs and poetry being written with worn-down pencils. Both sides had fought the fight, for the survival of freedom, which needed to be preserved, it had been for the same cause, but the after-effects would never let them forget.

Was the war really over for the boys who sailed back to Blighty with missing limbs, and facial disfigurements, coping with injuries that were just too painful for their families to acknowledge. Turning their eyes away from these poor soldiers seemed the only possibility for fear of showing disgust, which would not be appropriate and might appear disrespectful.

Many men carried a weighty guilt that sat like a slab of stone on their shoulders, a heavy load to carry. They had survived when their best mates, the pals they grew up with and shared secrets, were lying dead in a trench drowned in rat infested muddy water and with a bullet in their back! Alone and isolated with no tears wept over their bodies, cramped in crooked positions as they had fallen. Perhaps they were the true survivors, free of pain, free of guilt. Free of being called a coward. You had to be dead to be a hero. You had to be dead to survive this.

Harry managed to get out of bed and sat outside in the sunshine in the yard in the house in Chatham. He was feeling better. The August sunshine warmed his face and he made himself comfortable in the deckchair. He could smell the Medway in the air. The Chatham Dockyards, just a few streets away, were alive and calling to him. He wanted the smell of sickness and bed sheets off his skin and it did not take him long after that to feel the need to totally get out of the house. His mum was fussing and he felt like a drink. If he was patient, he could walk to the end of the road and onto the High Street.

'Mum!' he shouted, 'I'm off for a short walk.'

Mary Cornell peered out of the kitchen window and watched him walk to the end of the road. She knew where he was going because 2/- had disappeared from the pot in the kitchen.

It was about to disappear into the till of the Ship Inn at the end of the High Street.

ADA

The landlord had known she was trouble. There had been a rumpus a few nights earlier when his wife Annie had asked her and some forsaken old sailor, who was not getting what he assumed he was due, to leave the bar. A fight had started and voices had been raised.

'Oi! I'm a married lady. Keep your hands to yourself, you dirty old bugger!' Ada Quinn had hollered as she pushed him.

'Lady? I can't see a lady in ere.' It was the smirk on his grimy face that had fired Ada up - enough to punch him in the face and knock him to the floor, breaking a chair and some glasses. The landlord's wife, not scared of trouble, had pushed both of them out into the street. She dealt with trouble like this on a daily basis.

'All right!' Ada had said, 'I'm off home.'

The man had run after her as she strutted off up the High Street, following her like a lame dog. The landlady laughed to hear him groveling. She watched them as they disappeared up a side alley. *Ada will sort him out,* she thought.

*

The landlord looked at the tall woman in front of him with a thin, wide grin. Her hair was pulled back off her face and tied in a disheveled knot under her black velvet hat.

'Thought we'd barred you,' he said.

Ada slammed some coppers on the bar.

'That's for the damage I did - I'm sorry.' She grinned and put her arm on the bar. The striped sleeves of her blouse were rolled up over and above her elbows. There was a small tattoo. She pulled her sleeves over it.

'Me husband got me to do it,' she said.

'Is he on the ships then?'

'Army. Not seen him in two years. Can I have a beer?'

He pulled her a half pint somewhat reluctantly.

'No more trouble eh?'

Ada walked over to a table and sat down with her feet neatly together. Harry was sitting in the corner. He was already on to his third pint when three dockyard workers walked in, they ordered the landlord to bring drinks over as they made their way towards Ada's table. Ada's cheeks were flushed but Harry admired her composure.

'Give me a break guys, I just want a quiet drink,' she told them.

'A lady shouldn't be in a pub on her own or folks'll think she's offering something.'

'Oh really? And what would that be?'

'Your Bill wouldn't like it, Ada. Not when he's fighting for king and country.'

'Leave it out fellas. I can handle myself.'

'You can handle me whenever the fancy takes you, Ada,' said one of the men, laughing. Ada stood up to move to another table but, as she moved past them, one of the men pulled her onto his lap bringing his knee up between her skirts.

This annoyed Harry. He hated it when men treated women like that. He banged his cane on the table.

'I think the lady wants to drink alone.'

The men turned to face him and, at once, he regretted opening his mouth. Dockyard workers had the reputation of being tough bare-knuckle fighters. One of them stood up.

'Look at yourself,' said Harry. 'I've an injured leg, a war wound, and anyway I'm too pissed to fight you. Have some self-respect.'

At that precise moment, Ada could no longer resist the urge to punch the guy who had fumbled her across his face with her own bare knuckles. He fell to the floor, stunned and red faced. She had knocked him right out.

'Oh shit, I've done it again. Look, nothing broken,' she shouted to the landlord holding out her hands.

'Thanks, mister.' She turned to Harry and smiled. 'Blokes rarely stick up for me like that.' While the other two men attended to their friend, she ushered Harry towards the door.

'I owe you a drink – but somewhere else - for your own safety, love.'

'Where the hell did you learn to fight like that?' asked Harry.

'My husband's a fighter. He taught me a trick or two. Haven't seen him in two years, not heard from him neither. I guess he's not that bothered; he could be dead for all I know.'

'Don't joke,' said Harry

But Ada liked a joke; it kept her spirit alive. She needed a little black humor to lighten her day.

'Got a name, mister? You married? Got kids?'

That was a lot of questions.

'Yeah,' said Harry.

'I got a daughter. She's only a kid, nine years old.'

Ada did not choose to add that Lily, her daughter, was in the workhouse because Ada couldn't make ends meet. She tried to find work, did some cleaning, took in ironing, but, with the war on, it was hard. She took him to a small pub further down the High Street, where she propped her elbows on the scrubbed wooden table and they drank more beer and she cracked more jokes. She hated her life.

'One day,' she said, 'I am going to strike it lucky. You've got to try and see the good in your life.'

What a good attitude, thought Harry. He wanted to tell her stories that would make her laugh. Her grin seemed to take away the dark cloud that lived above his head. But although Ada brushed off her difficulties, he sensed that there was more about her that she refrained from telling him. And this was correct. Ada was a formidable character and a bit too outspoken for most, but she needed money to survive. If that meant a quick grope in an alleyway with some drunken sailor whilst she nicked his wallet then so be it. Life's cruel demands had led her down the unfortunate path of prostitution. Not through choice, far from it; she was well aware of where prostitution led and she avoided the other prostitutes and their pimps, who hung around the dockyards. She had seen the faces of those girls, old before their time, with bruised cheeks covered in cheap, pink powder and she loathed the idea of being answerable to any man and knew what happened if you ended up working under those dubious characters. She had only married her own absent husband, the fighter William Quinn, because she thought her daughter should have a father.

When William gets back, all will be well, she told herself when she felt life knocking down her spirit - but whom was she kidding? William Quinn had never paid much attention to her before he went away. She had had to learn to fight for her own survival. She had taken a few too many knocks when she was a young girl and vowed if any man would dare to hit her then she would get there first.

'So,' she said, 'you like a drink, love, do ya?' She had money that she had saved from the night before. It was tucked in a small satin purse between her cleavage, just where she could see it. They drank it and Harry forgot about the pain in his leg and the war in his head went away temporarily.

'Ada, I need to go home,' he said as they staggered out, his arm round her shoulders.

'Course love. Where d'you live?'

'You can sleep in my bed,' he told her and she did not refuse. He longed to have a women he could wrap his arms around, but when they got to his mother's house, she left him on his doorstep. As she walked away feeling sorry for him. He hadn't got a bean to his name. She decided she would come back and find him tomorrow. *Harry Cornell,* she mouthed to herself, *not a bad name,* as she walked back along the High Street pulling her shawl about her broad shoulders.

*

Harry did not see Ada Quinn until the following week when he ventured out to buy some tobacco.

'Hello again!' She tapped him on his shoulder. 'Remember me, lovey?'

They spent the next four hours drinking in the *Three Cups* on the High Street then Ada walked him back to her lodgings. She never usually took blokes back to her rooms and she looked up and down the street before putting the keys in the lock, hoping that nobody would see her inviting him in. Her room was small and bare. An iron bed stood in the corner, piled with blankets with rows of pots and pans stored neatly underneath. A scrubbed washboard sat beneath a line of stockings that she had draped over a piece of thin wire attached to two old rusty hooks.

'My daughter sometimes sleeps in there,' she said, pointing to a green-painted door slightly ajar.

Harry did not care about the state of her room; he was happy to be there.

'I have never brought anyone here before,' she added. She took a bottle of gin and two glasses from behind a floral curtain that hid some shelves.

Harry found a chair so he could sit and rest his leg and his cane fell on the floor. He took the glass from Ada closed his eyes and took a long breath.

'Loosen your collar, love,' she told him.

He felt tearful but he could not think why, meanwhile, Ada thought how he was not like any of the other men. They would have been all over her by now, groping and fumbling. He was playing it cool, she thought and it unnerved her slightly.

'You loosen it,' he told her.

She moved an inch closer; her shawl dropped to the floor and, as she bent forward to pick it back up, he grabbed the back of her neck.

'Loosen it!' he repeated.

She laughed but, before she could reply, he had pulled her towards him, glass of gin in one hand, kissed her laughing lips. With fingers that she was surprised to feel were trembling, she loosened his shirt collar and then undid the buttons on his shirt running her hands in over his chest. She felt his breath quicken and needed to reassure herself that all was fine and he wanted her and would not hurt her. Putting his gin down on the floor, he pulled her onto his lap. He wanted to feel her bare legs. Running his hands up underneath her black skirt, he searched for her suspender clips, opened then and slowly rolled down her stockings. She had never been treated with such care; it was clearly important to this man that she should enjoy what he was going to do her.

'Relax woman,' he ordered and guided her onto the bed and undid the buttons on her blouse.

For almost the first time in her life, she allowed herself to lose control of the moment and, as she did so, she realised that she wanted a lot more of him in her life. In any case, there was no point trying to steal money from him; he didn't have any.

And Harry - he felt alive again. She wasn't his Evelyn Anne and never would be but she was helping him to come out of the darkness. With Ada and Gin, he had found a place to escape to, a place that did not judge and look down on him.

*

'I don't trust that woman, Harry.' Mary Louisa said, sitting with him in the front room of their mother's house, Harry squinted at the diminishing light. 'And it's too much for Mum.'

'You're nagging. Ada's a kind soul; she means no harm.'

'How could you both let mum get so drunk? Her health can't take it. You were out of order!'

Harry shrugged. The Armistice had seemed like a good excuse to celebrate and Ada had dragged him and his mother into the *Globe* on Chatham High Street. People had been out in the streets celebrating and there had been a great atmosphere. For once, Mary Cornell had been happy to drop her Victorian composure and to raise a glass to *Peace in the World* – and, hopefully, peace in the minds of her children.

'It's too much for her,' Mary Louisa repeated.

Now that Mary Louisa had married and moved out of the house, she felt it was her duty to keep a careful eye. Their mother had aged during the war. Coping with a young grandson and then caring for Harry as he convalesced, had put a lot of stress on to her. Mary Louisa wrote to their brother William in Brighton and explained her concern.

Meanwhile, Ada was now a regular visitor to the house in Hospital Lane and Mary Cornell saw that Ada had some affection for her son. *A man needs a woman to support him emotionally,* she thought. After Harry's behavior towards Evie, Mary Cornell believed Ada would stand her ground. Ada was certainly a match for Harry and not a person to mess with. Mary Cornell had often heard them arguing when they were drunk. Harry would lose his temper over something stupid and Ada would be shouting in the street then, just as quick as things could kick off, all would be calm again. Mary Cornell saw an innocence in Ada who, with her arms wrapped around Harry's neck, would smile sweetly.

'Come on, Cornell,' Ada would say, 'time you got out of your chair and walked this woman down to the *Globe.*'

Harry never argued about going to the pub.

By Christmas 1918, the men were coming home but Ada's husband, William Quinn was yet to appear. Ada was now frequently seen with 'Cornell', as she called him, out in the pubs of Chatham and she was nervous about how William would react.

'You don't know him like I do,' she told to Harry. 'My life won't be worth living if he comes back. Hopefully he can stay missing.'

One Sunday morning the following summer, Private William Quinn walked into the *Ship Inn*, and asked the landlord if he knew where he could find Ada. The Landlord, kept tight lipped but William suspected he knew more than he would admit to. It wouldn't be long before he would find her. He had many contacts.

Fortunately, Ada heard that he had returned before he found her.

'I need to get out of Chatham, Cornell,' she told Harry, 'and quickly.'

15. Sixteen Bob a Week

Tommy Carter tried to mop up the wet footprints that marked the floor in the entrance to the hospital. Too many visitors and hospital staff were coming in and out of the rain, making it a pointless task as they criss-crossed their prints on the marble floor.

A group of sensibly-dressed ladies were assembled rather uncomfortably in the entrance hall. Tommy Carter had watched their grand cars arrive at the front entrance. He had watched one of the chauffeurs light up a cigarette as he leaned against the door of his big, expensive car. The chauffeur had winked at him like he was a small child but what Tommy Carter had really wanted was a cigarette.

Tiresome small talk competed between the ladies. Before the war they would have been greeted and ushered through to the meeting room opposite the reception desk; now they were inconveniently in the way of a flurry of personnel trying to get through their demanding work schedules. A huge, Victorian portrait hung over the ladies in a high position above the door. Its subject was the chairman of the founding medical board. His name, indecipherable from below, was on a brass plate embedded in the polished, mahogany picture frame. The ladies sensed they were being looked down on, and they discussed the bad weather and their husbands and their sons who were now at Oxford and how the hospital grounds were looking so lovely that year in rather subdued voices. Hearing Dr. Howard, they moved towards the corridor *en masse,* although hospital staff moving hither and thither, slowed their chaotic rush. Dr. Howard was accompanied by Matron. He might have been higher in rank but it was Matron who maintained order and guided the ladies into the meeting room.

Tommy Carter laughed, revealing bad and crooked teeth, and stood to attention as they passed. Harry had taught him to do this after Tommy Carter had told him that he would like to be a soldier. Harry had had him marching up and down the corridors with his rifle mop and taught him how to salute when an officer was approaching. They called the Matron the 'Sargent Major'; it was their private joke.

Once in the small meeting room, the ladies were joined by a couple of suited gentlemen. Digestive biscuits were displayed in on plain, blue, china plates on trestle tables and volunteers from the 'Friends of the Horton Cluster Committee' served tea in matching blue cups. Philip Cavanagh was one of the suited men. He had been on the board of trustees for twelve years and always put in an appearance at these meetings. He had done so ever since he had brought Harry to the Asylum all those years ago. He was greeted by Dr. Howard who made a beeline towards him. They were old friends after all.

'Harry Cornell hasn't long to live,' Dr. Howard whispered after exchanging pleasantries.

'Poor man,' said Cavanaugh, 'maybe it's for the best.'

Dr. Howard still resented the day he had been asked to get involved. Harry was a problem that hung over him. As for Cavanagh - Harry Cornell represented a time he would be more than happy to forget. Reputation was everything. After all, Cavanagh was born into the aristocracy and known in the art world as a talented artist and dealer, and as a respected philanthropist who showed a keen interest in up-and-coming talent. He had made mistakes regrettably, who had not? He could not help but feel a tad relieved that the one piece of the jigsaw that could still damage his reputation was near the end of its life. It was all such a long time ago, all that business before the war, but it still had the power to harm him –if Harry opened his mouth and Dr. Howard had better carry on keeping him quiet as had been agreed. Well, soon it would all be over by the sound of it. He smiled at the other trustees as they moved about the room greeting each other, and shook the gloved hand of a lady who was titled but he could not remember her name.

'Lady Margaret Littington,' said Dr. Howard.

'Lady Margaret, how are you? - and your daughter? We were neighbours in London,' said Cavanaugh.

'She's well thank you, Philip - and very busy with her career.'

Cavanagh moved on.

Tommy Carter had infiltrated the meeting room and stood to attention near the door with his bucket on the floor beside him. He saluted. Matron told him to disappear but not before he had had a good stare at the man in the smart suit talking to Dr. Howard and the posh lady - and not before Cavanaugh had had time to become aware that Tommy Carter was staring at him. The boy decided he did not like him.

Tommy Carter reached the door of the isolation ward and peered through the round window onto the corridor. Harry was propped up on a pillow with a blanket wrapped around his shoulders. Tommy gave a limp wave but saw there was no point in trying to get Harry's attention. Harry was staring out of the window, watching the rain.

I'll follow you, Ada, like I don't have anything left to lose.

*I'm running again, running slow. I can't see a destination –
I'm just following you without care or worry.*

*Mum, there's no point in crying, tell Patrick he'll be better
off without me in his miserable life.*

*My rucksack's heavy and my leg is hurting but I'm coming
with you. I'm giving up everything for you - and look how you
treat me. How can you do that to a poor old soldier like Cornell?*

1919

Harry and Ada ran from Chatham. The small amount of
savings they had scraped together would be enough to help
them find a room somewhere in London where it would be
easy to get lost. Huddled together on the train, all they had
was two brown suitcases and a duffle bag that Harry had slung
over his shoulder.

Once in London, they acted out their adventure like two
naughty school children playing truant. The first couple of
nights they slept rough. This did not bother Harry. It was an
improvement on the many nights he had spent sleeping under
the stars but never with a warm woman beside him. Her breath
warmed his face as she snuggled her head under his chin. She
hummed an old fashioned tune and wondered, as Harry did,
what brought them to this: a draughty doorway, a couple of
blankets and no fags. Life gave no indication of where it was
going to turn. Eventually, with the guidance of a street trader,
they found a couple of rooms in Kitchener Road, Forest Gate.
The room was almost bare but there was a bed at least, which
they christened happily as soon as they were handed the keys.

The landlady seemed pleasant enough.

'You can use the privy in the back yard,' said the landlady. Her rosy cheeks suggested she was partial to a drop of gin. 'It won't bovver you to share it with them upstairs.'

Harry had worked up a smile in her honour. He handed her the rent which she tucked into the pocket of her apron.

'You married?' she asked.

In the street, a boy was drawing pictures on the pavement with a piece of chalk. Harry watched as the boy drew the union flag on the paving slab. He saw the boy captured in his own world, drawing straight lines with caution and precision. He found that he wanted, for a brief moment, to step into that world.

'Well, no one will find us here, love.' Ada chirped, rubbing her hands together, when the landlady had gone.

'Yeh, we're safe.'

*

Harry stretched out uncomfortably under the sheets; his joints were aching. He suddenly felt cold and alone. Maybe Ada was in the hallway or out in the back yard. He lay still for a second then called out for her. He jumped out of bed and pulled on his boots; she was nowhere to be found. When she returned a day later, she found Harry cowering in the corner of the room trembling like a small boy.

'Hey, love,' she said, 'what's wrong?' She helped him onto the bed.

'Where were you Ada? I tried looking for you, I was scared he'd found you and taken you back to Chatham.'

'Don't be daft. I've bought you a beer. I had to go out and get us some money. You need to find a job; our money's not going to last.'

'Where did you go Ada?'

'Just here and there, looking around, you know.' She stroked his thinning hair. A crumpled ten-shilling note was tucked into her pink, satin bra and it scratched at her skin. She was tired and sore. She had warmed to her roguish boy because he needed her and she liked that. Although guilt was an emotion she had never experienced before, it was starting to fill her thoughts. *How could she have left him alone without any explanation?* She even felt a little guilty about how she had been earning her money.

The war carried on endlessly in his head. He tried to crawl into his shell but the images were so vivid. In his dreams they were there in the darkness, Teddy boy and Russell Cooper, Evelyn Anne and the kids. He would be shouting at them to get out the way and then there was his father washing away the mountains and trees he had chalked on the wall, where a soldier lay bleeding over the top. There was blood. It dripped down the chalked bricks, over the mountains, trees and green fields. Harry would wake sweating and Ada would give him whiskey.

'Here Cornell, this'll calm your nerves.'

- until the next time which might not come for several days. In those periods, there would be calm, and Ada would be relieved and then something would set him off again: a face in the crowd, someone shouting, a horse in distress, a woman walking with her children. Then Harry would be thrown back into the middle of chaos. Eventually, Ada had no choice but to seek out a doctor for advice on getting to grips with Harry's madness, which was how Ada described it, calling these periods his *mad episodes.* She had to get him better, get him working again; they had to be able to make ends meet.

The whole country was struggling to cope with the after effects of war. Change was embraced by the young. Women had found a new independence. Dresses were looser, hemlines shorter, flowing locks were cut into more manageable styles. The younger generation established new freedoms after the restraints they had endured before the war.

As men returned home, the need for change and celebration became evident. The horror of war was embedded in the back of their minds. For the wealthy and the middle classes, the practise of masquerading created a carnival atmosphere. This may have seemed sufficient for most, happy to lose themselves in joviality, drink and dressing up. The disguise only covered the surface, what sat beneath festered and bubbled away.

New dance halls, opened up and the young and able-bodied danced to new steps that enticed them to move beyond the old boundaries. There was music on the streets and a social revolution was creating liberalism where 'anything goes'. It was the beginning of the end for aristocratic, Victorian values. Stuffy, for those who could afford it, was out with the Ark. Freedom was what they had fought for and now it was meant to be there for the taking.

There was very little support for the soldiers who had returned home with injuries and for helping those unable to work, but war pensions were offered to all soldiers and Harry did receive a small one. It helped with the rent. However Ada wanted more and continued to supplement their income in her usual way. She suspected Harry was aware of what she was up to and was grateful that he turned a blind eye. It did trouble him slightly but he pretended not to care. He had enough to worry about and Ada could take care of herself. She was not his Evelyn Anne; now that would have presented a different reaction in him. He thought of her often, his Evie, her softness and simple voice. He could still almost smell her hair that had the little ribbon falling through it the day they had met outside the Empire in Brighton. He visualised her standing in the road with his little daughter, May, clinging at her long skirt as she curled herself around in the folds. Sometimes he imagined she was waving to him.

'*Bring back some coal Harry,*' she was calling.

How he missed her. She was better dead he told himself. Evelyn Anne would not live with a man who let her walk the streets, a man who cried like a baby whenever there was a thunderstorm. Dennis Scully must have killed her back then, before the war, or she would have come back for the children. Yes, that was it; Dennis Scully must have killed her then made some arrangement for the kids.

Ada already knew about Evelyn Anne. Mary Cornell had told her everything before they left Chatham.

'It was his own fault,' Mary Cornell explained, 'and he took it bad when she left. It did surprise me though, that she never came back. What sort of woman abandons her kids like that? It has been hard on them, on Patrick and May, and we're not sure what happened to the baby after he went to the workhouse. Florence and William think he was taken to an orphanage. None of us have heard hide not tail of Evie since, not one whisper.'

Ada promised her she would look out for Harry.

'A man needs a good caring woman, Ada,' said Mary Cornell and put her hand on Ada's as they sat at her kitchen table. 'Harry needs one more than most.'

The subject of Evelyn Anne fed Ada's curiosity.

'What happened to your wife Cornell,' she asked. 'Died did she?'

Harry looked up. 'Don't talk about her, Ada.'

But it annoyed Ada that Harry still held a candle for her. Brewing within the care she had for him was another emotion, alien to Ada, the green poison of jealousy. She told herself to ignore it but it ate away at her feelings. It pushed her to create a reaction in him, one that would show Harry that she was now the first person in his life. She wanted him to explode so she could see the truth, buried deep within him. She wanted him to shout out so she could stamp on his feelings and destroy them

'When men can't speak about their wives it's because there's some truth they want to hide,' she told him.

Harry said nothing so she rattled on about William Quinn.

'That old bugger,' she would curse, hoping it would lead Harry into talking about Evelyn Anne; if she could be open and honest, why couldn't he do the same?

'Wish we could get married, Harry,' she would say.

'I got a wife.'

'I know, lovey. And I got a hubby and I wish I didn't. What can we do about it?'

And there the conversation would end.

*

Ada had broached the subject of Lily, her young daughter. She wanted to go back to Chatham and fetch her up to London. She wanted Lily back so they could be a family and, also, she thought Lily might have her uses.

'We haven't got the money to look after her, Ada,' he would say. The child would be better off staying in the workhouse, he told her - just until they found enough work for them to survive.

Harry scraped enough energy together to find some work. There were plenty of jobs to be had in London and he was good at making contacts, mostly via people he met in public houses. But he spent the wages he earned on whiskey and ale and he found that holding a job was difficult. His temper and moods affected all who worked around him. The war going on in his head lead him back into situations where voices were raised, opinions declared, fights broke out and broken glass lay in puddles of ale. He was becoming a nuisance to society.

Ada marched him to a doctor because they needed a medical certificate to get his pension increased.

'You fought for your country, didn't you? You're due some payback!

At first Harry was adamant that there was nothing much wrong with him but then he gave up and agreed with Ada: he had suffered long enough and the government should cough up and offer some assistance.

*

In 1917, the government failed to take the mental illnesses bought on by war service with due seriousness and medical officers were instructed to avoid the term 'shell shock'. For the poor victims suffering from war-inflicted nervous disorders, it could be confusing. The army dealt with over eighty thousand cases of men suffering severely from wounds that were not visible. No funds had been allocated to support these men and procedures were set up which the men had to follow to determine the amount of pension they were entitled to. Following a medical assessment, the patient was diagnosed with a degree of sickness, described as a percentage.

Ada started to pass herself off as Mrs Cornell. She thought this would help their situation when she tried to get Harry some support, hoping nobody would ask to see their marriage certificate. They were passed from one authority to another and it became very stressful.

'How did you get on down at the British Legion?' she asked one evening.

'There's a bag of coal in the hallway,' he said and fell exhausted on to the bed. 'It's all they would give me.'

When his date to be assessed arrived, Ada walked with Harry to the military hospital where they saw a rather condescending medical officer.

'You smell of whiskey, Mr Cornell. Give up the drink and I'll give you a medical certificate.'

'But we've no money and you can see by the state of him, he can't work,' said Ada.

'Come back when you're sober.'

They left the hospital and the two of them walked into the nearest public house to drown their sorrows. They managed to arrange another appointment and this time Harry went along sober. They told him he was 60% sick and he could have 16/-per week.

'Now I can bring Lily home,' said Ada.

*

Harry didn't want Ada to go to Chatham to fetch Lily.

'Be careful you don't bump into Quinn. I should come with you.'

But Ada was adamant she could take care of herself; it would only make things worse if he came. She did not want

Harry bumping into William Quinn nor coming with her to the workhouse.

Chatham workhouse was a familiar place. Ada, abandoned by her own mother and with little knowledge of her father, had found her way to the workhouse when she was a child. Bruised and worn down, she was nothing but a waif, grateful of a bed and warm, if not flavorsome, food. She was not used to the regimented daily life of the place and rebelled unsuccessfully until she learnt how to manipulate those in charge. She was unable to read or write but her formidable character helped her to survive. Other girls and young women learnt to bite their tongues and steer clear of upsetting Ada Quinn.

Ada was made of strong stock but at the tender age of twenty, she was not physically strong enough to fight off the advances of a middle-aged laundry man who found his way into the workhouse courtyard where they hung the bed sheets.

'Scream you little slag and I'll hurt you bad,' he told her. 'Smile like you're enjoying it.'

He shoved her against the wall behind the damp, linen, bed sheets and lifted her tattered skirt. She didn't scream, and she performed as she was told, shaking her head silently at two young inmates who saw the back of the laundry man through the sheets as they lifted in the breeze. His trousers were crumpled around his ankles and he moved backwards and forwards, grunting and moaning and holding Ada's leg up with his grubby hands. They knew better than to say anything, better to not tell on Ada. Anyway it was better to leave him picking on Ada and not on them.

This happened regularly every week and at the same time for about three months whenever he came to pick up the laundry. Ada concealed the act, submitting to his demands and never uttering a sound. She did not know his name and never wanted to. She was more than grateful when she heard that he had been found dead at the bottom of a laundry basket, drunk on gin with a foul chemical smell on his clothes. She acted faultlessly surprised when they told her he had been found by hotel workers whose job it was to unpack the laundry baskets up at the Bull Hotel in Rochester.

A few months later, Ada gave birth to a little girl with a mop of dark hair and a sweet smile. 'Father unknown' it said on the child's birth certificate. Ada cuddled her baby and vowed they would leave the workhouse when she found a husband.

*

This was the fourth time in ten years Ada had collected Lily from the workhouse. Lily, pale and fragile in a brown, cotton coat and grey socks, creased and ruffled over her scratched shoes, hugged her mum tightly.

'I've a surprise for you,' said Ada. 'We've got a place in London - and you've got a new uncle.'

'What happened to my other uncle?'

Ada explained that William Quinn had come out of the army and joined the circus as a fighter. 'Now you can live in London with me and Harry.'

Harry was not at home when they arrived in Forest Gate. The room was empty and there was not even a note. Ada became worried when he did not appear that evening and took Lily with her to visit all the pubs in the vicinity.

Harry was nowhere to be found.

'I promise Lily,' she said, 'he'll be back. The daft old bugger can't have gone far.' That night, cuddled up with Lily in their bed, she worried about Harry. By morning she was convinced he must be in trouble. *Perhaps he has got himself arrested, been in a bar brawl maybe*, she thought. She left Lily alone in the room and went out to try and earn a few shillings, hoping he would be back when she returned.

Lily, not used to being on her own, soon became anxious. The room was sparse and she had nothing to do. When someone banged on the front door she almost jumped out of her skin. She looked out of the window hoping it was her mum, but could not see who was there so she ran and opened the door - to a policeman. He held out a note.

'I can't read, sir.'

'Is your mum in?'

Ada had clocked the policeman as she approached the corner of the street. Lily ran past him and out into the road where she hugged her Mother.

'Mrs. Cornell?' asked the policeman.

Ada looked at the note and he saw that she was not capable of reading it either.

'It says your husband's at Ilford Police Station and he's suffering from shell shock,' he explained. 'Can you collect him?'

'I'll come now,' she said. 'Go and lock the door Lily.'

The police station was less than a ten-minute walk and Ada and Lily ran most of the way.

'He's in No.3,' the officer pointed to the cells as they approached the front desk. 'The doctor's seen him, Mrs. He was found down on the Broadway - having a fit.'

Ada rushed to the cell. She hugged Harry.

'We wondered where you were. Come on lovey, let's go home. Come and meet our Lily.'

The policeman that found him had assumed he was drunk

but the doctor had explained that fits were common following shell shock and they should all be aware, with so many men coming out of the army, that they could happen anytime.

This one had been an epileptic fit and it had left Harry feeling washed out. He had cut his face from when he fell. But Ada was there now and, *bless him,* she thought, he had called her his 'wife'.

'I love you, you silly old sod,' she said.

FOREST GATE

Harry got on well with Ada's daughter Lily from the start. She called him Uncle Harry and he liked that.

'You look just like my little girl.' Harry remarked as she climbed up onto his lap

'What's her name, Harry?'

'May - she had brown eyes just like you.'

'Is she in the workhouse?'

'No, she has another Mum and Dad now in Brighton, near the sea. She plays with the fishes.'

'Is she a mermaid, your little girl?

Harry laughed; he realized how much he missed his little girl. The thought of not knowing where she was pained him.

'Will you take me to Brighton, Uncle Harry?'

'Yeh, I'll take you to meet the horses on the merry-go-round.'

'And you can go to the pub, Harry - with Mum.'

The new place they had found in Forest Gate had two rooms. Lily slept in the room with the sink and the cooker so Harry and Ada could have a bedroom and some privacy. They were able to survive on Harry's 16/- a week and Ada supplemented their income when she felt she could. They could not go without their drink, tobacco and a bag of fish and chips on Friday when they came back from the pub.

*

'You've got a letter, Harry,' said Ada, passing it over.

'It's from Mary Louisa.' He took out a penknife to open it. 'Mum's not well and she wants us to go back to Chatham as soon as we can.'

'It's the flu Harry,' Mary Louisa wrote, 'she has got it really bad. I have written to William and Florence in Brighton and the others. Maggie is coming over tonight with Blanche, Sarah and Amy,'

Blanche, Sarah and Amy were Harry's four other younger sisters. They had all lived in Chatham with their sister Maggie since before the war. Maggie was now married to a Christopher Redman, a sailor, and Maggie was glad that her sisters had married and were living nearby to help. Just as Mary Cornell had wished for, all of her four daughters were finding husbands. Mary Louisa, was now married to a William Dicker, Sarah Elizabeth had married another sailor, Hubert Wadsworth, and her youngest daughter, Amy, was soon to marry an Alfred Moon. Blanche was still single. Harry felt like the bad apple in their company but he wanted to see his mother.

*

'We're here, Mum.' Harry pulled up a chair

'Harry, you feeling better Son?'

'Much better Mum. It's you who needs to get better.'

'There's a lot of this about, Harry.' The colour had drained from Mary Cornell's face and she shivered, pulling the blanket up to her chin. *There's always illness in this house,* he thought, remembering his time in this dark room, where the picture of the Virgin Mary smiled down on you and never at you.

'Will you do something for me, Harry? It's something I've wanted you to do for a long time.' Mary's voice was rough and raucous.

'Whatever you want, Mum.'

'Go back to Brighton and find her. Your children need their mother.'

'But I'm with Ada now, Mum.'

'Patrick needs his mum; he asks about her all the time. You owe it to him, Harry, to explain.'

Harry sat nervously by her bed, lost in wandering thoughts.

'And, Harry,' she said, 'you should paint more pictures. You were always good at that sort of thing.'

A knot was forming in his throat. It blocked his air passage and he felt as if he would choke. He held her hand and they talked about the mountains and trees he had drawn on her wall. They had been for her, he told her, and he had been so proud he had drawn them. He told her how he had been so angry because she had not seen them and had made him scrub the wall. She told him how he had amused her but he always was a young ruffian. It made him smile and give his cheeky grin. He held her crumpled hands and kissed them. They felt hot and sweaty against his cheeks.

'Go find Evie, Harry - and don't let her go this time.'

With tears rolling down his cheeks, he promised to go to Brighton and try and find his children.

Outside, Ada Quinn stood indignantly in the hallway, listening, with her arms folded tightly against her chest.

16. Forgiveness

Harry had seen enough dead bodies but none of them had looked as peaceful as Mary Cornell his mother. There was so much more he would have liked to say to her. He regretted all the years he had walked away from the feelings he should have shared with her. Too late now. He left the room and walked out into Hospital Lane.

'I'll go and fetch Patrick,' said Maggie. 'Someone has to break the news to him.' Her black, curly hair was pulled back from her face revealing tear-stained cheeks. She let her mother's fingers slip through hers. She had been sitting by her mother's bedside for most of the night. Mary Louisa put her hand on her shoulder.

'Don't, Maggie. Harry's gone to him; I think they need this time together.'

Harry will only make things worse, Maggie thought. Ada was standing by the doorway and started to agree with Mary Louisa but Maggie gave her the stare to tell her: *this is none of your business.*

'He needs time with Patrick, the boy will be heartbroken,' said Mary Louisa. ' 'Whatever' he's done, he's the boy's father and you can't take that away from them.'

The priest had sat with them most of the night. He shook the hands of everyone left in the room. With him departed Mary Cornell's strong Catholic faith, as if he had wrapped it up in a black bag and was carrying it away with him because it was no longer needed. Mary Louisa had promised him that she would attend Mass but he knew her faith would never be as strong as her mother's.

*

If I could say to you this,
Would you offer me your forgiveness?
If I could tell you what I see,
Would you look into my heart and understand?
I see her in the way you stand, and the tears you've cried.
I see her when you shake your head,
And look at me with silent pleading.
I see her when you smile and then look in fear when I walk
into the room.
Son, if you could forgive me,
Do you think she would come home?

Harry stood gaunt and with his hands in his deep and misshapen pockets.

'Patrick, your grandmother has passed.'

Patrick, now fifteen, had turned into a gentle young man. He had seen it all during his fractured childhood and there was not much left that could hurt him, not this father who had denied him his presence and had allowed his son's childhood to slip by without him. Patrick did not acknowledge his father, just turned his head and stared into the branches of the overhanging trees in Hospital Lane, January sunlight streaming across his young face. He hoped his teary eyes would go un-noticed. His grandmother had been good to him, had kept him warm and safe, shielded him from his parents and their turbulent lives. He resented his parents for giving her that burden.

'It's okay, Dad, I know she has. Mary Louisa and William told me I can stay with them. They're going to move in.'

'That'll be good for you, son. Mary Louisa's a kind woman.'

Patrick shrugged his shoulders. He wanted to tell his father to bugger off, he wanted to thump him, he wanted to cry, he wanted to be hugged, he wanted a father who could love him and take him with him to London. This whirlwind of conflicting wants confused him so he said nothing. Mary had taught him to be polite and god-fearing. Out of respect for her, he smiled at Harry and remarked how sorry he was for their loss.

'It's hard to lose a mother,' he said. 'At times like this, families should stick together.'

Harry never took the bait; he just wanted to assume the boy was coping so he patted him on his shoulders. There were no hugs, not for Patrick - and not for Harry. Mary's suggestion, just before she died, that Harry should go back to Brighton silently nudged his thoughts. *What if I do?* he wondered, thinking of all the possible repercussions. Maybe now was the time.

*

'You crazy sod, why would I want to go back with you to Brighton?' Ada screeched. 'Harry, love, our rooms are nice here; I want to stay in London - I'm a Kent girl, Harry. Anyway, you have enemies down there; it's not safe.'

But thoughts of Brighton stayed on Harry's mind. They took over and dispelled the thoughts of the war. He was determined, and Ada suspected this was all about Evelyn Anne. She had heard him shout her name in the midst of his dreams and nightmares. Ada's jealousy bubbled up and overflowed. Not a woman for keeping her feelings under the surface, she made unreasonable demands on him. Arguments followed and fights broke out between them. The neighbours complained about raised voices coming sometimes from their room or the hallway and sometimes from outside on the street. Ada used her fists to thump at his chest, leaving him sore and bruised. She had her own bruises, not always from Harry but from their drunken binges, when the two of them turned to alcohol for solace. She was turning into a familiar figure in the neighbourhood, stumbling in doorways and on cobbled streets and kerbstones, with Harry clinging on to her shoulders. They could often be seen, pushing each other aggressively as they walked back from their local.

But Harry had the stronger will. Eventually he persuaded Ada to move to Brighton and they packed their suitcases. Taking Lily with them, the three of them boarded a train at Victoria Station and turned up in Brewer Street at the doorway of his brother William, to the annoyance of William's wife, Florence. Harry assured them it would only be for a week until they found lodgings.

'We're a Christian family, William,' Florence complained. 'They're not even married.'

'But he's my brother,' William sighed.

It's the air of freedom.
We've tasted the same, you and me.
Are you here breathing it in?
Can you sense I'm here?
Can you hear the children chattering, the sea gulls squawking overhead?

Are you humming to the seaside songs of the merry-go-round?
I'm close Evie.
Where are you?

Harry bought Lily an ice cream. She smiled; the sea air was going to be good for her. Ada walked along the front with them. Brighton was shining and on Harry's face she saw that he felt he had come home.

'Well I never,' said the landlord. 'If it isn't Harry Cornell. Haven't seen you since before the war.'

Harry leaned on the bar whilst Ada and Lily found a table. He ordered drinks but avoided conversation. He had no recollection of the landlord.

'She doesn't like me,' said Ada when he brought the drinks over. 'Who?'

'Your sister-in-law, Florence.'

Not this again, he thought.

'Lily and me are going to walk back,' she said after they had sat in silence for a while. 'You coming?'

But Harry said he wanted to walk by himself for a bit and this made her nervous. If the stories that he had told her were true, then some of his enemies were dangerous. Was he safe? She tried not to worry. There were plenty of people around, enjoying the fresh air, and the seaside atmosphere was happy. Lily tugged at the sleeve of her cotton blouse.

'Can we go to the pier, Mum? Can we buy some chips?'

*

Harry strolled up towards the arches. *What did he expect?* he asked himself. Everything had changed and so many good memories were steeped in sadness. He had walked here many times as a child and as a tearaway. Here he had been the love-struck young man, then the drunk whom his wife could not stand to live her life with. Now he was just a broken old soldier who could make no sense of it all. He walked down the steps that led to the arches, to where he had sat with Alf Goldwater and Dennis Scully before the war. He walked towards the sea, crunching over the pebbles, past the fishermen's nets and upturned rowing boats.

'Be careful what you say to fishermen Harry, they are not to be messed with.'

He had been such a foolish boy then. He remembered the day his uncle had given him that advice after they had hauled him out of the sea. He had held so many hopes and dreams. *I never got the big fishing boat I wished for*, he thought to himself. Life took control and you learned to give in to it and here he was again - on Brighton beach, thinking about survival, back at the Arches, as if it was yesterday.

If Alf Goldwater had survived the war, surely he would not still be harboring the old grudge that had panicked Harry into leaving Brighton in 1915.

He looked at a group of men congregating in one of the arches. It had been nearly seven years since he last stood outside this entrance.

'You looking for someone, mister?' a young fisherman quizzed him.

Harry pulled his cap forward.

'Just an old mate,' he said, 'name of Scully.'

An older man pushed himself to the front of the group.

'Don't know anyone by that name but we could ask around. Who shall I say is looking for him?'

'Cornell - just say Cornell.'

As he walked back up Lewes road he thought to himself that he must be crazy. What was he doing advertising his presence? But the war had changed everything. If they still wanted him dead, he didn't care; he was dead anyway.

And there was just a chance that Dennis Scully was still in Brighton, and if he was, then maybe he had some explaining to do about Evelyn Anne.

*

Ada felt annoyed that Harry had not wanted to walk home with her. The first month in Brighton was unsettling and Harry was withdrawn. In London he had relied on Ada more, but in Brighton he was a lost lamb unable to talk about his feelings. When she pushed him he closed down and said very little. This made her think he was keeping things from her. That evening, when he finally got home, she could not stay silent any longer.

'Where were you Harry?'

'Nowhere special.'

'But you must have gone somewhere; you were gone ages.'

'I was just trying to do a bit of business.'

'What business?'

The more she poked and pried, the more Harry became irritated. He turned and walked away from her and she whacked him across his back. He stared at her with a stare that looked out a thousand yards and then the war came back. He crouched down, cowering, his head between his arms. Bombs were blasting: one, two, three. He was back in that dark hole but Ada left, slamming the door behind her.

Next morning Harry returned to the Arches. The young fisherman said he knew a man called Scully.

'Where can I find him?

'I'll bring him to you,' said the boy and nodded towards some deckchairs.

'I'll wait there then.'

Harry walked over to the group of chairs, crunching his boots on the pebbles. *I'm dead,* he thought and sat down with eyes closed, facing the sun.

*

'Harry Cornell?' Dennis Scully loomed over him at the side of the young fisherman. 'What you doing here?'

It was a shock to hear Scully's voice. Harry was half-blinded by the sun behind Dennis Scully's back.

'My mother died. I've bought her back to bury her. '

The young fisherman left them to it and the two awkwardly caught up. They talked of war and old friends lost but neither mentioned Evelyn Anne.

'Alf around?' Harry asked, as casually as possible.

'Runs the manor, just like before. Work's building up. What d'you want, Harry?'

'Think Goldwater might give me any work? Set me up again? I want to be back in Brighton, Dennis, and I have links in London now, and in Chatham. I can make trips back and forth, no questions asked.'

'Dunno, Harry.'

Dennis Scully was perplexed; he was unsure how Goldwater would react. In the past Dennis Scully had always tried to put in a good word for poor old Harry. He promised him there on Brighton beach he would try his best. Meanwhile, Harry squinted at him, wondering if the bond was still there or had been blown away on the wind of the years.

'I'll ask him and let you know,' said Dennis Scully.

The young fisherman came back. He signaled with his eyes that he wanted to leave.

'Oh, by the way, Cornell, do you recognize my boy here, Dennis Jnr?' Dennis Scully asked. 'They grow up so quickly, eh?'

'Who's that bloke, Dad?' asked the young man as he and Dennis Scully walked back across the beach.

'No one you need to worry about, Dennis – well, not yet anyhow.'

'Seems like a bit of a loser.'

'Don't say that. He knew you when you were a kid.'

17. Lucky

The room was conveniently situated at the back of a greengrocer's shop in Middle Street opposite the synagogue, not far from the sea front and the Arches. Jewish women sheltered under the green-striped awning of the shop doorway, holding onto their baskets as they chatted, not drawing a breath between sentences. A constant flow of people went about their business to and from the Lanes and were much too busy to take any notice of the comings and goings of those who entered the small greengrocer's.

Dennis Scully smoothed down his brown hair with the flat of his hand. He took pride in his appearance. He went over in his head the words he had chosen to use for his meeting with Alf Goldwater. He needed to sound confident if he was to be sure that the meeting would go his way. His son however followed his father abruptly into the shop, pushing past the Jewish women. A green, canvas curtain hung over the doorway leading to the back room. The two men walked towards it in their shiny black shoes. Dennis Jnr. held the curtain back and let his father go through. The smell of rotting cabbage and fruit, festering from where it had fallen underneath the crates, made his stomach queasy.

Alf Goldwater sat enthroned in the back room on a rickety chair, gripping an enamel mug of tea with his large, work-worn fingers. He beckoned them to take a seat. Dennis Scully sat down at the table, ignoring a half-eaten bagel left on a saucer. He refused Goldwater's offer of tea.

'What is in it for you, Dennis?' Alf Goldwater asked straight off. ' I don't understand where you're coming from. I thought Cornell was long gone. Why would I want to find him any work, the little bastard?"

'He's desperate, so he is, and he has now got links in Chatham and Forest gate. We could make use of him, Alf.'

'And what sort of state's he in?'

Dennis Jnr. raised his eyebrows and Goldwater clocked him. He caught the tension in young Dennis's face. So Dennis Jnr. had his doubts about Cornell - but his dad had warned him to keep his mouth shut and keep his thoughts to himself. Alf Goldwater was irked. Dennis was up to something and he was not sharing it. What was he hiding?

'I will say the war has not been kind to him, so I will,' said Dennis Scully.

Alf Goldwater stared at the younger Dennis.

'What's wrong with you?' he asked. 'Cat got your tongue?'

The younger Dennis stayed silent and shook his head.

So Dennis Scully was up to something; Goldwater decided that he wanted to know what.

'So give him a job,' said Alf Goldwater. 'If he lets me down again, it'll be on your fuckin' shoulders.'

Dennis Scully nodded in agreement but Goldwater knew his technique.

'We can test him out,' said Dennis Scully. 'It's been seven years and the old sod has survived the trenches.'

'People don't change.'

'Better the devil, as they say,' said Dennis. 'We're short of someone to do transport; we can't rely totally on the trains.'

'He got transport?' Alf Goldwater asked.

'He would need help with that, Alf - I can sort it.'

Someone entered the shop and they stopped talking.

'All right,' said Alf Goldwater. 'Go and 'ave a word, then you can bring him in. And warn him - I ain't got time for no fuckin' grass on my patch.'

'You mad, Dad?' asked Dennis Jnr. when they were out on the street. Cornell's a liability, and you know it.'

*

Ada ran out into Brewer Street to see what Lily was shouting about. Harry was standing in front of a horse and cart and little Lily was already climbing aboard.

'What's this?' Ada yelled at him.

'This, my darling woman, is Lucky. Isn't she a fine mare? And she's going to take us all the way to Chatham.'

'Mum, come on, just up to the end of the lane and back.'

Harry climbed up and pulled at the reins and Ada was delighted. They had given up their rooms in Forest Gate and taken a couple of rooms in Old Brompton near Chatham and, meanwhile, Ada's estranged husband, William Quinn, had not been seen or heard of for a couple of years so they both felt more safely settled. Harry seemed to be coping better and was more focused. His nervous attacks were less frequent. His last medical exam had given him 40% of disability and he was able to live on his pension and the money he now earned from Alf Goldwater.

He coped with his continuous trips between London and Brighton and they came in handy for the Cornell family because they could join Harry on some of his trips and keep in touch with each other. Harry felt useful for a change.

It came as a shock though when, in December 1922, they received the sad news that following a short illness,

Florence, Williams's wife had passed away. Leaving four children. Williams's daughter Daisy who was only 15 years old at the time had to take care of the other children, it was going to be a tough time for his brother William.

WEST PARK

The rain started to clear, leaving a pinkish glow that illuminated the sky behind the clouds. Nurse McCarthy decided to move some of the beds out onto the terrace after the ward rounds. First she pulled her blue jersey around her shoulders, attached her mask and walked over to Harry's bed to check his chart.

'Morning Harry - get a good night's sleep?'

' Lucky pulled us all the way to Chatham, through wind and rain,' said Harry turning his eyes towards the window.

Nurse McCarthy wasn't listening.

'Nurse.' Harry raised his voice.

'What is it, Harry? Would you like some water?'

'My horse - is dead. The French have eaten her - my Lucky.' He hesitated. 'No - Lucky's fine. Lucky's with the Gypsies.'

'Make up your mind,' said Nurse McCarthy. She sat on the end of the bed which meant trouble if Matron caught her.

'So you had a horse called Lucky?'

'The gypsies took her. I got to know them on my trips between London and Brighton. They said they'd look after her and she's fine. They were fine people.'

'That's grand, Harry.'

'I painted a picture of them, sitting around the fire. They had a blue caravan and they let me eat with them. That's the picture he took it from my room.'

'What do you mean - *he*? Who took it?'

'The aristocrat – Cavanagh - yes, that was his name. I remember now. It was my other horse that died - in France. It fell in a ditch.'

He was talking steadily and concisely for once. Nurse McCarthy noticed the change. *Could he be improving?* She wondered.

'When was that, Harry?'

'In the war - before I got messed up.'

The door to the ward opened and Dr Howard entered; thankfully Matron was not with him. Nurse McCarthy stood up and smoothed down the bed covers. She accompanied Dr Howard on the ward round.

'You did say, sir,' she said, 'to let you know if there was any change in Mr. Cornell.'

Dr Howard tried not to show his interest.

'- *and*, Nurse McCarthy?'

'There's a marked improvement in his communication.'

Dr. Howard thanked her for letting him know. He wondered if he should go and talk to Harry but decided against.

'What's he been talking about?' he asked.

'About his horse in France and some gypsies - and some aristocrat. It's still very confusing but he was clear and concise, not like his usual ramblings.'

'Patients can get confused - particularly in their last few days.'

Dr. Howard walked back to his office. He had known it was a risk to take Harry off his medication and he had always thought it possible that Harry might start talking again once he was off the treatments they had used to keep him silent all these years. The mind was powerful and some things were never erased. One could only hope that the TB would do its work quickly. Maybe even - he could do something to aid it? Dr. Howard shuddered, shocked at his own cynicism. This was not why he had become a doctor; he hated himself for the thought.

1923 CHATHAM

Harry never discussed the deliveries he was making for Alf Goldwater to addresses in Chatham, Clerkenwell and now Pimlico, South London. This did not stop Ada from probing and asking questions.

'You forget Harry, I know a lot of people in Chatham. You tell me what you're up to and I'll make sure we keep our noses clean.' She wanted to be involved; she hated being kept out of the loop.

'It's better you keep out of it, Ada. It's better you're not involved.'

But if something dodgy was going on, Ada wanted to be in on it. She wanted to be in Brighton the next time he took a run down there.

'You need me with you, Harry. It wouldn't be good if you were on the road on your own. What if you had one of your episodes, lovey?'

He agreed she could come on the next run. His sister Blanche and her new husband Bill Perkins needed help moving their things down to Brighton. Earlier that year, they had received more shocking news. Mary Louisa had become ill and died and Blanche was now the only sister left in Chatham. It had been decided that she and her husband should move back to Brighton. Blanche was worried about her brother William living alone and coping with the children since Florence had died. They were to move into Brewer Street to look after him so his daughter, Daisy, could be relieved of taking care of the children and could find employment.

Alf Goldwater agreed to pay out for some digs in Brighton for Harry and Ada when they traveled down with the horse and cart and Lily was happy to tag along because she enjoyed the trips to the seaside. During the summer months it made for a pleasant trip and they all appreciated getting out of Chatham and its dirty streets and dockyards and onto the country lanes of Sussex. Harry had always loved the countryside. The trips could take up to three days and they would sleep under the cart on a huge piece of carpet which kept them dry.

He appreciated the company of Ada and Lily but he was also grateful when they stayed behind in Chatham. Then he could stop by a field and spend time with the gypsies; they seemed to understand how he craved solitude.

WEST PARK

Just you and me we breathe in this country air,
This field belongs to us, Lucky.
I'm striding through the long grass,
The bombs have stopped falling - only daisies and meadow
flowers survive.
I jump the fence,
I can paint you in this place.
Here I brush and stroke the undertones of me,
onto the shadows on your face.
I am falling onto my knees, in the grass,
I am shouting to the sky,

Please look at my face, Evie.
Forgive me. I know what I did.
Dripping the paint now.
The grey is awash on my canvass.
A lucid layer of anger distilled in oil,
On a graveled path of pain,
Muddied with our tears that will not leave my head.
I am painting my anger now,
And your hair is hiding your face,
I have tormented and tainted you,
I'm taking the blame, carrying the weight on my shoulders,
As in France, when God delivered his wrath.
I'm kneeling at your feet - begging you.
Please come home.
Tell my children I will paint them and together we can sing
a freedom song.
They can walk the lanes - jump the rugged walls,
Where velvet green fields of these South Downs entice them
to play on my canvass and the sky looks down and light plays
wistful games of hide and seek.

'You looked like you were having a nice dream there, Harry,'
said Nurse McCarthy.

Harry managed a thin smile.

'I'd love to hold my paintbrushes again.'

'Sure you would Harry, my love. Shall I ask Dr. Howard
for one; I'm sure it would do no harm to ask.'

Later that day she plucked up the courage to mention the
paintbrushes to Dr. Howard.

'I can't see what harm it would do to find a paintbrush for
him to hold,' she said.

Dr. Howard, preoccupied with another patient, nodded approval.

Perhaps Harry had some old paintbrushes in his belongings which were kept in the hospital store. She hurried down the stairs to the store which was on basement level. The store held all the belongings of the patients that they brought with them when they were admitted. Some of the items were kept down there for years and usually were given to relatives after a patient's death. The store was musty with shelves stacked three high, full of brown cardboard boxes, and old suitcases.

Charlie Wright, the store manager was listening to some rock-'n-roll music on his radio when Nurse McCarthy walked in.

'Henry Havelock Cornell, you say?' He pulled a pen out of the top pocket of his brown overall and looked down a long list of names for a reference number.

'I've only got a fifteen-minute break.'

'There's an old suitcase and some paintings.'

'Let me look.'

'Is he dead then?'

'No - see if there are any paintbrushes amongst his things, can you?'

Charlie found the shelf reference number and disappeared to the rear of the store. He returned carrying a brown suitcase, which he placed on the counter.

'Poo! It's a bit whiffy.' He rummaged through the clothes inside. 'There are some brushes and tubes of dried-up paints.'

'Put them on a tray, Charlie. I'll bring them back later.' She blew him a small kiss of gratitude and made her way back up to the ward.

Harry was awake when she placed the handle of a brush in his hands.

'I see your face,' he said. 'You have brown eyes.'

'I do.'

'My Evie's eyes were blue.'

'Like the moon?'

'Yes, like the moon.'

He lifted up the long-handled paintbrush and touched the bristles with his fingertips. 'She had soft hair,' he said.

Nurse McCarthy began to talk about his Evelyn Anne. He told her about the time they had met outside the Empire Theatre and how one day she disappeared because he had let her down and she never came back, not even to find her kids. Holding the brush in his hand opened up some memories that had been locked away for far too long. He was remembering and his dreams were real enough to express. Harry felt good that there was someone to listen.

'I have so much to tell,' he said, suddenly gripping her wrist.

Brighton 1925

Dennis Scully Jnr. stormed out of the pub in a temper.

'The bloke's nothing but a drunk,' he complained to his father outside. 'Why do you go on covering for him?'

Dennis Scully put both his hands on his son's shoulders. 'Stop it, Dennis! Leave it alone!'

'Dad, are you *crazy*? The police stopped him; they wouldn't have stopped him if he'd been sober and his lights were on. What if they'd searched the load?'

Dennis Scully told his son to go home but as Dennis Jnr. walked off down the street, he bumped into Ada Quinn.

'Oi! Watch where you're going!' she snapped, then she realised it was young Dennis Jnr. 'What's up with you?'

'Harry's in the pub and out of his brain as usual.'

Ada laughed but Dennis Jnr. grabbed her arm.

'I'm warning you,' he said. 'Your old man's going to drop us all in it. Take him back to Chatham. We don't want him here.'

'Where's your dad, little man?'

'Dad's a fool; he's covering up something for Harry and it's going to get us all in the shit.'

Ada ran towards the pub. Harry was un-conscious in a corner and Dennis Scully was trying to wake him up. He had a cut over his eyebrow.

'Did he fall?'

'I'm not sure what happened, Ada. He got in a fight. You need to take him home.'

Ada looked at Dennis Scully in the eye.

'Your son thinks you're hiding something from him. Are you?'

'Just take him home, Ada, and try and keep him away from Alf for a couple of days - until I have cleared the air.'

Ada walked Harry home. He leaned on her all the way up to Jubilee Street.

'He won't tell me where she is Ada.'

'Who Harry?'

'My wife, he says she's dead, you know.'

'Let's not talk about her; she's long gone; you've got me now, lovey.'

Ada frowned. The memory of Evelyn Anne hung in the wind and whatever Ada tried to do to convince herself that the woman was no threat, there she was, lurking on every corner of the Brighton streets. Ada wanted to go back to Chatham. Unfortunately they needed to wait for more instructions from Alf Goldwater.

When Harry sobered up he was in a foul mood. Ada's nagging did not improve it and he stormed out down to the sea front.

'Harry, stay out of trouble!' she shrieked after him.

He walked along the promenade towards the pier. The sun was shining and people were out in force. The war had changed their faces; it had changed everything. He held so many regrets and he blamed himself. To dwell on the past was not healthy for the mind so the doctors had told him. They thought he was a failure, just like Evelyn Anne had, and his mother, his brother and his father, and Mary Louisa and Florence. *Ada too,* he thought, *she nags and complains.* But he loved her as he had loved all the others, did he not? *Was there any point? Was there any purpose in loving anyone?*

He sat on a bench and looked out over the sea. Where could he sleep and find some peace that night, he wondered. To the front of him, there was just seawater. He felt very lost. Despondency enticed him; he would pour enough alcohol through his veins to take the pain away.

18. Poisoned Pens

The years that followed WW1, saw many men coming home with nervous disorders. How could they be welcomed as heroes when their wounds were not visible? How was a man, who had done his duty for King and Country, supposed to explain this condition? Many carried guilt due to leaving their fallen friends in some muddy French field. Like so many of them, Harry could not grasp that his symptoms were part of a medical condition and not something he should feel responsible for.

The term 'shell shock' was first, used in 1915 by Charles Myers who published an article in *The Lancet* when it was still a condition far from being understood. War neurosis, or 'neurasthenia' as it later became known, did not discriminate between what class of man it decided to attack. There were many in the country who still assumed that it was used as an excuse to disguise a coward whether rich or poor. Families were ashamed and found it difficult to cope with their sons and husbands, as they struggled to return to some semblance of how they had been in character before the war years.

The sufferers, unable to share the horrors they had witnessed, tried to cope by remaining silent, as if this was their only salvation. They buried their darkest thoughts and hoped they would dissolve over time. For a man like Harry, there was little sympathy. Especially since he appeared to have been unbalanced before he joined up. *'Shell shock'* who could see it? Who could detect it, stirring in the mind of a liar and a cheat? Britain only wanted 'heroes'.

The thought of being branded a coward was incomprehensible. Harry used clever words and the warm taste of whiskey to disguise the dark and senseless that was taking over his rational thinking. When the screaming in his head took over, his cries in the land of reality remained muted while he lost himself in drink and violence, lashing out in frenzied frustration at everything and everyone. He became unapproachable, a man to be wary of, to avoid and never to question. It suited him. And, unfortunately, the people who knew him, worked with him and worried about him were the very people who brought out the very worst of his character - by continuously judging his behavior.

He was slipping slowly off the edge of a cliff. He feared the next loud bang of a door, a horse bolting up a street or a face in the crowd that reminded him of young Teddy boy or Russell Cooper. Any such jolt was enough to make him fall or send him cowering to the corner of some closed courtyard. They had told him in the hospital, in 1918, that his pain would eventually stop, but they had lied and now his trust was destroyed. Five years on and he was still waiting to fall. Every day he wondered, would this be the day that would finally finish him?

BRİGHTON.

Harry crouched his resentful body and shivered in a doorway. It was pitch black and he could barely make out the walls of the yard in which he had sheltered. Lucky waited nearby unobtrusively. Her breath misted into the cold, early-morning air as she lowered her head towards the ground. Lucky sensed his impatience; Harry hated to be kept waiting and there were only a couple of hours left before daybreak.

Bloody hurry up, he thought. He pulled at a thread of wool on the end of his glove. The fingertip was fraying and there was a hole. He wrapped the thread two or three times around his finger and stuffed both his hands back in his pockets. Then he stood up and stamped his feet on the ground to increase the circulation. It was too early for a drink but, well, it would warm his chest so he took a small swig of whiskey from his flask.

Dennis Jnr. appeared from the shadows. A couple of other men stood behind him.

'Hope we haven't kept you waiting.' Dennis Jnr. sounded sarcastic.

'Where's your dad?'

'He's not doing this one, Cornell. You answer to me.'

'I don't answer to anyone, Sony Jim. Where's the stuff?'

Harry felt annoyed; Dennis Jnr. felt annoyed. Harry had no right to humiliate him in front of the other men. He clicked his fingers to get their attention. Harry took hold of the reins on Lucky and stroked at her mane.

'I'm not leaving the town in day light, it's too risky,' he said.

Dennis Jnr. held his tongue. He knew Harry was right.

'They're bringing it up now. I was down on the beach half an hour ago and it will be here on time; you'll have to wait.' Harry lit a cigarette, which he pulled from behind his ear.

Dennis Jnr. walked over to the gate of the yard and looked down the lane. The other two lads, bored of waiting, began to joke with each other. *Kids,* thought Harry, studying their immature faces, unaware of what they were getting mixed up in, probably too young to have fought in the war. They did not know anything. His eyes upon them, both instinctively pulled their caps down to shield their faces.

'They're here,' said Dennis Jnr.

The two lads ran across to the gate and slid it open. Two older men sat up on the front of a cart; the lines etched into their exhausted and leathery skin added hostility to their empty and inexpressive faces. Their load was transferred on to the back of Harry's cart quickly and silently and covered with blankets. Harry, relieved, was anxious to get out of Brighton. He and Lucky slowly made their way out of the yard in the direction of London Road. With luck, by the time it was light he would be out in the country lanes. He kept his lights turned off on the cart and Lucky pulled slowly; she knew the way.

The light in the lanes was beginning to change. The eeriness of the morning mist flowed up into the atmosphere. Meanwhile, Dennis Jnr. padlocked the gates then, reaching into his jacket, he handed the two men who had come up from the beach a couple of rolled-up banknotes. He shook their hands and left with the two lads. It was only five-minutes through the small lanes that ran parallel to the sea front to reach the greengrocers shop in Middle Street. Alf Goldwater was lifting a crate of apples and putting them outside on a display under the window when they reached him. Dennis Jnr. picked one up, just to show off in front of the other two lads.

'Get inside,' said Alf Goldwater, 'and, you two - get lost.'

'It all went off half an hour ago.' Dennis Jnr. told Goldwater in the back room.

'And Harry?' He asked raising his eyebrows.

'Yeh, he was okay.' It pained Dennis Jnr. to say so.

As Dennis Jnr. turned to leave the shop, Ada Quinn, bold and wearing a frown, blocked his way. She was sweating from running through the lanes and did not bother to wipe it from her red face.

'Where's Harry?' Her hands were flat against either side of the doorframe.

'How should I know?'

'Not very good at telling porkies are you?' She grabbed the neck of his shirt.

'Get your hands off me, you stupid witch!'

'Where is he? The cart's gone from the yard.'

With an effort, Dennis Jnr. pulled her inside the shop.

'We don't want her spouting in the street,' he told Alf Goldwater.

Alf Goldwater was happy to agree.

'You shouldn't try an' keep tags on your ole man, Ada,' he laughed.

But Ada was not one to be intimidated, not by men like Alf Goldwater and a young Dennis Scully Jnr.

'I don't give a toss what he gets up to, but if he's gone up to London, I could have gone with him. He's gone up to London, hasn't he?'

'Don't know about that, love,' said Dennis Jnr. mockingly.

'Don't be an idiot.'

'Maybe he's gone to find his long-lost wife. She couldn't hack him either but she had the good sense to clear off.'

'Well now,' Ada stood her ground, 'that would be a bit difficult - because your dad says he done her in.'

Ada was no fool. She had worked it all out. She had lain next to Harry night after night, witnessing his nightmares. She had often heard him cry out that Evelyn Anne was dead and had never been found. But also, she had seen the look on Dennis Scully's face whenever her name was spoken and now she wanted her words to evoke a reaction, to probe for the truth, and it seemed to work because Dennis Jnr. went pale. So there it was: Dennis

Scully Snr. held the missing link. He knew something concerning Evelyn Anne. And that was what Ada wanted; if she could find out the truth she would have more of a hold over Harry.

'Clear off, you old witch!' Dennis Jnr. tried to push past her but Ada punched him with her fist across the side of his jaw and knocked him over. He stumbled to recover his balance, wiped his mouth, and saw a small amount of blood on his shirtsleeve. Alf Goldwater offered his hanky, amused that Dennis Jnr. had taken a blow from a woman, but there was always a time and a place so he ushered Ada into the back room.

'Ada, calm down! Come through and let's try and sort this before it all gets out of hand. Dennis, it's about time you went home.'

She wanted to refuse; she didn't want one of Alf Goldwater's bloody lectures. She dropped herself onto the hard chair and rested her elbows on to the table.

'I should have gone with him,' she said.

*

Dennis Jnr. was sick and tired of Cornell; he never wanted to hear his name mentioned ever again. His father always dismissed Dennis Jnr.'s concerns when it came to the subject of Harry Cornell and this irritated young Dennis Jnr. more than anything. When he entered the hallway of the house he lived in with his parents in Carlton Hill, his father was in the back kitchen, waiting.

'It's done, Harry's on his way up to Chatham.'

Dennis Scully nodded.

'Hope he keeps to the plan,' added Dennis Jnr. 'He should get back on Friday. That's if you can trust him.'

'Why shouldn't we?'

'You tell me.'

Dennis Scully lifted a jug of water and poured a glass.

'There's nothing to worry about, Dennis. Harry will do what he's been told to do.'

Dennis Jnr. had been up half the night and sleep deprivation made him tetchy at the best of times.

'Ada said something about you and Harry's wife. Did you - do something to her?'

His father's face remained calm and expressionless. 'Go and get some sleep Dennis; you look dead beat. Cornell's a good worker, so he is. He has a small problem with drink, that's all.'

Dennis Jnr. climbed the stairs of the small terrace house and made his way to his bedroom. He had never liked Cornell from the moment he had set eyes on him. They had a good thing going here and he resented his father letting someone as crazy as Cornell, loose with the responsibility for transporting contraband goods between Brighton and Chatham. He had to find a way to get Cornell out of the way.

West Park

'There was a letter,' Harry whispered, 'come here, nurse. I'll tell you'

Nurse McCarthy, intrigued, sat on the end of the bed.

'A letter - where?'

'He told me he wrote a letter to the pension's office. He confessed it to me, years later. He said it was him that did it. He didn't like me you see. He was a bloody hothead. You listening, nurse?'

'I'm listening, Harry.'

'I got 16/- a week for me, Ada and Lily, and he wrote to the pension's office and they stopped my money. I fought in the war; I was sick, really sick, and I couldn't work. He saw to it and they bloody stopped my money. He told them I was a drunk and I took cocaine. Me – cocaine! Where would I get the money to buy cocaine? 16/- a week and they stopped it - because he bloody wrote lies to them about me. He confessed, yeh, I heard him say it to the others. He was glad he did it, he said it was because he never liked me. I never trusted him neither; he wasn't his father's son, no he was not.'

'Who?'

'Dennis Scully Junior, that's who. He told me he sent it - on the same day he killed his own father. I heard him say it over the radio transmitter. He knew I was listening, they all knew.'

Nurse McCarthy said nothing about this to Dr Howard. She felt there was no need to alarm anyone and anyway, Harry was a great one for storytelling. He was a dying man with much to get off his chest. She could hardly tell the difference between truth and delusional daydreaming, but she was his nurse and part of her job was to listen. Only God would know the truth when the time came. God could come and sit on the end of Harry's bed and be his judge. Nurse McCarthy crossed herself at the thought.

Where does truth come into it anyway? she thought. She had sat with too many patients recently as they faced their inevitable deaths. Their supposed innocence was not there at the end; they had no understanding of God. His protection was wasted on their poor souls and she witnessed their fear when holding their clammy hands. There were often no Padres to administer last rights and, in most cases, not even a family member to show up and show respect. *Would anyone come for*

Harry Cornell when his time approached? she wondered, *and who would be there to show him how to ask for God's forgiveness?* She could only hope that God would be there for him because all she had to offer was basic medical care.

She apologised to God under her breath as she moved on between her patients and she apologised to herself for letting her mind wander. What she did not know was that Harry had already faced his creator and aired his views, and that there was no room in Harry's heart for a God who had let him down his whole life, a God who had never been there to offer any comfort or guidance. The same God who had given comfort to his mother in her misery, and the God his brother William had relied on, and his sisters had looked up to, that same God, that should have taken him in, had only spat him back into a society that had been blind to any good he had in him.

No wonder Harry was angry with God. He had no need for any of it. Not now. He could peacefully go to his death, fearing no damnation. His innocence lay amongst the pebbles on Brighton beach where he had left it long ago, while his resentment remained for the stupidity of those who had judged him and looked down on him.

BRIGHTON

At the end of the war, the Cornell family had been touched by the death of the two brothers of Florence Cornell. Tears for these boys were justified, but the day Harry received the news that Heaven had taken away his beloved sister, Mary Louisa, and that the good lord had cut her young life short, he drank until he passed out in the gutter. *Why her and not me?* he thought. *He has made me face the guns and the shells and I have tasted and seen the horrors of hell, but what sort of God would take Mary Louisa?*

His tears fell offended but he felt that his family hated him for his own survival.

Harry had read in the newspaper about a woman who had taken her own life following the death of her sons in war; her grief had been unbearable and the story saddened Harry. Were her tears the same tears that the country cried when they talked of glory and heroes? he wondered. No, he told himself, her tears were for her own personal loss and she had found the courage to end her pain. He admired her and wished he could find that same courage. It was against her religion and the law to take her own life and yet the country hypocritically said it was glorious to send her beloved children to their deaths. One incident of many. Would England ever accept defeat? No, the country believed it was victorious, even though there were never any winners when it came to war. It confused him: so much death around him and no good reason that he could understand to explain it all.

Brighton

Harry and Ada lived between Brighton and Chatham over the next few years and the extra work he picked up from Alf Goldwater kept them going.

Most of their money found its way into the tills of the local pubs. Harry needed his drink. The alcohol was effective at numbing the emotional pain but it fuelled his anger, leading to outbursts of violence. Ada coped with that; she had learned to play him. She knew when to keep her mouth shut and when she didn't, Harry usually appreciated her judgment. Occasionally the restraint got too much for her and she would overstep the line. In particular, she was still kept in the dark about Evie Ann and fights broke out between them around the subject. It was a fiery relationship.

Ada started to drink more whilst in Brighton and in London she was able to dabble in cocaine. Harry had caught her taking it and asked her where she had got the money, accusing her of stealing from him. Although the Cornell family saw Harry as the bad apple in the cart, there was no sympathy offered to Ada from Harry's siblings, apart from Blanche, his younger sister. Blanche had been happy to move back to Brighton with her husband Bill Perkins and their three children from Chatham.

'He has always had a short fuse, Ada; he was like it with Evie.'

'He'll not talk about her, Blanche. If I mention her name he changes the subject and gets cross with me.'

Blanche couldn't tell Ada much about Harry and Evelyn Anne but she was certain that Harry was a good man regardless of his faults.

'Your mum said the same and I can see that too,' said Ada. 'I know he loves me - but I think he loved Evie more.'

'Evie ran away, Ada. Harry can't accept it; he can't understand how she could leave the children. It really upset him and then the war happened and he's never recovered. Be patient if you can.'

'If I could give him a child, he would forget Evie.'

'I think he is a bit old for that now.'

'Men are never too old.'

'Look to your faith, Ada. I know you want to do the best for him.'

'I'm a sinner. He won't marry me until he knows what happened to her even though he thinks she may have died.'

'Died!' Blanche was shocked. 'What on earth makes him think that?'

The two women spent a lot of time together in Brewer Street although Blanche's husband Bill thought Ada was a bad influence on his wife. Blanche pursued the friendship and heated words were spoken between husband and wife. Blanche believed, as her mother had done, that Ada was the sort of strong woman that Harry needed and she refused to hear anything bad said about her. When her husband called Ada a 'dockyard tart' it distressed Blanche.

'She's has had a really rough time, Bill,' she said. 'They think the world of each other.'

'It's not just her. I know what Harry did to Bertha Botting. Once a rogue always a rogue, Blanche.'

Blanche's relationship with Bill, her husband, was far from tranquil itself and Blanche began to confide in Ada. Then, one day, when Blanche was heavily pregnant with her fourth child, Ada saw Bill in the Park, leaning against a tree with another young woman. She didn't recognize the stranger but, a few weeks later, she came across her at the house in Brewer Street; the strange young woman was Blanche's niece Daisy. It was a horrible thing to discover. Ada mentioned her concern to Harry.

'Don't get involved, Ada.'

Blanche gave birth to a baby son, Michael, but her health was damaged and she developed respiratory problems. Ada often called in to help.

'You're good with him,' said Blanche as Ada rocked the baby in her plump, strong arms.

'I love little babies,' said Ada.

*

One day, out of the blue, Bill and Blanche received a letter from Warren Farm Industrial School, Brighton, an orphanage. It advised them that a James Cornell, fifteen, wanted to meet his family.

'How should we tell Harry, Ada?' Blanche asked. Ada was reading the letter for the second time.

'Blimey, he's been up the road all this time, just half-a-mile away.'

'He's fifteen, poor lad. How time flies. We owe him.'

*

Jim Cornell waited at the gate of the school where he had spent most of his young life. He shook hands with Mrs. Hollingdale, the head mistress, who wished him luck. He looked nice and he was wearing a flat cap. He had an infectious grin. Ada and Harry stood waiting. Ada was wearing a little, black, cloche hat and a purple, wool coat - she wanted to look smart when she met young Jim. Harry stood beside her, sober and solemn. The anxiety made butterflies in his stomach. What do you say to the son who was dumped in a workhouse at ten-months old? Who did he look like? Would he ask questions about his mother? Harry wanted to run but he stayed put and the moment he saw Jim close up, he was overwhelmed. This was his son all right, there was no mistaking it. He was the image of the young Harry, full of aspiration. It was written all over his face.

I always called you Johnny when you were tiny, hey son. I'm the father, the father who went out one night to the pub and left you to cry. I'm the Dad that they took you away from because I was useless and neglected you.

The words flew around in Harry's head but he just stared at the young boy speachless. Jim stared back with an eager nervous smile.

'Hey, boy, climb up on the cart,' said Ada.

Ada chatted meaningless talk as they clattered towards Brewer Street and Jim glanced back at the school where he had lived for far too long. Then he turned to stare at the man they said was his father. He looked at the lines engrained on Harry's face, at his deep dark eyes and the red veins running over his nose and cheeks. Harry avoided Jim's gaze. He had nothing to say, only lots to think about.

'It's better that the lad stays with us for now,' said Blanche when they reached Brewer Street. 'You can stay here for as long as you like, *Johnny.*'

It seemed strange to Jim when she called him by that name, but everyone seemed to insist.

'My school has organised a job for me on a farm but I'd like to visit you all, Auntie Blanche. I'm a keen worker so nobody needs to look after me.'

Harry was grateful. He didn't really want the boy complicating his life.

*

Blanche was very sick and had taken to her bed. Daisy, her niece, was helping with the children and Ada visited regularly, sitting with her for long periods.

'Harry,' Ada said one night on her return home, 'I really don't like the attention Bill is showing Daisy. Something's going on between them. It's not right with Blanche being sick as she is.'

Harry shrugged; it was none of their business.

Blanche's continuous coughing left her exhausted. Bill, had finally decided to call in the doctor. Blanche lay wearily in her bed and watched Ada cradling her baby son.

'Ada,' she said, struggling to speak, 'you're so good with him. If anything happens to me - you must take him. Bill will never cope on his own with all the kids.'

'Don't talk like that, Blanche love.'

But Ada was flattered to think that Blanche trusted her and Harry with baby Michael.

*

'I already have two sons,' Harry complained when Ada broached the subject. 'Anyway, Bill would never allow it.'

'Maybe he should stop getting cozy with your niece. If Blanche was made aware, Bill couldn't stop us taking the child as our own, Harry.'

It was too late by then. That evening, Blanche suggested to Bill that it would be good for little Michael to go to Harry and Ada if she never recovered. There was a huge row between them in the kitchen basement in Brewer Street. Later, Bill accused Ada of being a tart and Harry of being a drunk and it would be over his dead body that he would give his young son to either of them. Harry was furious and, in spite of what he had told Ada earlier, he stormed into the bedroom where his sister Blanche lay sick, followed by Ada. Blanche's deep and sorrowful eyes looked into his red face. She knew what was coming; she had suspected for a while now.

'It's time you knew, Blanche - it's about Daisy ...'

Ada stood behind him with her hand over her mouth.

Bill Perkins never forgave them.

Five days later Blanche passed away from TB and Ada had her way. In any case, Harry was adamant that they should stay in Brighton whilst he was working for Alf Goldwater. They took baby Michael home with them. He kept Ada and Lily busy fussing over another mouth to feed. Meanwhile Harry felt that his family was at breaking point and turned to his brother William. William was unsympathetic. He blamed Harry for Blanche's death and believed that Harry telling her about Daisy had been the straw that finally killed her. Harry kept trying.

'Daisy's your daughter, you should have a word with her, William.'

'You're a right one to talk - remember Bertha?'

'I never touched her.'

'And you're still lying, Harry. When are you going to face up to things? You look after that baby like Ada wants you to, and don't you dare let any harm come to the little mite. I'll never forgive you if you mess him up like you did your own kids.'

*

'He blames me for Blanche's death,' he told Ada later that day, 'but she already knew about the affair didn't she? How did she know Ada - did you tell her?'

The baby started crying. Ada picked him up and tried to console him. Harry left the room; whatever he said, he would always be in the wrong.

His neurosis still undermined everything. It kept him in a state of instability and paranoia. Convinced that Lucky was being mistreated at the stables where he kept her, Harry attacked a stable-hand with a bottle and fractured his skull.

He was fined 40/- and ordered to pay another 40/- in court costs.

WEST PARK

There is a tramp asleep on the grass in Park Crescent. Nobody takes any notice of him. I like coming to the park on sunny days. I can hear the kid's voices and the gulls. Ada does not notice him at first and then says we should buy him some drink. It is the last thing he needs but hey, why not? Ada wants to leave and go back to Chatham again. Brighton does not want me here. It is turning up its nose, each creamy-rich, regency terrace, sneering at me. Harry Cornell, poor sod. I don't give a shit. One day I will be laughing. Ada will learn that I am right and she is leaving me. Can't be doing with her leaving me.

My chest is hurting and I feel dog-tired. I'm struggling up the chipped and checkered steps to my front door. The handrail is rusted underneath my clammy hand. The woman next door says she's calling the doctor. Ada is supposed to be here looking after me. She's selfish to go like that. How the hell can I marry her if my Evie might still be alive?

That poor old bugger I left lying on the grass, is that me? It is me! The grass is all wet and I am now soaked through. Can somebody help me up please?

Harry shouted out and Nurse McCarthy glanced over from the nurse's station. Harry was gripping the bed rails.

'Help me up, I'm all wet. Please get Ada; she's left me here'

Harry gradually became aware that his bed was wet and that he had been dreaming.

'Calm down Harry; I'm here.' Nurse McCarthy was pulling the curtain around his bed and holding some fresh towels.

'I'm really sorry, nurse, really I am.

19. Art Therapy

Ada finally dragged Harry back to Chatham with Lily and ten-month-old Michael. Jim wanted to come too. Lily was growing up fast and had started courting. Living with Harry and Ada was troublesome and she was relieved when her young man proposed to her. Marriage should have made a respite for young Lily who never knew, from one moment to the next, what mood she would find Harry in. He would fall into deep bouts of depression, leading to terrible uproar and Ada would run off and not be seen for a couple of days at a time. But that meant that Michael, now a toddler, was left with Lily and her new husband, Mr. Lovell.

Jim also realised he had made a big mistake leaving Brighton to be with his father and Ada. He wrote to Bill Perkins in Brighton apologising for his father's behaviour. He wanted to retain some family links and had become good friends with his cousin Sidney, who was the youngest son of Florence and William, a few years younger than Jim. The two boys had spent a lot of time together when Jim managed to get time off from the farm. Jim, aware that those good times were now behind him, boarded a train to Watford where he found work as a salesman. His father was an embarrassment and he needed to put some distance between them. He vowed he would never be known as Johnny again and kept the name his mother had given him - Jim Cornell - and hoped that Harry would not come looking for him.

Work from Alf Goldwater became scarce and there was not enough money. Harry had returned Michael back to his father in Brighton. The boy had not eaten for a few days and was in a very poor state. He died a few days later, aged only four. The family decided not to call the police, but they blamed Harry all the same. They told him to leave Brighton and never come back. Brighton, the Arches, his childhood and Evelyn Anne – they were all about to be lost to him.

WEST PARK

There's a fire burning in the field and music playing. We're all there with the gypsies. The fire glows, warming our cheeks.

Ada's crying over a baby.

'Stop crying, woman,' I'm shouting. 'Johnny! You're alive! I thought for a moment you were the baby, just as you were in Jubilee Street but I see you standing behind the fire and you're handing me a sixpence.'

'Take the money, Dad,' you're saying. 'It's for the baby.'

'Why's Ada crying? Tell her to stop.'

There's a gypsy man. He's riding my Lucky. He's riding towards me.

'The baby's dead, Harry,' he's saying but, as he gets closer, I see he's a small boy.

'He needs a drink,' I'm saying. He takes the sixpence Johnny has given me.

'He's dead, Harry. There's no more I can do.'

When I look at the child, it's my sister Blanche's little boy, Michael.

'He needs a drink; that's all he needs. Somebody give him a drink,' I'm shouting.

'Harry love, let me wash your face; you're sweating.' Nurse McCarthy picked up a towel.

'I took the boy back to his father. I told him we've no money and he must take him back. We were so cold and hungry. We'd eaten nothing for two days. He died and I'm sorry, but Ada left me. She'd taken all our food; I didn't know what else to do.'

'Harry, stop fretting,' said Nurse McCarthy. Tears were streaming down his cheeks.

'I was sorry, nurse. They told me, "get out of Brighton!" or they would kill me. My own family said that. We had to run and I was told not to come back. I couldn't go back to Brighton so I'd never get to see my Evie again.'

'You've had a bad dream again.' Nurse McCarthy sat on the end of the bed. His time was near; she hoped his suffering would soon be over.

Following Michael's death, Harry and Ada did not return to Brighton; they settled in Old Brompton near Chatham. On 24th February 1932 a letter came from the Ministry Of Pensions saying that Harry's pension was to be stopped entirely due to his mode of life. He discovered that they had received information that he was unable to work because he was a drunk and a drug addict. Distraught, he started to write a string of letters to the Pensions Office, pleading his case. He had no idea who sent the anonymous tip-off.

Ada, at the end of her tether, marched him down to the nearest doctor's surgery in Old Brompton near Chatham. Dr. Myles Tonks listened carefully to how Harry described his condition and encouraged him to talk about what had happened to him during the war. It was difficult but Harry managed to talk about his fits, mood swings and, above all, his paranoia. Dr. Tonks needed evidence of trauma. Harry believed he was going mad and did not really understand the link.

'*War neurosis*, Harry,' Dr. Tonks explained. 'I believe your symptoms are brought on by what we call 'shell shock'. I think you've been badly treated because of it.'

Dr. Tonks agreed to write on Harry's behalf to the Ministry of Pensions. He was the first doctor Harry had seen who had offered him any understanding. Harry and Ada sat together in his consultation room and Harry put his head in his hands.

'Thank you doctor,' he said with tears in his eyes.

'I'll try and help, but you must be honest with me - and try your best to stay sober.'

Harry stood up and stared at a painting on the wall. It was a watercolour of a coastline. It was signed with the name 'Tonks'.

'Did you do this, sir?'

'It was painted by my uncle, *Henry Tonks*. He was an artist during the war. He was also a surgeon.'

'It's very good. I like the pastel colours.'

'Thank you. I also paint - my uncle inspired me. Are you fond of art Harry?'

'He loves it,' said Ada. She explained how Harry was always scribbling little pictures.

'I only have pencils,' said Harry.

Dr. Tonks had witnessed the effects of *shell shock* during the war and was interested in Harry's case. It was evident that this condition had produced a crisis in masculinity. Men like Harry who had grown up in tough environments amongst fisherman and railway men, were not allowed to cry and their only release was in violence and other self-destructive behaviour.

He wondered how many other lost men were hiding away within their families, struggling against shame. In April 1932 he wrote a letter to the Ministry of Pensions:

> *The Manor House,*
> *Old Brompton, Chatham.*
>
> *H. Cornell.*
> *This case appears to me to be an example of a gross attempt at evasion of responsibilities.*
> *This man was in the line (Driver RFA) for nearly two years. He got shell shock badly and is now a hopeless invalid. I regard his condition as being entirely due to his war service.*
> *Myles Tonks. MRCS, etc.*

In Harry's case, there was something else - a suppressed creativity. Dr. Tonks had a theory that this creativity could be the key to helping him deal with his trauma. Harry was on a merry-go-round. His only escape was alcohol and it was alcohol selling the tickets. As a doctor, Myles Tonks had been blessed with the ability to use his academic training but possessed a clear understanding that there was more to healing than what he had learned at medical school. As an artist he was able to develop different cognitive and emotional skills. His medical training led him to believe that Harry's condition needed insensitivity treatment: a short stay in an asylum to calm him and keep him safe, detox from alcohol and perhaps electric-shock treatment for his fits. Might this be the right action for a middle aged man?

'I'm a bad man,' Harry confessed. 'There's no good in me. I have no faith, sir'

'It will be the treatment that helps you, Harry, not your prayers.'

Dr. Tonks thought he would try something else.

'Here take this.' He pushed a large brown notebook across his desk. 'You may not think this will help but, as an artist myself, I can assure you it will. I want you to sketch whatever comes into your mind. When you've done that, come back and I'll prescribe the medicine that you need.'

Harry returned a week later and Dr. Tonks was amazed at the tranquility of the scene Harry had drawn.

'The South Downs, near where I grew up,' Harry explained. 'The horse in the lane is my Lucky, I've had her with me a few years now.'

Dr. Tonks sensed that he was onto something.

'Harry would you paint this sketch? Come to my studio and do it. You have talent.'

The studio was situated in an attic room above the Manor House Surgery in Old Brompton. Harry loved it. He had never experienced the smell of oil paints before. The mixture of light and smell awakened sleeping senses.

The light in here is fighting with my darkness; I could be in a small part of heaven, where even a man such as me is allowed some kindness.

I'm like a child who for the first time delights in the taste of treacle pie swallowing slowly.

Not a moment is lost as I linger in this room. I am given this brush to hold, it's a gift not from god, but from my own creative spirit.

The canvas is blank and this is my day, my moment. All belongs to me now as my mind recalls 'The Downs,' distanced, from the sea to the sky, where I can control the shadows, eliminate dark corners and bring life. Who would have thought it, me, Harry Cornell - bringing life.

When he returned to the surgery the following day, Tonks had received a reply back from the Pensions Office rejecting Harry's claim.

'I'm sorry,' he said. 'They say it's your mode of life that's the cause and not war neurosis. They're wrong, Harry; you must fight this.'

'I can't pay you; it's all pointless.'

Harry never returned to his studio and Dr. Tonks banged his fist down on the table when he heard the front door slam. But he kept the sketch Harry had drawn and put it in his file. Two days later Ada burst in.

'He needs to be in hospital, sir. He's sick and I can't look after him anymore.'

Dr. Tonks followed Ada to her lodgings and found Harry crouched drunk on the floor in a pool of vomit.

'Please clean him up, Mrs. Cornell, I'll go and phone for an ambulance.'

They took Harry to Stone House, a mental hospital and it was there that Harry first received electric-shock therapy.

Two weeks later he was allowed home. Ada had gone off again, leaving him with no food and no money. He went to the Globe pub in Chatham to see if anyone had seen her and was told she had been with a fellow who had a camera.

'She's gone back on the 'bong' Harry. Taking stuff again. You're well rid if you ask me,' said the landlord.

Harry searched for three days and slept rough on the common not wanting to go back to his empty room. Bedraggled and tired, he eventually made his way home. He was determined that she was not going to treat him like this anymore but he started to pine for her. When she turned up at their rooms a few days later, he opened his arms and hugged her.

'There are not many men would take me back after this, Harry - only you,' she cried as they sat with their arms around each other.

'I love you, Ada, and I can't live without you.'

She laid her head against his chest.

*

Electric-shock therapy was commonly practised in mental hospitals. The patients were taken to a darkened room where medical staff held them down in case they injured themselves during their convulsions. Harry was no exception, it scared him but he lived with fear every day anyway. The therapy left the intensity of his memory misted and confused. It memories were still there but his anxiety was muted.

Following the death of little Michael, Ada had hardened. The two of them terrorized the people they came into contact with. It did not take much to provoke them with a wrong look or an offending word. Ada was compiling her own list of convictions, mostly for being drunk or having arguments and violent fights with their neighbours. They struggled to keep up with their rent and there were days when they just lived on whiskey or cheap beer. Ada started to go back on the game although she hated it more than ever.

*

The trains rumbled over the tracks above the arches, making the walls vibrate. Ada had ventured up to Victoria and stood sheltering from the rain. *She would be able to pick up a customer here,* she thought, *maybe even a toff.*

'Bloody Cornell,' she mumbled to herself, 'he's brought me to this.'

She pulled up her collar and walked towards the station.

'Ada Quinn!' said a voice.

Ada stopped and turned to look behind her.

'They chucked you out of the dockyards, you old witch?'

'What you doing up here, Dennis?'

Dennis Jnr. loosened his collar and tilted his hat back to reveal his smoothed down hair. 'I thought we'd seen the last of you. Still knocking about with old Harry Killbuck are you?'

'Don't call him that.' She hated the nickname. 'What of it?'

'Alf often talks about you, Ada. It was you that showed guts Ada, not Harry.'

'So what? I could always hold my own.'

'We could use you, Ada.'

Ada laughed. 'And you Dennis, you making the decisions now? What about your Dad? I bet he's still keeping you in short pants.'

Dennis Jnr. grabbed her arm. 'So this is what you want - hanging around under these arches? And Harry doesn't care about you being up here - picking up punters?'

'I was just sheltering out of the rain.'

'You need some proper work, Ada. Come on I'll treat you to a cuppa.'

'What type of work Dennis? - we can't come back to Brighton, so there's no point in asking.'

*

'They're hungry enough to do most things we ask.' Dennis Jnr. told Alf Goldwater back in Middle Street, Brighton, later that evening. 'They can start taking deliveries to Chadwick and Lillington Street.'

'Can you trust them?'

'I trust Ada. She controls Cornell. She says he's lost it - he's been in the loony bin.'

*

Dennis Jnr. handed Ada a small parcel when he met her on Brighton Station.

'Alf needs this back to London - the address is on it.'

'Tell me what it says.' (Ada couldn't read.)

'It needs to go to a Mr. and Mrs. Kelly in Lillington Street. SW1.'

Kelly was an Irish name. 'They relatives of yours?' she asked.

'Yeh – they'll give you something to bring back here tomorrow. Here's money for your train fair.'

*

'I've no idea what's in it,' she said later to Harry, 'but it feels like papers. I don't know what they're up to but he said he would pay us well if we deliver it quickly.'

Harry was feeling really low and was suffering with anxiety. He was receiving treatment from the Medway hospital and had been staying for short stays. All they could offer him were sedatives and more electric-shock treatment leaving him confused and drowsy. He sat slumped in a chair, clutching a bottle of ale. He did not want to be back in the clutches of Alf Goldwater and Dennis Scully. He had been assigned a probation officer in Chatham and this man, James Bray, had tried to get him to look for honest work, but it was hard in his present condition.

'Be careful. Ada. They'll suck you in. I don't care what they're up to - I want nothing to do with it.'

But Ada liked the excitement and the money was good. She was fed up with looking like a tramp and had bought herself a new hat and coat. She enjoyed her brief meetings with Dennis Jnr. when he had come up to Victoria Station. She saw her chance.

'Let's leave Chatham and go to London. There's a better chance of you getting work there and Goldwater says he can get us some digs through some friends of his. That old horse of yours is on its last legs, Harry; it's ready for the knackers yard.'

Bill Redman opened the black gate to the courtyard in Chadwick Street.

'No. 39 is yours; you can pay your rent weekly.'

He was an overweight man, balding but clean-shaven, his trilby hat cocked to one side. A contact of Alf Goldwater's, he lived in Chadwick Street with his wife and son Joe.

Harry and Ada moved in. Unknown to Harry, Ada kept making deliveries for Alf Goldwater. Harry did not like her being away for long periods which caused more rows and eventually Ada had had enough.

'He's driving me up the wall,' she told Dennis Jnr. when they met on Victoria station. 'But I deserve my own piece of happiness. I want out.'

'Always said he was a liability.'

'It was different then. I thought he would get over his problems. But it's hard; I don't know how I'm going to leave him, Dennis. He won't survive without me.'

Ada had money in her pocket and she wanted to spend it

on nice clothes. They made her feel special. She wasn't going to let Harry drink away her earnings.

'What's in the parcels, Dennis?' she plucked up the courage to ask.

'A mixture of stuff - most of it's coming over from France.' Dennis Jnr. was not going to give much away.

Back in Chadwick Street Ada decided to steam one of the packets open.

'I wouldn't do that,' said Harry.

'I can seal it up again, love. I just want to see what they're up to.'

She help the package to the steaming kettle and gently unglued it. There was a bundle of files inside.

'It's just a load of old documents!'

Harry took one of the files and undid the string.

'They're property deeds and death certificates. Wrap them back up, Ada; it's not good to poke your nose in.'

'I've got to take them to some bloke in Vincent Square.'

'You're playing with fire, Ada.'

20. The Pavement Artist

The day that Dr. Tonks opened Harry's eyes in his small studio and showed him how to embrace and be at ease with the creativity, that Harry had always believed was something to be ashamed of, was a day of enlightenment. Someone was on the side of the light that was fighting his darkness.

Dr. Tonks would never know what doors he had opened that day because all he foresaw was that the fight would get harder for Harry. Perhaps, he thought, if the Ministry of Pensions was aware of the damage they caused this man when they rejected him, perhaps they would not be so judgemental.

Harry wanted a chance to get off this treadmill, which kept him living on the rough edge. When he slammed the door on the surgery in Old Brompton, that day when he discovered that the Ministry of Pensions had turned him down yet again, he actually chuckled to himself. He decided to find the nearest pub and toast the Ministry of Pensions; he wished he could tell them to *stick their money*. The sight and smell of Dr. Tonks's studio had showed him that he was missing out on something that had been calling him his entire life - something that might help him to survive.

WEST PARK

I left her back in Chadwick Street.
And I walked to Piccadilly.
It's so cold and I think I've been here all night.
There's a man standing, he's wearing a khaki coat.

He must be some old soldier.

Our eyes have met. He has chalk in his hand and he's drawing on the pavement.

He's creating a picture of Eve in the Garden of Eden.

It's not very good and I feel annoyed.

Her face ain't right; the features are all wrong.

I think of Evie. I think of her face.

There's tuppence in my pocket and I need a drink.

I'm walking towards the newspaper kiosk,

Through the London smog and greyness.

The man in the kiosk smiles at me; he knows my name.

He hands me a small box of chalks and charges me tuppence.

I don't feel cold now or see the smog.

I look again at the picture of Eve and see the man has now drawn the serpent.

People are throwing him money.

I say to myself, 'you can do better Harry.'

And I do.

There in the grey mist of Piccadilly, there in the darkness, I am in mountains and trees.

'What have you done to my wall, Harry?' I hear mum shouting.

'It's just a picture mum. I've painted it for you.'

Nurse McCarthy started her shift in the dark. She went through her notes, illuminated only by her night-light and caught a glimpse of Harry. His eyes were wide open and he looked content. His time was near and she wondered how long. She walked over and sat on the end of his bed.

'Want anything, Harry?' She had ten minutes before she started with bedpans and ward rounds.

'Did I tell you about the Duke of York? He liked my paintings you know.'

'You've told me many times.'

'Me, Harry Cornell, who would have thought it? I had an exhibition; my paintings sold for fifteen quid. Who would have thought it, eh?' He glanced towards the window. 'Then they brought me here - because they wanted me to stop saying things. They knew I wouldn't shut up. Patrick - my son - he came back for a while and then I didn't see him again. There were people who said bad things about me, but it was them - they were the bad ones.'

'Did you have a big family, Harry?'

'Not one I was part of. None of them wanted me around, not even Ada. I'd tried to be good to her, she betrayed me after I left. All Ada ever wanted was money - it found her and changed her.'

Harry stopped speaking and looked at the door. Tommy Carter was grinning at him through the window.

'Tell that boy to clear off. I don't like him staring at me like that.'

Nurse McCarthy glanced up but Tommy Carter had disappeared.

1935

Warwick Square. London SW1
Philip Cavanagh

Dear Cousin Philip,
An artist working under the arches in Piccadilly has come to my notice. This poor man is an old soldier who has been suffering from war neurosis yet I have been most taken by

his talent. It would be a great injustice for this to go un-noticed. His style is simplistic and naïve. His subject is the countryside and country folk. I would be most grateful if you could approach him at your earliest convenience to see if he would benefit from your assistance. His name is Henry Havelock Cornell.

Yours faithfully
Rt. Hon Colonel Collins.

VICTORIA STATION

'Where is he; you got any idea?' Dennis Jnr. Asked Ada outside the main concourse.

'Not a clue, Dennis. He comes and goes. I've not seen him for three days. Sometimes he sleeps at Chadwick Street; sometime he doesn't. I can't spend my time worrying about him; I have enough to do working for Alf Goldwater.'

'Are you and Harry over with?'

'I'm not sure. He says he loves me but then he just clears off again. He's never been right - the war saw to that.'

Dennis Jnr. scraped the bottom of his boots on a metal grate.

'Think you still have a hold over him?' he asked. 'He listens to you.'

'Why?'

'Harry can have his uses, Ada.'

Dennis Jnr. walked into the station towards the turnstiles and Ada's eyes followed him curiously. 'Make sure you find him; Alf wants him,' said Dennis Jnr.

PICCADILLY

It was strange that a gentleman should breeze by and comment kindly on Harry's work. He had been sitting on an old deckchair that he had found and fixed, the perfect solution for his aching limbs when the gentleman approached, and he was still sitting there, chatting with the artist next to him, when the gentleman came back and again viewed Harry's picture, in chalks on the paving stones, of a castle on a hillside.

The gentleman liked the way Harry had made his figures simplistic and out of proportion. They belonged to the picture and were not out of place. The man wore an expensive suit but it was a warm day and he had neatly draped his jacket over his arm. His cravat, a little bohemian for a normal city gent, led Harry to think he was an artist – but you never saw many dealers, or 'toffs' as Harry called them, not around the street artists or the *screevers* as they were known, not down here in Piccadilly. Apart from the general public and the other pavement artists, you only saw the racketeers asking for protection money. They were a real problem. They started by knocking over your oils and causing damage to your pictures but it could get worse. Some even had the monopoly over selling chalk. Generally they left Harry alone, but it didn't stop him feeling annoyed at the injustice towards his pals working their art on the pavement.

'Do you paint on canvas?' the gentleman asked.

'No sir, just chalks.' Harry opened his hands to revealing his white chalk sticks and jumped up out of his deckchair to stand politely.

'You should - you obviously have some talent.'

It was the first of many such conversations. Mr Philip Cavanagh returned to Harry's pitch in Piccadilly and sometimes he caught sight of him outside the National Gallery. Cavanagh came from a completely different world but Harry sensed his compassion and interest. Cavanagh understood the creative mind and Harry, sensing this, was undaunted in his presence and never intimidated by the conversations they shared. Poor Harry was so damaged that it was only creativity that gave any light into his dark world and their conversations marked the beginning of a period when Harry gained insight into his own developing creativity and, together with the insight, some confidence in himself. Cavanagh, for his part, was consumed by the intrigue of stepping into Harry's dark underworld. He wanted to taste it; his curiosity wanted a peek into a lifestyle reminiscent of a Dickens novel and very different from anything he had encountered before. Cavanagh was fascinated by Harry whom he described as: a person locked in a vault, his artistic creativity hanging just out of reach above his head. Cavanagh wanted to be the person who finally brought that creativity within Harry's grasp.

In time, Harry felt confident enough to tell Cavanagh of his troubles. Cavanagh learned that Harry had been moved on from a place outside the Duke of York's residence.

'I'm sorry they stopped your pension.' Cavanagh leaned back on the park bench and handed Harry a cup of tea he had bought from the café in the park.

'So am I.'

'I have a friend who lives close to me in Warwick Square. She could possibly help you. She's the daughter of Lady Margaret Littington. Her name's Miss Eleanor Littington and she works on the local War Pensions Committee.'

This subject was still raw. Throwing restraint to the winds, Harry explained about the injustice he had received regarding the wicked anonymous letters sent to the Ministry of Pensions. But why was this man, a well-respected gent in his field, taking time to help him? Cavanagh explained how he had studied at the Grosvenor School of Modern Art and was taking an interest due to Harry's talent.

'You have great natural talent, Harry; you paint from your soul. I'm going to give you some paints and canvasses. They're a gift; no need for any money.'

Was Cavanagh playing a game? It was a slow process gaining Harry's trust. His usual paranoia and caginess would return frequently and then he would think about HRH the Duke of York and how he looked through his binoculars from a window high up in his house in Piccadilly, down on to the pavement artist, working humbly below. But then he would think how HRH the Duke of York was admiring his work, created on a paving slab. And then there was someone else apart from the Duke of York, looking down on him from high - an angel, and the angel began to assure him that maybe, indeed, he had something special, a gift.

Harry accepted the gift of the paints. The different medium was going to be daunting but this did not deter him from experimenting on a cheap board on his pitch on the pavement. He was used to people watching him work; in fact he quite liked an audience. The box of metal tubes of oil paints looked up to him, waiting, when he opened it. The creamy colours looked flat on his palette. But there was a picture in his head that needed to be placed. He thought of Eve and the Garden of Eden. If Eve could break the rules then so could he. His chewed the cigarette butt balanced carefully between his lips and lost himself in concentration.

He looked at the greens, the yellows and the browns and started to play with them. Captured by his own creativity, a new world opened up for him and a picture started to take shape. In flowed the calm and tranquility of a sort of paradise: the power of shadows and light, the mystery of what existed behind a tree or a bush of flowers. His animals and people he placed in the air with no sense of exact proportion but, for once, the things he had always been told had mattered, he now had the power to change. He felt himself free to paint a picture that came from the most precious part of his mind. Eve knelt on the ground and the serpent coiled around a branch over her head. She was not beautiful but she was free to smell the flowers.

*

'I have a buyer for some of your work, Harry. A gallery have shown some interest and I want to take some of your paintings over to them.' Cavanagh was excited to give Harry this news.

The £12 the gallery paid for two of his paintings, gave Harry a boost. He arrived back at Chadwick Street and Ada found him asleep on a chair with a bottle resting on his lap in his hand.

'Gawd, look what the wind has blown in! What you doing here?'

Harry woke.

'Come here and let me kiss you, Ada.'

Ada shoved him away from her.

'I've sold two paintings - for 12 quid!' He grinned. 'A gallery up West, real posh place - and they want more.'

But Ada was not impressed. She had bigger plans nowadays than what a few pictures might bring in.

'Where've you been, Harry?' she asked. 'Goldwater has work for us.'

'I'm finished with him.'

'No you're not. He's been looking for you.'

'Yes I am. This is the work I want to do. It's honest work - and I'm good at it.'

'You're some *smart arse*, painting pictures on pavements. Yeh, I saw you with all the other down-and-outs. You're a worthless piece of shit - and you still stink.'

He pushed her against the door and she slapped him across his cheeks. Composing himself, he searched for the right words.

'Do what you like, Ada, but I've met someone who's going to help me.'

'Who's going to help you ?' She moved away from the door. 'One of your screever friends, eh? Will they keep you in booze and players like I do?'

'I've the chance for honest money, something you wouldn't understand, a tart like you who's had most of Chatham Dockyard.'

Bill Redman appeared in the doorway holding a large, brown packet.

'It's quite heavy,' he said, interrupting. 'Alf Goldwater wants it in Brighton by tonight. He wants you to take it up to Victoria, Harry.'

'Why me?'

Bill handed Harry the heavy parcel, which he had placed in a potato sack.

'Dennis Jnr. will meet you in the usual place about six. Good job you showed up, Harry.'

'Hey wait a minute,' Ada said after Bill had gone back to his own apartment, 'I want to take a gander in that parcel.'

*

The house in Warwick Square had a black-painted front door with a brass lion's head knocker. Harry felt nervous standing on the front step and as he knocked lightly on the door he expected a butler or a maid to answer. Eleanor Littleton who eventually answered the door was slightly abrupt in her manner.

Harry handed her the note he had folded neatly in the palm of his hand. She saw the signature of her neighbor, Philip Cavanagh, and gave Harry a friendly smile. They walked into a wide hallway and she showed Harry into a room on the side.

'Can I offer you some tea, Mr. Cornell?'

'No thanks, miss.' Harry glanced over the painting above the fireplace.

For over an hour, Harry explained about his war pension and why it had been stopped, that he had suffered an injustice because an unknown person had sent unkind letters to the Ministry of Pensions telling lies about him. Miss Littleton said she couldn't promise any results but she would certainly write to them to find out more information. This was a result for Harry; he had written so many letters and was just not being listened too.

'Harry what was on those documents?' Ada asked when he got home. She had not given up.

'Death certificates.'

'Whose?'

'I've no idea, Ada. I didn't read them but it's what they looked like.'

Ada poured some tea and sat down on the bed next to him, using her finger to wipe away the lipstick stain from the cup

'That old Jew is forging ain't he?' she sighed, 'and we are getting a pittance for the risks we're taking.' She stood up and walked towards the window. 'They must have a printing machine or something - here in Chadwick. Street.'

*

Alf Goldwater raised his eyebrows and wiped his brow with his hanky.

'Ada knows about the certificates,' Dennis Scully reported, 'but I think we can trust her.'

'You can't trust anyone, Dennis. Harry must have looked at them. Are they asking questions?'

'Not yet, but it won't be long before they work out the amounts involved. Redman, Fred Allen and Ted Ming are all working out of Chadwick Street now.'

'Find out what Harry's up to,' Alf Goldwater frowned, 'and get your Dennis to keep an eye on him. In fact, you ought to go and see him yourself, see where we stand with him. If he should go spouting his mouth off on one of his benders we'll all be in trouble.'

*

Ada stood on the concourse at Victoria Station, her arms folded across her chest.

'We want more money, Dennis. You owe us. We know what you're all up to - and I've seen the printing machine in Chadwick Street.' She held her chin up; she knew it was dangerous to push Dennis Jnr. but it sent an adrenalin rush through her veins. Dennis admired her guts but Harry, as always, was an irritant. Dennis Jnr. was miffed about his Dads brief visit to Piccadilly which was an insult, he thought. Why did Alf Goldwater not trust him to sort Cornell? This had caused arguments between him and his father. Dennis Jnr. could never accept his father's lack of trust in his ability. He pushed and pushed for recognition and rows inevitably lead back to the subject of Harry Cornell and the way his father would always cover for him.

*

'It's been a long time, Harry,' said Dennis Scully. He squinted in the bright sunlight, his face bleached out by the strong morning light.

'Day trip to London is it, Dennis?'

'You could say that, Harry. Good to get out of Brighton sometimes.' Dennis Scully's voice was cold despite the soft Irish accent.

'I wouldn't know, Dennis. Haven't been back in a long time. What are you doing here?'

The ageing Dennis Scully, crouched down to get a closer look at the picture Harry had drawn on the pavement. Small canvasses were attached to the metal railings and Harry stood in front of them as if to shield them from his view.

'You're not here to look at my work,' he said.

'Well that's where you're wrong. We never realised how talented you were Harry. Matter of fact - we need your help.'

'Not interested. I'm doing all right.'

'And how long will you survive painting pavements Harry, what about the winter months when you will be frozen to the bone, so you will? Alf needs someone with an eye for detail. You're just the man; look at it as promotion.'

Dennis Scully stood up and Harry moved in close to him, close enough for Dennis Scully to smell the whiskey on his morning breath.

'I've seen what you're up to, Dennis,' he said. 'I've seen those forged documents. If you're not careful, you'll be inside for a very long time.'

'That may be,' Dennis Scully held his gloved hand up to his mouth, 'but if I told you about the money involved, I think you'd take the risk.'

A woman walked passed and threw a penny into Harry's cap on the ground. Dennis Scully smiled smugly and his eyes followed the woman as she walked away.

'Out of your league, Dennis,' said Harry. 'We get more skirt up in London.'

Dennis Scully ignored him.

'You have a friend, Harry, a Mr. Philip Cavanagh. He's a wealthy man; you know that don't you, Harry?'

'So?'

'He's also an engraver.'

'I don't know anything about engraving.'

'But you'll learn, Harry - and learn quickly. You have the perfect opportunity.'

'I'm getting help with my pension and then I'll have enough money to live on. I'm not interested in getting involved, Dennis.'

'Well, that's a great shame my friend. Only - I have to tell you – you're already involved; you're up to your neck in it. You're a dead man, Harry, it's just you don't know it.' Dennis looked round to make sure nobody was in earshot. 'Your death was registered in 1916 - yeh, you never came back from the war.'

'What you on about?'

'And guess who claimed the six hundred quid insurance money?' Dennis Scully asked triumphantly.

'Who?'

Dennis Scully kept his head down. Harry would either blow or cave in with what he was about to find out.

'Mrs. Evelyn Anne Cornell of course - widow she is now.'

Harry sat down onto the kerb, the colour draining from his cheeks.

'She's alive?'

'What's it matter, Harry? What's more important is that you're alive. And if anyone should tell the Prudential Assurance Company that you're alive – well, let's just say you could be in a sticky situation, so you could. Have a think about it - it really would be in your interest to do what Alf asks. I would stop pushing for that pension too.'

'My Evie,' Harry whispered. He wanted it to be true. 'I must find her, Dennis. Tell me where she is.'

'Look, my friend, you must never return to Brighton. You'll be arrested and so would Evie. Do what we ask for everybody's sake and I'll see you get protection. I've already set you up with a new address, at 118 Lillington Street in Pimlico. You can use it as a studio if you want. Stay in Chadwick Street for the present but use the new address to store your paintings.'

Dennis Scully handed him the key.

'I have some friends already living at 111,' he continued. 'Mr. and Mrs. Kelly will make contact in a few days. In the meantime, speak with your friend Cavanagh, tell him you want to become an engraver.'

'You blackmailing me?'

All the Irishman could do was smile - *poor old Harry,* he thought, *if only he knew.*

Dennis Scully left Harry on the side of the pavement. His world was raining uncertainty. Evelyn Anne's face was back in his mind and his heart thumped. All he could think about was her and that she was still alive. He looked at the key in his hand. He had no choice but to do as those bastards wanted.

*

In a small pub, off Vauxhall Bridge Road, Dennis Jnr. sat with a beer and Ada sipped on a sherry.

'Alf says he'll cut you in but he needs assurance. Tell Harry to stay off the booze – and you too, Ada. We're not willing to take any chances.'

'Did he believe your dad about Evelyn Anne?' Ada smirked.

'Does it matter? You'll get some of the six hundred quid. Get yourself some new clothes and tart yourself up eh?'

'Hope I can do a bit more than that Dennis.'

21. Lillington Street SW1

I'm not dead; I'm alive and well – and they said I died in 1916.'

'No you're not dead, Harry.' Nurse McCarthy tucked and smoothed his bedclothes.

Harry coughed into a cotton hanky.

'I had no choice did I,' he said, 'but to do what they wanted?' Tears formed in his red eyes.

'Don't get distressed. It's not good for you.'

'But you need to understand, nurse. It's very important.'

She wanted to sit on the bed but there would not be time this morning.

'He came back to my room,' said Harry, '- the aristocrat. You know him, nurse; he was here in the hospital; he took my pictures; I trusted him; I thought he was my friend. He said he liked my work and he was going to show it to people who knew about paintings and how to sell them.'

'Nobody's been here to steal your paintings, Harry.'

'Not here, not here.'

'Harry, please calm down. Dr. Howard will be here soon and he'll give you another sedative.'

'I want you to know,' he looked at her intently, his head slightly raised from his pillow: 'the aristocrat stole them from my studio in Lillington Street - and he was here in the hospital. I'm not mad; I saw him.'

'Harry, I've a lot of work to do this morning.'

Dr. Howard had appeared outside the ward. He was about to start his ward round and spotted Harry through the window. Matron walked up behind him.

'How's he doing, Dr?' she asked.

'He's not giving us any trouble, Matron. Well, none that I'm aware of.'

Dr. Howard entered the ward and Harry watched guardedly as he and matron walked towards him. Harry's hands began to flap against the sheets.

'I am sorry doctor, he's been like this all morning; I'm trying to calm him.' Nurse McCarthy grabbed Harry's hand and tucked it underneath his blanket.

'Don't let them get me!' Harry gasped. 'They've come to kill me.'

'Harry, it's just Dr. Howard with Matron.'

Nurse McCarthy needed both her hands to restrain him.

'You cannot silence me! I've told the police, and they're coming to arrest them - all of them! And you, Ada,' Harry looked at Matron, 'I knew it was you who killed my Evie; Scully told me. He told me he murdered those other women, those poor four women; he told me where he'd put them and you can't shut me up any more. No more electric shocks, no more pokers in my brain. You're all fucking liars, blackmailers, murderers!'

Matron was quick to administer a sedative and as Harry fell asleep, Nurse McCarthy looked at Dr. Howard's face, which looked pale and fraught.

'I'm sorry, Dr. he really does get confused.'

'He needs to be kept calm. For god's sake, he's on his last legs. Keep him sedated from now on.' Dr. Howard walked away unsteadily.

Once they'd left, Nurse McCarthy could not stop thinking about Harry's outburst. In his moment of clarity, he had made some outrageous accusations and they troubled her. That evening when her shift ended she gained access to Dr. Howard's office. She knew where the patients' files were kept; it was not unusual for a nurse to refer to a patients notes. She sifted through them and found Harry's file. To her surprise, she saw that it only contained notes from the past year. *That's strange,* she thought, *where are his admission notes.* She wandered back to the ward where the night staff sister quizzed her.

'You still here?'

'Missed my bus. The next isn't for another hour. I thought I might sit with Harry; he hasn't got much time'

'He'll be lucky if he makes it to the end of the week,' said the night sister.

For a moment I thought you were still living.
Walking the South Downs with the kids and me.
Hang on to your hat, Evie.
Do you remember the lights on the Palace Pier, my darling,
and the pebbles under our feet?
They said they had killed you in Brighton and I couldn't
come and find you or know where your body lay.
Then for a sweet moment you were alive again, a brief and
happy moment. I wanted to come and find you, to tell you, Evie.
I never gave up on you.

LILLINGTON STREET 1938

Lillington Street curved towards Pimlico. The wide road gave easy access to a flurry of motor vehicles and trundling

carts pulled by horses, mostly for rag and bone. It was a busy
street with four-storey buildings on both sides that housed large
families in cramped conditions. It was a convenient fifteen-
minute' walk from Chadwick Street.

Cavanagh had never been in a building such as 118 Lillington
Street and he felt awfully uncomfortable. The slums in London
held the ghosts from the influx of people past. Since the industrial
revolution they had poured into the city, eager for work, eager
for prosperity. The buildings had wrapped their walls around
the cries of the poor who dealt daily with poverty, and their
rooms offered themselves as breeding rooms for crime wherein
the tenants did what they could to survive in a city which made
unjust demands, where nature had no place nor gave structure.
Each floorboard creaked in the same way as it had done for
a hundred years and the comings and goings of people were
dark in thoughts, dark in mystery. No music flowed down the
shabby halls, only the sound of doors slamming and raised voices
followed by whispers and silent sobbing.

But the love of art made sense of this visit. Cavanagh crossed
the threshold, bringing with him some of his engravings. He
wanted to advise and show Harry how to set up his studio. Ted
Ming, a stocky man with dark and oiled wavy hair and eastern
eyes inherited from his Asian grandfather, stood with his arms
folded in the hallway leading to the studio. He clocked every
visitor, making a mental note of how long they stayed.

'Who's the man in the hallway?' Cavanagh enquired
nervously once he was in.

'Nobody,' Harry replied, but he knew Ted Ming was
watching them. Dennis Jnr. had put him there.

'I've bought you this, I thought it might cheer you up.'
Cavanagh handed Harry a newspaper.

'What is it?'

'Read it .'

NEW LIFE AT FIFTY

Artist Who Believes In Miracles

Artist Henry Havelock Cornell believes in miracles. Five years ago he shuffled along The Embankment, in London, a middle-aged man, down and out and finished. Now he is holding his first one-man show at the Leicester Galleries and selling, his paintings at £15 a time. That is Cornell's idea of a miracle, states the 'People.'

It was the King who helped him and inspired him. Had Abraham Lincoln died at 50 he would have died unknown and, at that age, Cornell was spending his nights among the homeless in St. Martin's Crypt, thin, dour-faced, wearing a cap and muffler.

Cornell described to a London reporter, the lucky chance that brought him fame.

'I stood In Piccadilly,' Cornell said, 'gazing at the pictures. If a pavement artist can do that, I thought to myself, I can do better than that. I had 2d in my pocket, 2d to satisfy hunger or ambition. Ambition won. I bought chalks and started to draw on the pavement opposite the King's house - he was then Duke of York - at 145 Piccadilly.

'I did well until a burly sergeant moved me on, so it was back to shivering on the Embankment again. I wrote to the Duke and he sent his equerry to see that I got my old place back. Often, after that, I saw him at his balcony window, looking at my work through binoculars. "Royal patronage," I thought to myself. "Fancy poor old Cornell getting royal patronage!"

That was enough to work the change in Cornell's character. Back In his room he found inspiration. Scenes from his wandering career as riveter, newsboy, soldier, hawker and boot-repairer came back to him. He remembered the gipsies he had camped with, the down-and-outs he had met. And he started to paint these memories, to paint and paint till his dreams came true.

At 50 finished; at 55 a success.

There's a moral in that for all of us.

Harry had never seen his name in a newspaper other than in a police report. A warm and proud feeling worked upwards from his stomach. 'Can I keep this?' he asked. 'I'd like to send it to my son.'

Harry made a good student and as the weeks passed Cavanagh watched how he became captivated with the intricate detail he needed to work the fine designs. His large, stubby fingers were not work shy and from the precision of abstract to free-flowing, stylized lines, he could work them together. He embraced the rules where there were no rules. Cavanagh introduced Harry to an unfamiliar range of tools and a new medium. This new skill allowed Harry to focus and work with the part of his brain where he was in charge, where he was the master.

*

Mr. and Mrs. Kelly lived further down Lillington Street. Dennis Scully had introduced them to Harry when he first arrived. Both were in their forties. Mrs. Kelly was bigger than her husband with a rounded face and eye sockets, dark from late nights and probably a diet of gin suppers. One day, after Cavanagh had left, Harry became aware of them talking to Ted Ming in the hallway. Their voices were quick and sharp. Intrigued, he moved softly towards the door to see if he could hear what they were saying but it was difficult to make sense of it.

Later that same evening he watched Mr. & Mrs. Kelly accompany an old lady, across the street towards her doorway opposite. It was dark but he could see in the lamplight that the old woman was wearing a long black coat and a hat and that she walked tensely between them. The Kelly's left moments later and Harry didn't think much of it until he heard screams from a woman's voice in the early hours. Pulling back the curtain, he got up from the floor mattress he was sleeping on. A young woman was screaming outside on the street. Candles flickered in nearby windows and a man run out of the house opposite to grab the woman. He put his hand over her mouth and pulled her back inside.

The next morning a doctor arrived at the house and left shortly afterwards and, about noon, Ted Ming arrived and sauntered into Harry's studio followed by Ada.

'You didn't come home last night, Harry,' Ada said.

'No, I stayed over.'

Her eyes wandered towards the mattress on the floor. Meanwhile Ted Ming picked up a small bottle of oil from Harry's table.

'Don't touch my stuff!' Harry snapped.

Ted put the bottle down.

'Get a good night's sleep, Harry, did you?' he said. 'It can get a bit noisy in Lillington Street.'

'Not much disturbs me,' Harry lied.

'Really, Harry?' said Ada. 'That makes a change; a pin dropping would normally send you jumping out of your skin.'

Ted Ming looked at him suspiciously. The front door creaked open and a woman's voice shouted in the hall.

'Pull her in here and quick!' Ted Ming ordered and Ada went out and shortly after her long arms pushed the woman from the hallway into Harry's studio.

It was the woman who had ran into the street during the night. She stood in the doorway of his studio and her eyes were red from crying. She took a piece of paper from inside her threadbare cardigan, pulled tightly around her shoulders, revealing a hole in her sleeve.

"Here,' she said, 'the doctor signed it.'

Ted Ming took the piece of paper then he put his arm around her. 'Ellie love, go home and grieve, like the dutiful daughter you are. We'll take care of the rest. Would you like Ada to walk you home?'

The woman shook her head and ran back down the hall.

WEST PARK

Nurse McCarthy missed her bus because she nodded off in the chair by Harry's bed. It didn't matter; the night sister wouldn't say anything. Harry stirred as he fought the effects of the sedative and when he opened his eyes he felt comforted to see her there.

'Hello, Harry, how are you feeling?'

'Sad - I was dreaming about Ellie King.

Nurse McCarthy leaned forward, looking puzzled.

'Tell me.'

'Ellie King needed the money. She came up from Chatham with her elderly Mother. Ada found them rooms in Lillington Street. They insured her mother. She was a frail old lady and then the Kelly's killed her. I saw them from my window.'

Nurse McCarthy shivered but did not say anything.

'I wanted to tell the police and I wrote it all down - all that happened. But I couldn't find the guts to tell them. I was no grass and we were all involved.

Poor Ellie, she regretted what she'd done. She must have seen what they did to her mother – and she never got to keep any money. Poor cow lost her nerve - Scully finished her off in Lillington Street, Scully Jnr. He strangled her and hid the body under the floorboards in Stanford Street. I heard them talking about her.'

'Did you tell *anyone*?'

'I tried to tell them I wanted out, but they wouldn't let me and then Patrick turned up out of the blue. That's my son, he was worried about the war starting and I didn't want him to go. It was a shock him turning up then. All I could think about was how I could stop him joining up. I didn't want him to go to war like I did. War is a terrible thing, nurse, you see things you wouldn't want your children to see. Scully said he could help me get Patrick to Northern Ireland; he had contacts in the racecourses there. I couldn't tell anyone about Ellie King because I needed Dennis Scully to help me get Patrick away. It was the one thing I ever did for him.' Harry smiled. 'He was really good with horses, nurse. They turned him into a jockey in Ireland.' His voice quickened. 'Nurse, can you write to him for me? Get him to come here. I want to tell him about Evie, his mum. There are things he needs to know.'

'Of course, Harry.' Nurse McCarthy reached into her small handbag and took out a notepad and pen. 'Do you have an address?'

It dawned on her what she was asking of him. Here was a man who, only a couple of months ago, was admitted to her ward. A man, who shuffled as he walked and flinched when you spoke to him; a man who struggled to know his own name at times and where he was. Now he was about to give her the address of his son whom he had probably not heard from for twelve years. His brain was unraveling, resembling a ball of string and she had found the end of the twine and was pulling out the knots.

Harry gave her his last known address for Patrick and then gave her an address in Watford.

'My son Johnny lives there with his wife. They have children. But don't call him Johnny; he changed his name to Jim.'

Do you want me to call him too?

Harry struggled with his thoughts.

'No - no point. They told me to stay away when I went there. I wanted to tell Johnny about what happened to his mum - that was why I went - but I couldn't do it, I couldn't tell him. I've got a granddaughter though, at least I found that out. I can't remember what they called her but she was feisty like my Evie.

Nurse McCarthy looked at the clock on the wall. The next bus was due in fifteen minutes.

'Let's do this tomorrow, Harry,' she said and put her pen and notebook back in her bag.

Lillington Street

Harry liked his studio. He liked the smell of the room. Alf Goldwater had paid him for the work he had done on the plates, and he had opened a bank account with Barclays in Victoria. It was the first time in his life he had a bank account. They told him not to brag to anyone about the money he was receiving. He was to remain the hard-up artist to the general public.

Ada however was beginning to look more affluent. She appeared one morning in a grey *barathea* suit with a silver fox fur draped around her broad shoulders and Harry thought she looked out of proportion. She had aged in the past months but was quite unaware of the change in her appearance. The glint in her eye said she was enjoying an element of power and it gave her pleasure to cast this power over Harry. She strutted into his studio.

'It's time we had a chat,' she said, sitting down at the table and pouring herself a small glass of cheap sherry.

'Spare your words, Ada. I've seen you. You may think I'm barking mad but it doesn't take a madman to work out what you've been up to.'

She fidgeted on the rickety chair.

'I couldn't wait forever, lovey. God knows I tried. You never come home for days on end; a woman can't live not knowing if her fella loves her or where he's sleeping.'

'At least I cared for you. Not many blokes would put up with what you did, Ada. I left Brighton because of you.'

'No, Harry - you left Brighton because nobody wanted you there, not even your family. And you don't want family, Harry, you've made that clear.'

It started to rain against the window and the light in the room cast darker shadows. Harry picked up a piece of cold toast and shoved it in his mouth. He was hungry. It was nearly lunchtime and the pubs would be open. He shrugged his shoulders in a gesture of indifference that he hoped Ada would notice. He hoped she would think, 'well, enough said' but he was not that lucky.

'And Ted,' she carried on, 'he ain't a bad bloke.'

She was referring to Ted Ming. Harry was angered by the insult she made to his intelligence by even breeching the subject of Ted Ming, but Ada was hoping it would provide an opportunity for her to justify her actions.

Harry's temper could flare unexpectedly, especially when fed by alcohol or by insults directed at him. He took a deep breath because he felt his nerves bubbling to the boil.

'Ted Ming is a con and you know it but, hey, what do I care?' His hands waved dismissively in the air. He had seen them together: the small, knowing looks when Harry was in the room and the flirtatious touching on hands and shoulders; the extra make-up Ada plastered on her face and the perfume to disguise the stale tobacco-smell that lingered on her clothes. *What did he care?* he asked himself. *Was it worth losing his temper over?*

'We're getting married, Harry.'

He laughed.

'And you think that'll make you respectable?'

Ada stood up while she searched in her head for a response. Dressed as she was, she could not indulge in her usual reaction and slog him one. She sat down again.

'Harry, love, you couldn't give me the love I wanted. It was hard for me living like that.'

He suspected the subject of Evelyn Anne would soon come up. It was her last card. It still pained her to talk about his wife. Her jealousy was ingrained.

'So this is nothing to do with the money, Ada?' he said, 'the new clothes and flaunting yourself up and down the street like Lady Muck? Why not? It's better to believe it's all the fault of Evelyn Anne. For Christ sake woman, I lost her years ago.'

Ada saw the tears in his eyes and longed for a knife to stab him with, for her years of uncertainty, anger and sorrow.

'No Harry - but you carried her around with you and you placed her on a pedestal all these years. How was I to feel? And all the time she was up the road in Eastbourne - laughing at you, laughing at the sad, old drunkard that you are. You were quite unaware, but they knew, all your so called friends and family knew, they always knew.'

He put his hands in his pockets and turned his back on her.

'Dennis Scully knew too,' she said. 'It was old man Dennis Scully who sent her away. Thought you could have at least worked that one out. He was probably closer to Evelyn Anne than you ever realized. I could tell - women have the knack of picking up on things; we read it in people's faces.'

'Stop it!' he muttered under his breath.

'Face it, Cornell, you're on your own. She didn't want you back, in fact Scully told me she remarried; she's living on a nice little payment from the Pru following the death of her poor old hubby. It bought a nice little café in Rottingdean. You didn't know that either did you Harry?'

Harry rushed towards her, lifting her from her chair and pushing her towards the door of the studio. Ada lost her footing and her shoe came off and flew across the floor. Holding onto her fox fur which had slipped down her shoulder, she picked herself up from the dusty floorboards and checked quickly that she had not ripped her stockings. She picked up her shoe and squeezed her foot back in.

'If I had it in me to kill you, I would,' he said.

'It was time you knew.'

Ada was not ready to leave. She wanted the last word.

'We have had too many lies, too many secrets,' she said, her voice quivering and tears in her eyes.

'Well, now that I know, I'm going to go back to Brighton - to see my wife. For the sake of my kids, I owe them that.'

Ada took a deep breath.

'There's no point in you doing that.' She coughed a little

uncertainly. 'Dennis and me, Harry - we did it, we killed your precious Evelyn Anne. It was Alf who told us to do it. We did it together. I dressed up as a nurse. It was for the money; she'd become quite a wealthy woman. Scully and me finished her off then we emptied her bank accounts in Brighton. Take it from me, Harry, she ain't there.'

During a moment's stunned silence, Ada finished the sherry. Suddenly, without knowing that he was about to do so, Harry picked up the empty bottle and threw it at her. The bottle smashed against the door and fell on to the floor breaking into half-a-dozen pieces, shards of glass spraying in all directions - but the glass missed Ada as she ran down the hallway. Picking up a piece of cloth Harry wiped his hands and walked over to a canvass he was in the middle of working on. He stared at it. He wanted to throw it out of the window but resisted the urge. He felt oddly sure of himself; this was his future, his hope, his purpose and what he had to live for.

He put thoughts of Evelyn Anne to the back of his mind. Cavanagh was arranging an exhibition for him. There had been no more sleeping under the arches. If he could get his pension back and sell some more of his work he could look forward to better times. He threw on his overcoat, felt some coins in his deep pockets and closed the door behind him. He walked down the long hall and out into Lillington Street. There was a pub on the end of the road and a pie shop.

*

Eleanor Littleton had written to the Pensions Office but she needed information about why Harry's pension had been stopped if she was to take matters further. For Harry to get his war pension re-instated the Pensions Office had to be convinced that he could not be employed due to his war neurosis. The letters she had received from Dr. Tonks made her feel hopeful. She decided that she should find out more about his character. She looked at the pretty, painted tray that sat proudly on her hall table that Harry had sent her as a gift. What a lovely thing. She wanted to do her utmost to help this poor soldier. She decided to go to Chatham to make enquiries. She already had the address of his old doctor, Myles Tonks, in Old Brompton, and Harry gave her the address of Ada's daughter, Lily, now a married woman.

Ada was visiting Lily at her home the day Miss Littleton came to visit.

Miss Littleton asked a lot of questions and Lily began to feel sorry for Harry as her mum described with gusto his problems with the police and with alcohol to the smartly dressed lady from London. Ada described a loser and a drunk. She even told Miss Littleton that they had taken cocaine together,

'War neurosis,' Ada laughed. 'Harry Cornell never did a day's work in his life, the only thing he ever did was lift a bottle or his fist. I'm so glad he finally left me, miss. I don't have the bruises anymore.'

After they had both gone, Lily thought about the conversation and she became so angry with Ada that she decided to write to Harry and tell him what Ada had said to Miss Littleton, and to apologise.

Eleanor Littleton returned to London, furious at how Harry had lied to her. She sent him a note saying she could no longer justify his case to the Pensions Office. In fact, she told him, what she had learned in Chatham would greatly go against him. She wrapped up the painted tray in brown paper, tied it with string and returned it to his studio in Lillington Street along with the note.

Harry was devastated. He sat on his bed and stared at the wall for what seemed like hours. It was unfortunate that later that same day Dennis Scully appeared at the studio in Lillington Street holding a large envelope which he handed to Harry.

'That's for your troubles, Harry.'

Harry opened the envelope; it was stuffed with five-pound notes.

'Don't worry - they're all legal tender,' Dennis Scully added. 'If anyone asks – you've sold a painting.'

'Some of my pictures are missing.'

'They've been sold, Harry. Paintings can be quite valuable when they're in the hands of the right people.'

But Harry could only think about what Ada had told him, about what she and Dennis had done to Evelyn Anne – and yet it wasn't so much the murder, if true, that disturbed him as the fact that they had kept him in ignorance of Evelyn Anne's whereabouts. *All these years,* he thought, *you knew where she was. She was my wife, the mother of my children.* He could hardly open his mouth to speak, which Dennis Scully took as meaning that he was overcome with gratitude. Harry watched from the window as Dennis Scully crossed the road to No 113 where Ada and Ted Ming had taken up residence. Dennis Scully Snr. had aged and the lines on his weary face displayed a need for a slower pace. Now in his mid-fifties, his energy was taking a dip and the added pressure that Alf Goldwater was putting on him did not help. His son was pushing for a much stronger role and Harry had become aware that Dennis Jnr. was undermining his father's authority within the Goldwater family. He exerted his power using terror and force. Harry stayed out of the way of Dennis Jnr. There was never any love lost between them.

His thoughts drifted back to the days on Brighton beach before the war, when he had poured his heart out to Dennis Scully about Evelyn Anne. Humiliated and bitter, he stared at the money in the envelope. Was this meant as payment for his troubles? Dennis Scully, Alf Goldwater, Ada - how could any of them understand the pain that tormented him?

He felt no desire to count the money in the envelope. The five-pound notes were only sheets of printed-paper. The money, however they dressed it up, represented very little, were it not for the intricate designs from the engravings he had painstakingly produced; he had no interest in it. This money did not in any way represent the freedom he craved, freedom from worry and hardship; this money bound him tighter. He was caught in the middle of criminal activity and there was only one way out. He looked at the notepad on his table and picked up a pencil. He hated himself, it went against all the principles and rules he had learned to follow but, across the top of the page he wrote:

These are the names of the people I accuse of blackmail - forgery, and breaking into my room and stealing within the last six months.

22. The Grass is not so Green

Ada Quinn (alias) Ada Adams of Chatham
Dennis Scully of Brighton also his son Dennis Scully of Brighton
Mr and Mrs. Kelly of Lillington Street, Victoria SW1
Ted Ming of 39 Chadwick Street
Mr and Mrs Stevens, also 2 sons
Bill Redman also wife and Joe Redman of 39 Chadwick Street,
Victoria SW1 where the transmitting station is.
Mr Spree of 51 Vauxhall Bridge Road
Mr and Mrs Stevenson of 111 Lillington Street
All these people can be found in 118 Lillington Street, 51
Vauxhall Bridge Road and 39 Chadwick Street SW1 and the
others in Chatham Kent.
~~Also Mr Philip Cavanagh... of Somerset...~~ (Harry later crossed
this out)
Dennis Scully says that Mr Philip Cavanagh (artist) is also in
this and that he is a forger and had 5,000 pounds of my money.

Harry hesitated as he was about to add Alf Goldwater's name to the list. Fearful of the consequences, he put the pencil down on the table and turned the list face down.

Alf Goldwater had dropped in on Harry only a few times within the past year. He was bent and nervous, unlike the hardened Alf Goldwater Harry had known in Brighton, the

Alf Goldwater who had worked on the railway, enforcing his rule with muscle power, the Alf Goldwater young Harry Cornell had looked up to and respected. Now he looked as if he would explode from the mere pat of a hand on his shoulder - although Harry knew not to cross the man, regardless.

Harry feared they had all got into something that was too heavy for them to handle, even Alf Goldwater. If war was to break out it would put an end to it all. Uncertain of what might happen to them, Harry walked over to Chadwick Street. His newspaper rolled up under his arm.

After writing the names in his notepad, Harry felt better but nervous. The guilt he felt poured out from the end of his fingers with the ink. He had placed the notepad between some sketches and tied them within a folder. The sun was shining and he decided to walk up to Pimlico market. It was its usual hive of activity as he weaved in and out of the shoppers and market traders but there were signs of strain on people's faces. Many seemed lost in thought. Reports of German militarism rearing its monstrous head again was in all the newspapers. Thoughts of war clouded the air.

It was too early for a drink so he bought a newspaper. He had been following events with interest and still hoped the world had learnt its lesson in 1918. He was on his own in this with his 'friends' or colleagues. The war was not up for discussion amongst Dennis Scully and the others. Living on the edge and their involvement in criminal activity sent their stress levels firing out in all directions. Those involved in crime, in the thick of it, floated on quicksand. Any unnecessary movement, mistake or word out of place would take them under; they had no time for larger issues.

Harry was on the edge of the group, keeping his eye open for the escape hatch. Two murders had been committed, maybe three if it was true about Evelyn Anne. Ada was sharp with him, her manner, marked with impatience. She had married Ted Ming on receiving news that William Quinn had died following a nasty beating. Harry felt sad at the news of her marriage but also relieved; he was better off without her.

*

A black Rolls Royce pulled up outside the studio in Lillington Street and the chauffeur opened the door for Cavanagh. From the window, Harry saw Ted Ming exchange a few words with him and Cavanagh looked slightly agitated when he entered Harry's room.

'Sorry I am late – I've been to the Gallery.'

'What did he say to you?' asked Harry.

'Who?'

'Ted, I just seen you talking.'

'Oh wonderful,' said Cavanagh, catching sight of a finished painting on his easel. 'This is superb. This must go in the exhibition, Harry.'

'I sold it to your cousin, sorry to disappoint you. It is being sent to Guernsey.'

Cavanagh sensed Harry's mood and it made him anxious.

'Well we still have a few months yet, Harry. You've a lot of work to do.'

'Things get in the way. I've other business to deal with.'

Cavanagh knew what he meant, he knew what was going on. Torn between his interest in developing new artists and in exposing the talents of Harry Cornell, he was also caught playing a more dangerous game and he was in danger of being blackmailed if he pulled away. They had got to him.

'You should never have got mixed up with the likes of us, sir,' said Harry.

Cavanagh made no reply. The conversation was going nowhere.

'My son Patrick's coming to visit,' Harry added.

'I didn't know you had a son.'

'There's a lot you don't know about me.'

West Park

Tango music – it's playing on a radio from a room upstairs.
A French woman has moved in. She has a radio.
She plays it all bloody day.
I like this music. It reminds me of France.
Of Claudette and Eloise, the flirtatious Mademoiselles.
Scully Jnr. and Ted Ming have gone up there.
I'm sitting at my table and writing it all down.
It's not good what they're doing.
I put my hands to my ears. Stop it. Stop it.
The French woman is groaning and has stopped singing.
I know what they are doing to her.
Their filthy fingers will be all over her.
There are more footsteps on the stairs; another man goes up there.
They are doing it to her again.
And she is groaning some more.
I should go up there and stop them.
I cannot move. My body is shaking as I hear the music.
It's a faster dance and there is blood on the floor.
It's dripping through the ceiling and down my wall.

It falls on my hair like the mud and bits of men.
So I write it down on the paper lined with my tears.
I write it down for the French women.
For Claudette, Eloise and the girls in Le Havre.
The French woman, she's groaning no more.

'Turn off the radio!' The night nurse shouted at Harry. 'Go back to sleep, Mr Cornell. You'll get me in trouble if you say we have music on in here. You're dreaming again.'

'Where's my blanket?' Harry patted his hands on his bed covers. 'Scully took it. He wrapped her up in it. Tell the police, tell them about the radio and the French woman!'

LILLINGTON STREET, SUMMER 1939

Patrick Cornell banged on the door of 118 Lillington Street. His brown suitcase decorated with travel stickers felt heavy in his sore fingers. He had carried it from Victoria Station. Patrick, weary but relieved he had made it thus far, was apprehensive about seeing his father again. It had taken an effort to track his father down and Patrick had discovered his whereabouts from Lily in Chatham, after getting her address from his Uncle William in Brighton just before he had died in March. Patrick had gone to see William in Brighton and had ended up staying until William passed away. It was sad that Harry had not been invited to his brother's funeral and it would not have surprised Patrick if Harry had never been informed of William's death at all. His name was not mentioned in any favourable way amongst the family.

Patrick had been delighted to make contact with his younger sister, May, while he was in Brighton. They arranged to meet up in *Clarke's Creamery* on the corner of North Street and took to each other straight away. May, who had not seen her brother since she was three years old, was now a young, married woman. She was like a bird, Patrick had thought, her sparrow-like features framed by a mop of dark, curly hair. She resembled Mary Cornell, their grandmother, whereas Patrick had inherited his father's blue/grey eyes and golden red hair.

He felt an urge to link to his family. Another war was coming and he was expecting his call-up papers. As the two of them drank tea and ate lemon cake that spring morning in Brighton, they agreed that they should seek out James, their younger brother too. Patrick had been told that he was now married and had a couple of children.

'I believe he's living in North London or Hertfordshire,' he said. 'I'll make enquiries.'

'That would be wonderful - my other brother!'

'We'll have to find Dad; he may know something. He's somewhere in London.'

May had looked sad.

'I don't think I can,' she said. 'It wouldn't be right for me to see him, not after all these years.'

'That's all right. You look after yourself. I'll write, I promise.'

'I hope you don't get called up.'

He kissed her cheek and walked her to where the buses stopped outside the Royal Pavilion. He looked towards the huge white building and the long stretched out green lawns bordered by a spring burst of floral displays.

'I'll always come back here, May, war or no war. It's where we come from.'

*

Patrick knocked again on the door of 118 Lillington Street. He hoped his father would be pleased to see him. There would be so much to speak about. He ran his hand over his thin, red hair after removing his small trilby.

Small in stature at only 5'7" high, he prepared his smile of confidence, which propped up the body that really was a bag of nerves. The door opened and two men pushed past him and down the tiled steps. As they glanced at him they pulled their brown trilbies over their faces. Patrick tried to ask them about the whereabouts of Mr Harry Cornell but they brushed him aside with no wish to make conversation. A voice spoke softly, from the shadows down the hall.

'Patrick, is that you?'

'Dad? I hope you have the kettle on, I am parched.'

WEST PARK

Harry was pleased to see Nurse McCarthy when she came back and started her shift.

Tommy Carter was hovering outside like a child waiting to come in out of the rain. She had promised he could come and visit Harry. Harry needed a visitor, she thought, and she had asked Dr. Howard if it would be okay. Tommy Carter was pushing at the door as Harry woke and opened his eyes.

'Okay, Tommy,' she said, 'come in but be quiet.' She handed him a mask to cover his mouth. She did not want him to risk infection.

Tommy Carter put his finger to his mouth. 'Shsh!' He said.

'Yes, Tommy, we must be quiet in here.'

'Harry mate,' he whispered, 'we going marching later?'

'No Patrick, you can't join the army,' said Harry.

'You come with me - marching like soldiers.'

'No son, Dennis Scully has arranged for you to go to Northern Ireland. You can be a jockey there. It'll be okay, No one will find you there, and no need to worry about your old Dad. I'll still be here when the war's over.'

The mad leading the mad; Nurse McCarthy shook her head and chuckled. Another insane day of confusion. She let them to talk for about half an hour as she moved around the other patients changing bedclothes and taking temperatures. Harry seemed calm enough but Tommy Carter would have to leave before Dr Howard or Matron came. Later that morning, after Tommy Carter had gone, Harry called her over.

'I wrote everything down for the police. I had to tell them what was going on.'

'Is that so, Harry?' She sat on his bed.

'I wrote down everything they said over the transmitter, I could hear them over the air, so I wrote it as they said it, I stayed up for three nights. I could hear every word and I wrote it all down for the police. They had a machine in Chadwick Street. Every one of us had war bonds. Alf Goldwater said we would all have six figures in the bank.'

'Goodness - that's a lot of money.'

'Goldwater stole mine back - and then they took my paintings - and Scully took my blanket and wrapped a woman in it, a dead woman!'

A chill worked its way down Nurse McCarthy's spine.

'You must get my notes and tell the police. You must tell them that they took my money and killed my wife, Evelyn Anne.'

Harry started to sweat and Nurse McCarthy worried that he was becoming agitated. She offered him a small glass of water. He pushed it away.

'Ada Quinn and Ted Ming moved a dead body from Lillington Street to 10 Stanford Street. They said it was Ellie King. And then Alf brought up 5 pistols from Brighton. He said he would shoot me if I told the police. It doesn't matter now nurse; I know I'm not long for this world.'

'I think it's important you get some rest now, Harry.'

'Yes, I'm very tired, but please give me your promise Nurse. You must tell the police; it's important.'

LILLINGTON STREET, SEPTEMBER 1939

Harry waved goodbye to Patrick and was grateful to Dennis Scully Snr. for his assistance. He thanked him on the day Winston Churchill made his famous announcement that Britain was 'now at war with Germany'.

'He is the same age as my Dennis and I feel the same,' said Dennis Scully.

'Will Dennis join up? He should, and get out of London, get away before he gets caught.'

'We've come a long way, Harry.'

'Did they kill her, Dennis? My Evie - did they do what Ada said they did?'

Dennis Scully sighed.

'Just be grateful can't you? You and Ada have plenty of money. We can all disappear when the war kicks off and nobody will be any wiser.'

Harry still trusted the part of Dennis Scully that he believed protected him, the man who told him to run off to war in 1914, when he had been given orders to kill him.

'You made a promise to Evie didn't you?' he said. 'She said you should protect me and you did it for her.'

Dennis Scully stayed silent.

'I know about the other women too,' added Harry, 'and I don't want any blood on my hands. I heard your Dennis; I heard it all over the transmitter.'

Later that day, Dennis Scully told Alf Goldwater that Harry had been listening in. He had no choice; too much was at stake. If they were caught they would all hang, including Ada. Alf Goldwater decided that it was time to put an end to it all.

'People need to start disappearing and we'll start with Harry Cornell,' he said, loading some pistols into the boot of his car.

*

That night, Dennis Jnr. argued with his father in a back room in Lillington Street. Ada and Ted Ming were there too.

'He'll grass us up,' Dennis Jnr. Shouted. 'We should have got rid of him a long time ago.'

'We can send him back to the loony bin,' said Ada. 'It would be easy; Cavanagh said he can sort it.'

Dennis Scully agreed but Dennis Jnr. went crazy when he felt all the others were covering for Harry. All reason went out of the window and the atmosphere became tense. Dennis Jnr. hated being wrong; he felt he was losing his grip on the power handle. Why was his father always against him? This argument, disagreement, difference of opinion blew with the pressure gauge on max. For a last moment, Dennis Scully Senior saw the hatred in his son's eyes, the hatred of a boy who had lived too long in his father's shadow. It took just a flicker of one crazy moment but it was enough to bring a final end. Harry heard Ada scream out: 'Dennis has shot his old man!'

WEST PARK

'They never said where they took his body, nurse. They must have buried him somewhere. Alf sent young Dennis away; kept him out of my way. We were all worried after that. Dennis Snr. kept it all in order, you see. He kept the law away and protected everyone. I couldn't cope with it. I met a woman who was sweet on me. She wanted me to go down to Portsea and retire in the sea air, and I said I would after my exhibition.'

'That was nice.'

'Cavanagh came back and took all my pictures up to the Leicester Galleries. He had some money and probably a load of those war bonds. But they knew I could blow at any time. That old Jew, Goldwater, sent Dennis Jnr. and Ada to my room in Lillington Street. They put me in Cavanagh's shiny black car and brought me here to West Park. They thought I would stay silent once I was here. But I told Dr. Howard the truth - and Cavanagh told him to say I was delusional, a delusional old drunk.'

Nurse McCarthy frowned. She liked Dr Howard; this was hard to understand.

'It's all written in my notes. Between *Eve and the Garden of Eden* and the *Green Grass of the Happy Valley*. I painted it for my mum. *Mountains and Trees*. It's all there.'

Nurse McCarthy felt exhausted at the end of her shift. As her bus pulled away from Horton she stared at the red brick walls of the asylum. It had been a long week. Tomorrow, she decided, she would go down to the stores and look at Harry's paintings. She needed to see if the notes were there as he said they were. What a day. Raindrops streamed down the window like the tears of a man drowning. Crossing her legs and clutching at her bag she changed her mind, *just let things be and do your job.*

*

The moon shivers its way across the sky, grey clouds held back the rain. Harry peers into the darkness and his dreams crowd around him. He feels the cold running through his veins. In a far-away field in France the bombs stop falling and in the silence between the trenches he hears the voices of a couple of mademoiselles singing French songs. He hears a seagull squawking above his head and a child sobbing. He hears the chattering of merry drinkers in the pubs of Brighton and sees, through the misty glass windows, the cheery welcome of the landladies calling with outstretched arms. He crunches across the pebbles on the beach, the sun streaming down his cheeks, music from the merry-go-round filling the air, and runs across the duck boards from the Arches. Beyond the upturned fishing boats, two lads sit in deckchairs in their khaki uniforms.

'Teddy boy,' says Harry as one of the lads jumps up to pat him on the back and Young Russell Cooper lifts his hand to shake it. Looking up, above his head, a straw boater flies up into the air and a ribbon gets taken on the wind as he lifts up his arm to grab it.

'BRIGHTON!' he shouts with all his might. 'I'm home, Evie! I'm HOME!'

End.

Note from the Author.

In every human being there is a yearning to be understood. We all have different ways of expressing ourselves and most of us find a positive route. I have come across many young people in my life working within the arts that need their expression to be channeled. It may be through music, art, writing, acting, designing etc. All these avenues are there to let life and light emerge. Society has a duty to understand and value the creative mind. Deny creatively driven people this recognition and their very soul is in danger of being crushed and de-valued.

When I first looked at the notes that were written by my great grandfather Harry Cornell, this was the issue that screamed out from his pages. What was it that turned him into the character that was so lost and angry? My family tree has creativity running through its branches, we are artists, writers, poets, actors, dancers, musician's seamstresses and designers. I understood straight away.

I have not been able to find any record of the crimes Harry talks about and can only assume that if there was truth in his story, the beginning of WW2 shielded what was going on in Lillington Street. However parts of his story seem less than delusional and some of the names he writes about I have been able to prove existed.

I can only use my imagination to bring this story together. I will probably never know how close I have come to revealing truth. I suspect it resides between the lines where it is left for us all to decide what parts we choose to believe. I am sure the spirit of Harry Killbuck could forgive us for doubting him